Almost
NEVER

Britni Hill

This is a work of fiction. All characters, places, businesses, and incidents are from the author's imagination. Any resemblance to actual places, people, or events is purely coincidental. Any trademarks mentioned herein are not authorized by the trademark owners and do not in any way mean the work is sponsored by or associated with the trademark owners. Any trademarks used are specifically in a descriptive capacity.

Editing: Word Nerd Editing
Cover Image: Depositphotos.com
Cover Design & Formatting: Britni Hill

First Edition
©2016 Britni Hill

Britni Hill

For my sister, Morgan, one of the strongest and
most independent women I know.
You may be younger but I look up to you every day.

Britni Hill

Prologue

Nothingness coursed through me.

I hated it. Hated feeling empty.

"You know how I know I don't love you?" I spat.

I waited for the usual rush, the thrill that came with hurting him. It never happened, though. I felt … numb. The second I opened my mouth, I knew the words sitting on the tip of my tongue were the absolute truth.

"Because it doesn't hurt anymore. I'm not mad or sad. I'm nothing when I look at you." My voice trailed off, losing momentum as those words really sank in. "I feel nothing," I finished weakly.

Seconds ticked by where I repeated the words in my head and brought my gaze up to meet his.

His face went carefully blank before he turned, without a word, to leave. The only sound in the house was the echo of our front door slamming while I stared at the spot where he'd been standing.

Later that night, he crawled into bed with me, pulling me close. He agreed. It was done. We were done. It would be better that way.

That was the last time I saw him.

When I woke in the morning, he was gone, preparing to be shipped across the world without so much as a goodbye.

"Mrs. Daniels?" a soft voice draws me from my thoughts. Memories. Our last fight.

Confusion muddles my brain.

Mrs. Daniels? No, not anymore.

I shake my head to clear my foggy mind.

Sounds filter in slowly.

A consistent beeping registers, along with too bright lights overhead. I squint, trying to see. My throat is painfully dry when I attempt to swallow. Agony rips through my abdomen and I curl into myself. A soft, warm hand grasps mine, gently pulling my palm from my stomach. A slight tug in my skin lets me know I have an IV.

"Honey, I need you to rate your pain for me." I focus on the voice, pulling myself out of the pain and apprehension. A woman with dark brown hair pulled into a bun leans over me, a soft, sad smile on her face. I nod at her, letting her know she

has my attention and swallow around the thick lump in my throat. "On a scale of one to ten, ten being the highest, where are you?"

It all comes flooding back, crashing down on me.

The ambulance. The hospital. The blood.

I'm losing the only thing *he* left behind.

Britni Hill

1

A car zips past me as I step off the sidewalk, but I don't slow down. I'm on a mission and as far as I'm concerned, pedestrians have the right of way. Horns blare behind me as I dodge a few more vehicles.

Damn. Is everyone in town here—on this street, the street I'm trying to cross?

I finally make it, my focus on my destination, Brunette Brew. However, keeping my eye on the prize doesn't stop me from raising my middle finger behind me. These small acts of defiance make me feel way too good and I know it's not normal, but I really don't care.

I blame my bad attitude on my lack of caffeine.

Everyone else would probably blame it on grief.

What the hell do they know?

Caffeine withdrawals are serious business.

Aunt Ginger assured me Brunette Brew was the best place to get a cup of coffee in town. It was also the best place to get a muffin or a scone. The place was great.

I'd heard it repeatedly.

Ginger had kept talking until eventually I'd walked away and headed out the front door. I wasn't trying to be rude, I just really needed my morning fix before I could be that chatty—or chatty at all.

Another car zooms by as I step up onto the curb and a scowl creeps onto my face. I don't care how good this coffee is, making this trek every morning isn't worth it. I mentally add a coffeemaker to my shopping list. It's probably time to settle in anyway, to replace all the things I sold when I moved home. I hadn't thought that through very well. I'd packed my clothes and a few keepsakes into boxes and shipped them off to my parents, sold my car and furniture, then I'd hopped a bus and found myself back in the town where I grew up. Back at my parents' house.

With nothing.

That was six months ago. Six long, lonely months with no one to talk to but my mom and Aunt Ginger. No friends. No one else.

My dad isn't much of a talker on a good day. And now ... well, he seems to be thoroughly disappointed in his only daughter. Not that he'd say so, but I know.

I just know.

I can see it in his eyes every time he looks at me. He gave me a month to find a job and get out on my own in an apartment. It took me three, and the apartment came first.

I know I need friends and a life, but meeting people is hard when you don't want to rehash the dirty details of your life. It's easier to hide from everyone, to stay locked in a nearly empty apartment.

I push the door to the coffee shop open, surprised by the amount of people inside. Patrons reading the paper or typing away on tablets and laptops sit at a few of the small, round tables. There's a large fireplace with overstuffed brown chairs placed around it. An older woman is hunkered down in one of the chairs, playing a game on her phone. I can't help the smile that cracks my lips at the sight of her purple-rimmed glasses sliding down her nose while she squints at the screen. The curve of my lips feels stiff and foreign.

The café is nice, warm, and surprisingly

modern, with dark brown, tan, and cream hues. Artwork is scattered along the walls and a few plants stand in the corners or on random tables. What looks like garage doors make up the whole storefront. Handwritten chalkboards boast the menu and a handful of daily specials along with the usual coffee shop staples.

My mouth waters as I look over my choices. I may have found my new favorite place.

Damn the crazy walk here.

The line moves quickly and by the time I make it to the counter, only a few people remain behind me. I order a large, black coffee and step to the side to wait. At the last second, I stop the girl behind the counter and add something sweet. Knowing I will have caffeine in my hands in a few short moments, I finally breathe a sigh of relief.

My eyes roam before landing on the older woman still perched in front of the fireplace. Something catches the woman's attention and a small smile curves her lips. She's so cute, I can't help but follow her gaze to see what has peaked her interest. My eyes land on a man, who doesn't look too much older than me, wiping down tables. My heart stutters in my chest.

My brain can't even find the right words.

He wears a t-shirt boasting the coffee

shop's name. It clings to his shoulders and the worn jeans covering his bottom half hang just right off his hips. The fluttering I feel in my stomach takes me by surprise. He's ... wow. He's just wow. The thought sneaks through before I can tamp it down. Inhaling deeply, my lips purse into a thin line and I force my gaze away, but I can't seem to stop looking.

My eyes betray me and wander back. He works quickly, his lips moving along to the song playing overhead. His hair is a little shaggy and sticks up in that perfectly messy way guys try for, but something tells me he doesn't try too hard. His arms flex as he wipes, and I bite my lower lip.

As if feeling my eyes on him, he looks up, his gaze colliding with mine. His lips twitch, and that damn fluttering in my stomach is back. A lump forms in my throat when he flashes me a killer smile—a smile that probably gets him whatever he wants. He's hot and sexy and probably everything a normal twenty-four year old would want, but he's not for me.

I'm not normal.

I frown and turn away, mad at myself for even looking.

I say a silent prayer for the girl behind the counter to hurry with my order. Staring ahead, the burning gaze at my back unnerves me, causing my skin to flush hot and my heart to beat faster. I don't give in to my body's urge to turn and look. I refuse.

Instead, I focus on the day ahead of me, letting my mind wander to my new job. A bitter taste builds in the back of my throat and my stomach clenches at the thought of what I'll be doing. My heart speeds for a very different reason this time. I try to swallow past the lump in my throat, but it's suffocating. I'm terrified to do this, terrified to go to a job, and that's just depressing.

My mom and Ginger pulled some strings and before I knew it, I found myself accepting a teaching position for beginner classes at the dance studio I'd taken lessons at growing up. It's been a long time since I've thought about dancing in a classroom, let alone done it. I don't doubt for one second that I can teach people to dance, though. There was a time I'd excelled at it, wanted it even, but that dream had died along with many others. So while I was nervous for my first teaching experience, I was more anxious about the age of most beginners. The thought of being surrounded by little kids has me sweating.

A ragged breath brushes through my lips and I clamp my eyes shut, counting from one to ten

slowly. My attempt to calm my rapid mental spiral is failing just as the barista calls my name, dragging me from my trip to darker places.

Hot coffee and cookie in hand, I head for the door, keeping my eyes forward and downcast. I want to chance a look toward my mystery guy, but I know better. The words *not normal* and *not for me* echo in my head.

Unable to wait, I bite into the gooey warmth of my cookie and almost moan. I take a careful sip of my coffee and savor the flavor. Aunt Ginger was right. I might knock the coffeemaker off my list.

Maybe.

Just as I reach the door, beginning to juggle my coffee and cookie, a large hand shoots out, propping it open for me. I don't need to look. The thrill riding down my spine tells me exactly who the manly hand belongs to. *Him.* Refusing to acknowledge the electric charge in the air, I avoid his gaze until I can't anymore—until he invades all my senses and clouds my judgment. His spicy cologne fills my nose and I finally look up. Clear, sparkling green eyes meet mine and I nearly trip over my own feet. I'm not sure how I'm still upright, but my cheeks burn.

"Have a *nice* day." He flashes that bone-melting smile again and something about the way he says 'nice' makes me stall. The sound of his rich, smooth voice starts a flood of goosebumps along my arms. I fight the shiver that would be far too telling and clear my throat.

"Thanks," I say to be polite, my voice practically a whisper.

The instant the words leave my mouth, I rush through the door, staying as far to the right as I can so I don't accidentally brush up against him.

I hurry across the street, pausing when I catch a glimpse of myself in a store window. With a horrified gasp, I lean closer. When was the last time I looked in a mirror? I mean, have I really looked at myself recently? Dark circles rim my sad eyes. I haven't bothered with makeup in longer than I want to think about. My hair is dull and limp. I look tired and run down, maybe even strung out. Since my life changed a year and a half ago I've lost weight, and I need it back. Rubbing a hand across my face and pulling my fingers through my shoulder-length auburn hair, I attempt to give it some body and make myself a little more presentable. With one last glance at myself, I vow to dig out my beauty products when I get back to my apartment.

It can't hurt, right?

I finish making my way to my new place of employment and stare up at the building, heart pounding once more. A sigh escapes my flattened lips. *You can do this, Cora.* Mentally pepped up, or at the very least pretending to be, I put some steel into my spine and square my shoulders. I won't let anyone else down. I can do this.

Britni Hill

2

I'm back at Brunette Brew, this time at a table with a crossword puzzle. I couldn't stay away. It beats the loneliness of my small, quiet apartment. Sometimes I can't handle the silence. Sometimes it's too much. So here I am, dragging my spoon through my fruit and yogurt bowl while trying to figure out this last clue.

I tried not to come back. I've been to three other places in an effort to avoid coming back here. My awareness of *him* doesn't sit right. The fluttering in my stomach when he smiled at me, such a simple thing, doesn't sit right with me either. Unfortunately, nothing in Farley compares to the coffee and muffins at Brunette Brew. It's also steps away from the dance studio.

I haven't seen him yet, and I'm holding out hope that I won't. He has to take a day off sometime. Deep down, I know it's inevitable. And if

I honestly didn't want to see him, I wouldn't be hanging out here, where he works. No matter how good the coffee is.

And it's so good.

I shift in my seat, trying to ignore the direction of my thoughts and concentrate on the paper in front of me, but my leotard is itchy under my clothes and my tights are too hot. I wish I hadn't gone the traditional dancer's route when I got dressed this morning. I try to hold in a sigh, but fail.

From the corner of my eye, I see someone winding through the tables, hovering in my sightline but just out of reach. Without turning my head, I sense the figure shifting closer. A tingle runs down my spine, giving me a pretty good idea of who it is.

That's a lie.

I know it's him.

My whole body tenses, but I refuse to look up. I won't allow myself that luxury, that freedom—I can't.

"Are you a teacher or a student?" His deep voice drifts in my direction.

Keeping my head lowered, I glance around, hoping he's talking to someone else even though I'm the only one in this part of the café. My brows furrow. I don't want to be rude, and that leaves me no choice but to look up and answer him.

Taking a deep breath, I brace myself. I'm still unprepared for the stunning color of his green eyes or the handsomeness that is his face. I mean, really, this guy is too sexy for his own good.

"Uh …"I cringe. In the last year and a half, along with my weight and fashion sense, it seems I've lost my social skills. On top of that, I don't really know what he's talking about, or why he's talking to me.

"At the dance studio?" he clarifies, gesturing out the window behind him. I glance over his shoulder before meeting his gaze again.

Ah, yes, that.

The curve of his mouth draws my attention and I get stuck taking him in. His lips aren't perfect, or overly full, but they do look soft, and when they curve upward in a knowing way, my breath hitches. I have to remind myself I'm not supposed to be looking. Again. I don't stop, though.

My eyes roam over his face before darting back to his mouth, and my tongue runs over my bottom lip. I'm trying my hardest to focus on what he asked me, but being this close to him is seriously messing with my head.

I really have been out of the loop for too

long. Socially awkward doesn't even begin to describe me. I manage to get a few brain cells working and drag my gaze away long enough to muster a response.

"A teacher." It comes out choked and rusty sounding. "How did you …?"

He chuckles before I even get the words out and the sound skims over me, tightening my skin in a delicious way. Tossing the white towel in his hand over his shoulder, he steps up to the table next to mine and spins a chair around. He lowers himself gracefully, sitting on it backwards, his long legs spread out before him, arms resting on the top, his eyes never leaving mine. Everything about him is at ease, and I wish I felt that way for even one second on any given day.

Instead, I feel like I'm about to jump out of my skin. Butterflies riot anxiously in my stomach because there's a man within a few feet of me. I lost myself a long time ago, I don't think I'll ever find *me* again. I watch him watch me and something about his quiet confidence speaks to me. It's impressive, and something I long for.

Discomfort washes over me when I realize I've been staring for a while. I shift, crossing my legs. His eyes follow the movement, heat flashing in his gaze. It's been a long time since someone

looked at me the way he is, it ruffles my nerves even more. My fingers grip the edge of my seat tightly.

"Pink tights. Last time you left here, you headed across the street." His gaze is steady as he studies me, waiting for an answer. An acknowledgment. Anything a normal person would give in response.

I squirm under the weight of it, hoping he doesn't notice.

My heart pumps harder when I meet his eyes. Something that feels suspiciously like excitement flows from my head down to my toes. I want to hate it, but I can't. It feels too good. It feels vital. I try to keep the smile from my face, but my lips turn up all on their own.

His eyes flick down to my mouth.

"You watched me?"

Am I flirting?

He chuckles.

It occurs to me that if this guy weren't so good-looking, it might be creepy that he watched me then approached me to talk about it. But his handsome face and the curve of his cocky smirk makes it flattering, endearing. It's also a bonus that he doesn't give off the creeper vibe.

If I stare at him much longer, I'm afraid I'll

end up stuck in a trance and look like even more of an idiot. Shaking my head to clear my thoughts, a spoonful of fruit and yogurt makes its way to my mouth. The movement feels stiff and jerky. I don't know why I'm attempting to be a normal person. It feels off and awkward, and I'm surprised he hasn't noticed my social ineptness. I should just send him on his way.

"Maybe. Maybe not. But you'll never know, will you?" He raises an eyebrow and gives me a wink.

A laugh bursts forth, but as soon as it hits my ears, it dies on my lips. I can't remember the last time I laughed at something because it was funny. I've laughed ironically plenty over the last year or so—most of the time my laughs are fake, and sometimes I don't even bother.

Blonde and Handsome leans forward and I get the sense he's trying to get closer. That realization sobers me. Blood thunders through my veins, burning as it goes. It lands in my ears with a *whoosh,* drowning out everything else for a moment.

I need to leave.

To get away from all the things he's stirring up inside me with his innocent conversation. He's flirting, and I don't want him to.

Or do I? I don't even know.

What I do know is that I shouldn't.

Uncrossing my legs, I take a deep breath, willing myself to calm down. The urge to scoot away from the table is strong.

I want to run.

I *need* to run.

I stand too fast, my sweaty palms slipping on the table. The chair scrapes too loudly and my cheeks heat. I try to hide my flinch, but I'm sure I fail. Digging in my purse, I toss a few ones on the table without looking up to see his reaction, the need to get away consuming me.

I gather my coffee and zip my fleece jacket, keeping my eyes on my feet. Not wanting to engage him any further, I step away from the table, but his voice stops me.

"What's your name?" he asks as he stands and moves toward me.

Air hisses between my teeth as I inhale sharply and freeze. He scratches the back of his neck and I can't help but notice the way his shirt tightens and moves as his muscles flex. I hate myself for noticing, but how could I not? He's ripped in a lean sort of way.

I try my hardest not to look at him and urge my body to move, but it's not listening. My feet won't obey, they're rooted to the floor.

He's too close, invading all my senses. The scent of his cologne fills my nose and the heat from his body seeps into mine. Craning my neck, I meet his gaze. Those gorgeous eyes of his stare back at me, waiting, seemingly unconcerned with my bizarre behavior.

"I need to go." I sidestep him, but can't bring myself to look away. "Cora," I blurt without thought.

Relief and victory flash across his handsome face and I allow myself to give him a full smile, my lips stretching wide. His eyes widen fractionally before he returns it.

"Brady," he says, gesturing to himself.

I let myself have a second to absorb his name, the sound of his voice, the smile turning up the corners of his mouth. If I only have this, it's okay. I take it all in, admiring his strong features and shaggy hair. The brightness twinkling in his eyes. For a few moments, I forget all the bad things that have happened. I pretend I'm a normal twenty-four year old woman.

"Nice to meet you, Brady." My voice is quiet, timid. I know this is it, the last moment I'll let these thoughts and feelings flow through me. It makes me sad, but it's how it has to be. I'll lock it all down when I leave here today. I take a deep breath, flash him another real smile.

Then I bolt.

Heart thudding in my chest, sweat beading on the back of my neck, the sick feeling in my stomach crawls up the back of my throat steadily. The higher it crawls, the quicker my feet move. I need to put more space between us. I'm a tornado spiraling out of control, threatening to take out anything in my way. Swiping my trembling hands on my jacket, I desperately want to look back, to take him in, to get one last glimpse, but I don't. I can't. That part of me is supposed to be dead.

My chest heaves with the rapid-fire thoughts that flip through my mind. Mental fingers finally manage to grasp onto one of those fleeting thoughts and I'm sure I'll lose my breakfast. Brady was making me feel things. I liked his attention. I felt that spark and attraction you feel when you want to get to know someone. It's something I haven't felt since my husband.

So wrong.

It's so wrong.

Making my way across the street, I manage to gulp down the sour taste in my mouth and slip into the studio, leaning my back against the door.

"You okay, honey?" Miss Kaye asks from

where she sits on the piano bench, startling me.

I groan internally. My boss witnessing one of my panic-induced breakdowns isn't high on my list of things to do. In fact, I could do without it ever happening. I move away from the wall.

No. "I'm fine," I lie, smoothing a few stray hairs back toward my bun.

"You look rattled to me." She peers at me over the top of her glasses. It feels like she's looking right through me.

A panicked laugh slips out and I quickly rub a hand across my mouth to smother it.

"I'm good. I promise." *Lie. Lie. Lie.*

Taking a deep breath, I head to the small office in back where I hang my coat and stash my purse. Gripping the waistband of my skirt, I slide it off and adjust my tights. *Deep breathe in. Deep breathe out.* My eyes drift shut. Stretching my arms above my head, I bring them out in front of me and give them a good shake. I take it all and tuck it away—no more feelings, no more hope, no more flirting.

Another minute, a sip of water, and the tremble in my hands is gone.

I've managed to push it all down. Again. Another dark box locked away in the recesses of my mind. I have quite the collection already.

3

The sun dips low in the sky, painting the clouds orange and pink as I flip the light switches in the studio off. Everyday I'm here it gets a bit easier to interact with people. It feels good to be doing something again. I smile as I grab my things. With my hip propping the door open, I dig for my keys. Heavy footsteps draw my attention just as I snag the set from the very bottom of my purse. As I twist the key to lock the door, I glance over my shoulder. Brady jogs easily across the street, heading straight toward me. With a longing look in the direction of my apartment, I find myself turning to face him. I can't bring myself to be rude and ignore him, even though I should.

"Hey!" His lips rise in a half-smile, but his eyes are cautious as he approaches me. Everything about him is more reserved than he'd been days before in the café. He holds two brown paper

31

coffee cups from the coffee shop. One moves in my direction as Brady raises an eyebrow. "Peace offering?"

I reach out and grasp the cup carefully, making sure my fingers don't graze his. I don't think I could handle touching him, even in a simple way.

"Thanks." I offer him a small smile.

Brady scratches the back of his head and looks down at his feet. I take the moments without his intense gaze on me to run my eyes over him. His work shirt is tan today, with dark brown letters and the Brunette Brew logo gracing the left side of his chest. His sandy hair is mussed, as if he's been running his hands through it. There's a worn spot in the right knee of his faded jeans.

"You ran from me last week."

Startled, I look up, meeting his gaze. His words are matter-of-fact, and I search his face for something more, but I don't find anything. Not knowing what to say, I wait for him to go on.

"I just wanted to apologize. I didn't mean to freak you out."

He looks so contrite, and it tugs my heart. I feel a little guilty for running, and for avoiding him since. It isn't his fault I'm a psycho. It isn't his fault I feel so much guilt I can't let myself be normal.

"You don't need to apologize," I say, my voice barely above a whisper. My eyes fall to my feet. I don't know how to handle this.

"I just ..." Brady shifts, "I know what it's like to be new in this town."

"I'm not new. Not really." I smile when I looked up at him, appreciative of the gesture. He's trying to be friendly. Looking back, I wish I'd had the courage to stay and talk to him instead of running.

Brady frowns down at me. "Oh."

He seems genuinely curious and I bolted on him before, the least I can is offer an explanation. "I grew up here. I moved away shortly after I graduated ..." I shrug, feeling uncomfortable giving him even that much. I know this information could jump-start all the questions I absolutely don't want to answer. Looking up, I find him studying me closely, his brow furrowed in the cutest way, like maybe this isn't going at all how he planned.

"Well, either way, I thought you could use a friend." His added wink melts something inside me.

"I don't know," I mumble.

My words are weak, not carrying any of the conviction they should. The thought of letting anyone in scares me. The thought of explaining my past is too much. But there's a longing inside me for something—something more.

"You can't just say no. You at least have to give me a chance. I can be pretty charming." Brady flashes a boyish grin, as if to emphasize his point.

I gulp.

A friend?

I know I could use a few of those. I pushed everyone away long before I came home to Farley. I've been alone for a long time. My gaze focuses on the sun setting in the distance instead of on Brady.

"Are you hungry?" he asks, hesitant.

I shake my head immediately. Dinner is too much like a date and it can't be like that. The only problem is deep down I know I don't want him to go away.

"I was just going to say we've got stuff for sandwiches at the shop. We can talk. Be friends." He hooks his thumb over his shoulder in the direction of the café, grinning again.

I chew my bottom lip, eyes darting between Brady and the building. I want to say yes, I want to be that girl, but I'm not, and the word gets stuck in my throat.

He watches me, his eyes hopeful. I don't want to disappoint him, so I decide to take a chance. I'm going to take him up on his friendship offer. It has to be my way, though—on my terms.

"Can we walk instead?"

"Sure." He nods, rocking back and forth on the heels of his worn Chucks.

Relief rushes through me.

****

We're quiet for a while, walking side by side. I haven't spent time with someone who isn't obligated to be concerned about my well-being in a while. It's nice even if it's a bit quiet. My mom and Aunt Ginger are always trying to fill the void with mindless chatter, gossip I don't care about, and I usually end up tuning them out, which can be exhausting.

I like this, having him next to me without the constant chitchat.

I know he's watching me, though. From the corner of my eye, I can see it. I scour my brain for something to say, something safe and non-committal, but small talk escapes me. Brady clears his throat and relief floods my veins. If he's talking, I don't have to, right?

"Where did you move from?"

His question has the effect of ice-cold water washing over me, killing any ounce of relief comforting me.

"South Carolina," I answer, already fighting to keep my voice normal.

An angry knot of emotion swells inside of me, threatening to cut off my air supply. Where I came from is not something I want to discuss. Why I came from there is something I can't talk about. I was foolish to think I could have a friend.

His husky chuckle draws me from my anger. It's a happy sound, as if he's remembering something fondly. The sound soothes me a little, easing the guilty ache inside me. I watch him raptly.

He quirks a light eyebrow.

"It's beautiful there. And you traded it in for this?" He gestures around us. "Soybeans and humidity."

I shrug. It's all I can give him. I'm not about to explain why. The pain, the anger, the guilt—those are mine to keep, they're for me and me alone.

He's watching me again. When I look up at him, his eyes are soft. He knows there's a story there. My heart beats in triple time, waiting for him to ask, but he doesn't. He understands. I can see it in his eyes. His gaze drifts back over the skyline.

It's quiet again, and this time, I don't enjoy it so much.

"So, when did you move here?" It's a weak attempt at changing the subject, but if I can keep

him talking about himself, maybe he'll forget to ask anything else about me.

"I grew up here."

What?

My face scrunches. "But you said …"

He laughs and I turn my narrowed gaze on him.

"Yeah, so I don't really know what it's like to be new here."

He lied to me? Was it to talk to me? To seem less creepy?

But he didn't actually lie. We're working with half-truths.

"Hey, I moved away and came back," he soothes. "I've been in the same boat you are."

He's the one shrugging now.

His half-truth rubs me the wrong way, but it's most likely because my life has become a series of omissions. I'm flattered he twisted the truth in a harmless way so he could get closer to me, it makes me happy. But at the same time, I don't like this feeling he's causing inside me.

I watch my feet shuffle across the sidewalk, ignoring his probing gaze.

"You okay?"

"What? Yeah." I've sunk so deep into my own head, I almost forgot he was there. I force a smile.

"Hey, wait! How have we never met before?" Farley isn't small, but it isn't huge either. I guess it's possible we've never met.

Brady tosses his coffee cup in a nearby trashcan as we pass.

"Well, it's not that small of a town. Maybe we did and we just don't know it."

We round the corner, turning down Maple. Brady looks like he's thinking hard.

"How old are you?" He gives me a cocky look that holds way too much excitement. He's getting his way by asking these *get to know you* questions, and he knows it.

"Twenty-four."

"Mmm," he hums. "That may be why," he smirks down at me. "You're a baby. I'm twenty-eight."

My lips part in surprise. I never would have guessed he was that much older. The age difference isn't that great, but still, it's unexpected.

"What's your last name?"

My heart sinks.

This should be an easy question.

It's not. I hate the instant lump in my throat.

My breath comes faster, so I force a deep

one in and hold it. Resisting the urge to blow it out hard, I release it slowly.

"Daniels," I finally manage, hoping Brady hasn't noticed my near anxiety attack.

"Nope. Don't know any Daniels," he says, not missing a beat. "Mine's Maxwell."

He looks at me expectantly, but it doesn't ring any bells. I'm afraid of what questions will come next, so I keep my mouth shut and shake my head.

"Which school did you go to?" He seems to be enjoying this.

"Lincoln."

"Farley High." He points to himself, looking a little disappointed at our inability to find a connection between us. I expect him to continue with his line of questioning, but he stays quiet.

For some unknown reason, I feel a little sad, mourning the loss of something that never existed. A tiny bit of guilt creeps in, tugging at my subconscious.

I gave him a half-truth of my own. Yes, I'm a hypocrite.

He asked for my last name and I gave it, but he wouldn't know me by it. Not if we're talking about high school. I clear my throat, unsure of what I'm about to reveal, whether I'm ready, but if

I keep waiting, I may never be ready.

"My dad's last name is Thompson." It doesn't make me feel the way I expected, saying those words. I feel oddly numb.

Brady's brow furrows and he glances my way. Something in his gaze tells me he knows it's not what it sounds like. The way I phrased it could be taken a few ways. Maybe my parents weren't together. That's not the case. They're happily married. Unlike me.

I can't bring myself to say it was my maiden name.

I can't bring myself to look at him.

I'm praying he doesn't ask for details. The very thought has my palms sweating. Crossing my arms tightly across my chest, I curse myself for wanting to give him something to go on.

"Greg Thompson?"

My eyes jerk to Brady's in surprise. They twinkle back at me telling me he's found a connection between the two of us. I nod cautiously, not knowing exactly how he knows my dad.

"Our dad's play cards together on Thursday nights."

He laughs triumphantly, and I can't stop myself from smiling. In the back of my mind, I'm

wondering if he's met my dad, if he's heard about me.

My lips twist in a grimace.

I hope not.

We turn another corner. My apartment is down, just a bit, on the right, above the bakery. I'm ready to reach my sanctuary, my quiet. I'm just about to make an excuse when my phone buzzes in the back pocket of my jeans. I ignore it, assuming it's my mom checking in. Let's face it, I'm not Miss Popularity these days. But the urge to know who it is has me reaching into my back pocket. If it's an emergency, I'll regret not looking. The screen lights up, showing me a number I don't recognize.

Frowning, I swipe my finger across it.

Unknown: OMG! Why didn't u tell me u were home? It's Melanie!

A wide smile pulls up the corners of my mouth.

Melanie and I were attached at the hip when we were younger. We grew up together, did everything together. Until the day I left. Best friends is an understatement for what we were. She was my sister. Thinking about her now brings me nothing but good memories.

When I first left Farley, we kept in touch, but after a while, we drifted apart. I was responsible for that. Too caught up in my own drama to put in the effort. And since I've been back, I've kept myself isolated. I haven't reached out to anyone.

Out of everyone, I should've reached out to Melanie. She should've been the first person after my parents to know I was coming back. A horrible feeling consumes me. It's time for me to get out of my head. And get my head out of my ass.

With a few quick motions, I save Melanie's number in my phone and tap out a text of my own. Nerves make my fingers shaky. This is a big step for me.

Me: It slipped my mind. Didn't think you'd still be here. How'd you hear?

I probably look like an idiot. This has been the most emotional walk I've ever taken. If Brady's been paying close enough attention, he probably thinks I'm crazy. I'm surprised he hasn't run yet.

"You look awful happy." *Seriously, run!* My brain is screaming at him but he doesn't.

"Sorry. I didn't mean to ignore you." I wave a hand around wildly. "Old friend. I haven't really gotten ahold of anyone since I've been home. I didn't know she still lived here."

I'm talking way too fast. My mouth and my head are on completely different levels and I can't

make myself slow down.

"Two friends in one day. You are quite popular, Miss Daniels." *Miss.* My stomach drops.

Brady's arm brushes mine and the anxiety I've become so accustomed to threatens the tingle that wants to race through me.

I try to forget.

But it's always there.

The thing I want so badly to forget but never will.

He has no way of knowing what two simple words like Miss Daniels do to me.

I open my mouth to say something. What, I don't know. My phone alerts me of another text, so I snap my mouth shut and tune out the crazy inside my head.

Mel: Saw you walk by. Called your mom. Come back to Sal's.

Sal's is a bar on the street we just came from. It's the perfect opportunity to make my exit, to save Brady from any more of my crazy, even if it makes me a coward. I don't want to hurt his feelings, but I think I need to keep some distance between us.

"So, I'm right down here and my friend is right here around the corner at Sal's. She wants to meet up," I explain as my phone buzzes again.

Something flickers in Brady's expression. His eyes move to the hand wrapped around my phone.

Mel: Bring the man candy. Yum!

I almost choke. Leave it to Melanie.

The corners of Brady's lips lift in amusement.

I hate the disappointment I saw creeping onto his face when I started to blow him off. Pulling my bottom lip into my mouth, I chew it as I think over my options. The sadness in his expression killed the need to get away. Not completely, but it isn't as strong as it was moments before.

"And apparently you're invited, too." I flash the text at him.

A chuckle escapes him as he reads the words.

We turn and head back toward Sal's.

"I'll pass. You should catch up with your friend."

He's giving me an out. The one I wanted just minutes before. It's like he knows. I'm getting a strong sense that Brady sees all the things I think I'm hiding so well.

His arm bumps mine and the warmth of his skin sends a rush to the tips of my tingling fingers. I draw back, separating us, and take a deep breath before looking up into his green gaze.

We reach the entrance of the bar and I don't think I'm ready to say goodbye, but I'm going to. I feel a little bad that I was so obvious about wanting to get away. I turn to face him, not sure of if, or when, I'll see him again. My gaze sweeps over him and again I can't get over how handsome he is. I mean, holy hell hot. He's casually sexy. And I shouldn't be noticing that, but I am.

"Are you sure you don't want to join us?" I don't even know if I mean that, but it's out there. And he's refusing. I think I'm relieved.

I don't know anymore.

He stuffs his hands into his pockets and awkward silence ensues.

"So, how about another walk sometime?" He smiles warmly at me, waiting for my answer.

My mouth flaps open and closed while I try to sift through the tangled web inside my head. This is why I stay home—away from people. My social skills are shit. I apparently left my ability to think clearly in South Carolina. Or maybe I never had that ability.

One look into his clear eyes and I know my answer.

"I'd like that." *Even though I shouldn't.*

"Good." A boyish grin graces his lips as he

steps closer.

I hold my breath as Brady brushes a piece of hair that's blown across my forehead behind my ear.

"See you soon, Cora," he calls over his shoulder as he walks off.

The feeling of his fingertips brushing against my skin lingers. I touch the spot with my own, but my touch pales in comparison to his. My throat feels tight and I'm rooted to the same spot, unable to budge, as I watch his broad figure walk away from me.

Just as he reaches the corner, he turns back to find me staring

Shit.

Diving into Sal's and pretending I haven't been standing here like a dumbass watching him sounds like the best idea ever, but it's too late for that. I wave instead. He waves back, and I finally pull the door to the bar open.

9

The door to Sal's creaks open and a bell dings overhead. I look up wondering if I've imagined the sound. A bar with bells on the door would only happen in Farley. My eyes roam over the interior of the bar, searching the dimly lit area for Melanie. I haven't seen her in about four years, but I can't miss her. She's behind the bar smiling at an older man as she sets a drink in front of him and takes his cash. Her dark brown hair is cut into a pixie, the messy layers looking effortless. She's tall and thin and looks perfect. I suddenly feel tired. Very tired.

Backing out of the bar and heading to my apartment before she sees me crosses my mind, but I'm desperate for some interaction with someone who doesn't make me tingle and isn't over the age of fifty. Girl talk sounds nice.

I think.

I press forward.

Melanie sees me as soon as I take a few steps, her face lighting up, her mouth stretching wide in a smile. She squeals as she ducks through an open space in the bar. Before I know it, her thin arms are wrapped tightly around my body, squeezing.

She's hugging me and I don't know what to do. I stay stiff for a moment. How long has it been since I've had human contact? Warmth floods me and I eventually return her hug. Tears prick my eyes and I give her a squeeze, sniffling as we break apart.

Keeping her hands on my arms, Melanie leans away and looks me up and down. Her smile slips a little, her lips pursing. I try to ignore the furrow of her brow, but it has me worried. I know I've let myself go.

"It's been way too long." Melanie's eyes flick over my shoulder. "Where's the man candy?"

"Uh ... he left."

Melanie pouts.

She reaches for me, tugging me toward the bar.

"Well, fine, but you have to tell me where Mason's dumbass is."

Icy fingers of dread crawl down my spine,

wrapping around me and digging into my heart.

I snap my hand back, out of reach.

The constant weight that threatens to crush me enlarges. It's heavy, suffocating. Desperately, I try to drag air into my lungs, but it gets stuck. I'm panting, my chest heaving up and down, and I can't stop it.

Control is slipping through my fingers fast.

A quick glance around shows me how crowded the bar is, more so than I thought. I'm about to lose my shit in front of all these people. The thought only increases my panic.

The hot rush in my ears burns away all sound. Melanie's lips move, but I have no clue what she's saying. A lump the size of Texas tries to choke me. My eyes burn, but tears never come. They won't. I know it. They never do when the heavy weight of panic descends on me. I'm stuck in some dumb limbo, my penance for all the things I've done wrong. I used to be okay with that, relished it even, but now I'm mad about it.

Melanie's eyes widen. Grasping my arm, she gives a tiny shake.

"Cora, are you okay?"

I shake my head, the movement so small I'm barely moving. It's all I can manage.

With a hand on the small of my back,

Melanie pushes me forward. The warmth of her touch seeps through my shirt, but it does nothing to kill the chill taking over my body.

"Deep breathes, in and out," she murmurs near my ear, her voice low and soft as she guides me forward.

My body feels stiff, my movements robotic. I can't make my limbs react the way they should as I settle onto a barstool.

On the other side of the bar, Melanie watches me with a weary expression.

The concern and horror I see in her gaze as she places a glass of water in front of me make me sick to my stomach. She looks curious, but also like she's afraid to ask.

I brace myself and swallow thickly.

"He's dead," I finally manage to whisper.

So many things come crashing down on me with those two little words. Words I haven't said much since I found out.

Pain. Anger. Guilt. Fear.

Her expression doesn't falter, and I know she didn't hear me. There's too much noise from the bar patrons.

My tongue feels thick and clumsy.

"He's dead," I repeat, louder this time. I flinch, unable to hold it back.

I know the exact moment my words register. Melanie's eyes widen dramatically and her perfectly glossed mouth forms a small 'o' for just a second. She quickly wipes her expression clean, but she can't seem to erase the sadness from her eyes.

It makes me angry. I don't want her pity. I don't want anyone's pity. I don't deserve it.

She opens her mouth to speak, but I cut her off.

"Don't say you're sorry, please?" I plead. The anguish in my own words tears my heart in two.

"Okay." Melanie holds her hands up in surrender, another worried look crossing her face. "I won't tell you I'm sorry."

I settle back in my stool, trying to relax. My mind is racing, and I want it to stop. I haven't had a full-blown panic attack in months. Even a near one makes me feel twitchy, as if my skin is too small for my body. I've had too many close calls lately.

I sip my water, but the stupid lump in my throat isn't going anywhere.

"Can you tell me what happened?" Melanie finally asks with caution.

My lips purse as I study my friend. Before, I'd always been able to tell her anything. She knew every secret I ever had.

Her expression is carefully blank, none of the pity from before evident.

A sigh slips from me.

I don't want to rehash the painful story, but she is my oldest friend. She's bound to find out anyway. It amazes me that the news never got back to Farley. Then again, Mason didn't have anyone in town who cared. He'd been in the foster system since he was a toddler, and to top it off, he wasn't really an upstanding member of the community. My family kept quiet because of me.

"It was a deployment," I say, practically choking on the words. I don't know if I can go on.

I hate the way I react to his name. It shouldn't still be like this. I grieved him. I went through all the stages. I saw a grief counselor, I let him go, but thinking of him makes me think of other ... things—things I could never let go.

That's a story that won't be told.

I can't stand the thought of how Melanie would look at me if she knew.

"Well, he always was a dumbass."

I laugh, and I hate it, but can't seem to stop it from bursting forth. She's right. He was.

Melanie shrugs and smiles at me.

"Want a beer? It's on me."

"Sure, just give me whatever." I rub my

forehead, trying to ease the ache forming behind my eyes.

A pint glass lands in front of me. Condensation runs down the side and pools on the cardboard coaster Mel put down.

Taking a sip, I watch Melanie make her way down the bar, giving refills and chatting with people. Everything about her is calm and welcoming. She's always been laid back, and she carries it well. She looks happy and I wish once again that I could be normal.

Once she reaches me again, she grabs a towel and starts to wipe down condiment bottles.

"So, did you move back?"

I nod, swallowing a cool mouthful of beer.

"Yeah, I've been back for about six months. I should have called you. I just didn't even know where to begin. I'm surprised you're still here."

Melanie shrugs and grins as if there's nothing to say about why she never left Farley or why she ended up back here.

"So … who's the man candy?" Mel's raised eyebrows and eager expression makes me laugh.

"Brady. I actually just met him last week." I sigh wistfully, which earns me another quirked brow.

"And he asked you out?"

Melanie pushes the wisps of her short bangs to the side as she concentrates on an extra grimy ketchup bottle.

"No," I say, shaking my head, the move far more aggressive than it needs to be. Realizing I don't need to deny her question so adamantly, my cheeks warm. Or maybe it's the thought of Brady asking me out.

"When he introduced himself, I ran. Seriously, out the door and across the street. So, I'd say, I thoroughly embarrassed myself and he won't be thinking about asking me out."

Melanie giggles, but quickly tries to stifle it. I drop my head into my hands.

"Not that he was even going to ask or that I want him to," I tack on.

"But you were walking together. I saw you through the window." She gives me a skeptical look. "And from what I could see ... you want. He's hot."

I chew my bottom lip and shrug, reaching for my beer.

"Yeah, I don't know. He found me leaving work and apologized for scaring me. He wants to be friends." Thinking about Brady tangles my insides. "I could use a friend," I add lamely before clamping my lips shut.

Melanie makes a non-committal sound, something like 'uh-huh' as she pulls the condiment bottles from the bar and places them in caddies to be set back on the tables. I don't know what to say, so I just sit and stare at her.

A few moments tick by.

"Where are you working?" she asks, making it seem as though we weren't just talking about me dating or not dating someone. A part of me is relieved, but a part of me is a little disappointed too. I'm all over the place, bouncing around in ping-pong ball fashion.

"The dance studio across town. Miss Kaye's."

I roll my now empty glass back and forth in my hands, so I have something to focus on.

"You always were a great dancer. I bet you love teaching the little ones."

I freeze, keeping my eyes trained on the bar.

"I'm just doing adult classes right now and some bookkeeping. Maybe closer to summer I will pick up some of the kiddie classes." I'm not sure if that's true, but it sounds good. Better than the truth. Better than telling my friend I can barely stand the sight of a child. "Tell me about you. What have you been up to all these years?"

"You know, community college, a few deadbeat boyfriends, more bartending jobs than I can count, and now, one seriously sexy and sweet fiancé and this place. Not much to tell. I'm really happy, though."

Her dark eyes sparkle at me. There's no mistaking how happy she is. A pang of regret slices through me at the same time my heart swells for Melanie. I smile at her, even if I can't smile for myself. Just like I'll settle for being happy for Melanie, even if I can't be happy for myself.

We chat easily about old friends and our families after that. It's much better to gossip with Melanie than it is to listen to my mom and Aunt Ginger go on and on.

The entire time we're talking, I can't escape the memories of Mason floating through my mind. I don't usually let it happen. Trying to keep the memories of my dead husband at bay is easier than delving in and opening up other doors.

When it gets to be too much, I drain the last of my beer and toss some money onto the bar top. Melanie comes out from behind the bar to give me another hug. She pulls me close, and I can feel something different in this hug. I don't think too much about it, though. It's another one of those things I can't think about.

I leave the bar feeling more refreshed than I have in a long time. I needed my life back, or to have a life at all.

Step one: get an apartment. Done.

Step two: get a job. Done.

Step three: become friends and only friends with Brady. Still working on that one.

Step four: get reacquainted with an old friend. Done.

Britni Hill

5

Locking up the dance studio, I look over my shoulder for Brady. We've been taking our walks for a few weeks now—three, to be exact—two or three times a week. I'm still surprised every time Brady jogs across the street to meet me.

Just like now.

He takes long strides, coffee in hand. I know it's for me. He almost always brings me one. It's a sweet gesture.

Every walk we go on, Brady's a little more bold. He walks a little closer, his arm brushes mine more often, and he's been finding more reasons than there really are to brush my hair from my face. I like his company, but his attention makes me uncomfortable. More so every day. We talk easily about music, movies, and places we've been. We laugh and tease each other, but I see the gleam in his eye when he thinks I'm not looking. I'd never admit this aloud—hell, I don't even like to admit it in my head—but the want in his eyes makes me want too. What, I'm not sure. But something … something more, and it's getting harder and harder to keep him at arm's length.

The more I get to know Brady, the more peace he brings me. He keeps me grounded. He's helping me put distance between the past and the present, but some things can't be forgotten. I'm not sure I want to forget. I don't deserve to forget. I don't want to lose the calm he's given me, but I think I have to, before he asks me for something I can't give.

He smiles widely as he steps up on the curb. *God, he's sexy.* It's unfortunate that's he's so attractive. If he weren't, this would be so much easier.

"Hey," I say, tucking my keys in my purse.

"Hi." He hands me the coffee he's carrying. "I thought we could go to the park for a bit today."

He's smiling again. He's always smiling and it fuzzes up my brain.

Greedily sipping the warm drink he brought me, I nod. I'm distracted when Brady reaches out and tucks a strand of hair behind my ear. The tips of his fingers are warm and slightly rough as they brush my temple. A tremble moves along my scalp

and I wish I could ignore it, but it only enforces what I have to do today.

"Your hair's shorter." He tugs lightly on the ends, making me a little lightheaded.

Self-conscious, I run my hands through the strands. I'd gone the day before and had it cut. I needed a change. The front still hovers just above my shoulders, but the back is shorter, brushing just below the nape of my neck.

"I like it," he adds.

I glance up at him. I've somehow stepped closer without knowing it. We're almost touching and I don't think he minds at all.

"Thanks," I squeak, jerking myself back.

I take another step away to be safe, shaken by the fact that he makes me forget myself.

He chuckles and nudges me with his elbow.

"Ready?" he asks, his expression playful.

"Yep."

****

Brady reaches for my hand, his warm, large fingers twining with mine. The action steals my breath, freezing me in place, making him stop too. He looks at me, concern filling his gaze, and my heart aches.

My eyes drift downward to our hands and Brady's follow. I take a shuddering breath. My mind and body are at war.

After a long second, he let's go of my hand and I inhale a much needed breath between suddenly dry lips. He looks frustrated as he runs his fingers through his sandy hair and turns his back to me. He doesn't say anything, though. He just keeps walking until he finds a bench overlooking a small pond where ducks and geese swim.

I follow behind him, my body numb.

What I'm about to do makes me sad. I feel the loss of yet another person, but after the reaction I just had to him touching me, I don't know what else to do. He thinks we're going somewhere—somewhere down a road where he and I become a 'we' but we can't.

I'm stuck.

Forever.

Plopping onto the bench sends a thud through my body. My stomach twists, anticipation making me hot. I grip the edge of the bench tightly as I swing my feet back and forth, my shoes scraping against the ground.

I try to relax, to ease myself back, but my body won't listen.

Brady finds a couple rocks on the ground and tosses them into the water, watching them skip and sink before he joins me. As he sits, he slings an arm across the back of the bench, brushing against me. His fingers graze my shoulder and I shift my weight away, uncomfortable with the sensations crawling over my body. I wish he didn't have an effect on me. This would so much easier.

Once I sever our connection, I turn to face him. Brady watches me from the corner of his eye as silence settles around us. I'm stalling, unsure of exactly what I'm going to say.

Clearing my throat doesn't work, it only brings his startling green gaze my way. I've been practicing all these things I'd say in my head, and now … now they're all gone.

Why is this so hard?

"What's up, Cora?" Brady prods, his voice soft. "I know you want to say something, just get it off your chest."

He moves his hand from the back of the bench and squeezes my shoulder in a comforting way. It warms me, and finally, I reach deep inside for the courage I need to press forward. To be honest. To let him in on all the things I've been hiding.

Most of them, anyway.

Biting back a sigh, I turn to face him further, folding one leg beneath me. My side rests against the back of the bench. My fingers twist in my lap.

Out with it, Cora.

"I enjoy our walks and spending time with you, but I can only be your friend."

I meet Brady's gaze, keeping my eyes on his.

His forehead wrinkles as his eyebrows rise in surprise. Suddenly embarrassed and wondering if I've imagined his interest in me, my lips thin into a flat line.

What if I'm totally wrong and he isn't into me?

"I … I don't know if you want more than that, but sometimes I think you're flirting with me, and …" I stutter, then give up, my face flaming to the point that my ears are burning right along with my cheeks.

"I am," he interrupts, his expression open, un-guarded, and honest, making me wish I were a different person.

I want to laugh at his matter-of-fact tone, but I manage to keep a straight face. Laughing probably won't help get my point across.

"It can't happen," I say, my voice firm.

I halfway expect him to tell me it can. He doesn't, though. He just watches me.

"There are things you don't know. Things I don't know if I can tell you, and I'm just not ready

for more than friends. With anyone."

My throat feels like I've swallowed my food without chewing and my stomach is making plans to crawl up there and join the massive lump. I search his face as I rub the muscle above my knee.

"I feel like this is just a blow off," Brady sighs, frustrated, and shoves his fingers through his hair. "What things, Cora? You can talk to me. We all have stuff." His eyes plead with me, telling me he understands. Telling me I can divulge my truths and he won't run.

He's right, we do all have stuff. My stuff is pretty fucking heavy, though.

The value I base on this new friendship makes me feel like I owe him something, some sort of explanation. Another deep breath. I hold it in my lungs until it stings slightly, then blow it out.

"I was married. My husband was a marine," I start. My voice is flat, lacking any of the emotion you'd think would be normal to hear. I feel myself going numb, shutting down, and I stare out over the water, unable to look at Brady. Not while I tell him this. "He died," I say, and my voice cracks.

Brady moves next to me, and I pray he doesn't try to touch me.

"That's why I moved back here. That's why I gave up beaches and beauty for soybeans." I finally flick my gaze his way and give him a small smile.

He nods and the corner of his mouth tilts up just a bit at my words. I'm deflecting, stalling some more.

Maybe I'm trying to erase the things I just told him from his mind.

Brady does the last thing I expect.

He grabs my hand, brings it to his mouth, and presses it to his lips. They're soft and warm, just how I've imagined, and my skin tingles with the contact. He lets go just as quickly as he snatched my hand up, like he knows I can't handle too much of his touch. The softness in his gaze flays me open and I think I might cry.

I shrug, even though he hasn't said anything, shaking off the overwhelming emotion.

"It's been a while now. I'm fine. It's just— complicated. I don't want to go into the details. They're too much, but I don't think dating is the right thing for me."

My eyes burn. For Mason. For Brady. For everything lost. For the things I did wrong. For the guilt I feel every fucking day.

He leans forward, prop his elbows on his knees and keeps his eyes on the water.

I wait, fearing he won't want to be my friend. With the potential for more off the table,

maybe my friendship isn't that appealing. His quietness goes on for a bit and I shift impatiently, crossing my legs.

His gaze swings my way, pinning me to my spot.

"I won't push you, Cora." The low thrum of his voice is smooth. "But I won't lie. There's something about you ..." he pauses. Watching with fascination as his Adam's apple bobs, I lick my lips. "I think you feel it, too." His voice drops lower, taking on a husky quality.

Opening my mouth, I have every intention of saying it isn't true, but he leans in before I can and runs his thumb across my lower lip. My mouth slams shut as a shudder works through my body and my denial dies on my lips. There's no way I can say I don't feel it too. There's also no way I can admit out loud that I do.

"I'll still be your friend, and like I said, I won't push you."

Brady leans back on the bench, keeping his eyes on me. Mine dart around everywhere, unable to handle looking at him for too long. He's persistent, and I can see something in his gaze when I do meet his eyes. He thinks if he hangs on long enough whatever we're feeling for one another will outshine my need for space.

I'm afraid he's right.

And I can't let that happen.

The only way to make him see, to make him understand, would be to tell him all of it. The horrible toxic relationship I had with my husband, the end of our relationship, his death, and everything that happened after. It's the after that holds me back.

I can't tell him, and the thought of it causes something dark to grow inside me, clawing at my chest. It burns and I don't know how to stop it. I have no control over the monster trying to rip me apart from the inside.

I stand hastily.

"Walk me home?"

Brady follows my lead, nodding.

We walk toward my apartment, both of us quiet, his arm brushing mine every so often. Even after all we've just talked about, his skin touching mine spreads goosebumps across my arms and a zing up my spine. I still can't stand that I like it. But at the same time that I'm hating it, I'm thinking how easy it would be to reach out and lace my fingers with his. I wonder if his palms are soft or rough.

Guilt and grief, they fight for their rightful place inside me, just beneath the surface, waiting

to tear free.

The red door leading up to my apartment looms ahead. A few more steps and we're there. I face Brady, my friend. His eyes are full of sadness.

"See you soon?" I know I shouldn't ask, but the words are out before I even think about it.

"Of course." The corners of his mouth lift in a smile, but it doesn't quite reach his eyes. I can't stand that I've ruined his smile, his general happiness, with my darkness.

Without really knowing why, I step forward, stretch up on my toes—my five feet and four inches nothing compared to Brady's height —and lean in, pressing my lips to his cheek. He inhales sharply, air whooshing between his teeth.

Brady wraps his big hand around mine and squeezes. So many emotions fill me. There's no way I can sift through them. Before I get too lost, I jerk my hand away from his. Without looking at him, I open the door and head up to my apartment.

"Bye, Cora," I hear behind me, but I don't turn, and I don't respond.

Britni Hill

6

By the time I reach the top of the stairs, my chest is heaving, and it's not from exertion. My breath comes in quick, short pants that I have no control over. Telling Brady about Mason has brought up too many bad feelings. Too many things I work so hard to keep buried. And on top of that, the way Brady makes me feel messes with my head even more. My hands tremble so badly, I fumble getting the key into the lock. Taking a deep breath, I try to steady the trembling in my limbs. When my bottom lip shakes too and my hands slip again, a frustrated growl works its way from my throat.

Biting down on my lip hard enough for it to sting, I finally get the door open, but the small amount of relief I feel does nothing to lessen the storm inside me. The thumping of my pulse tells me what's coming. This is it, the inevitable—the tears that haven't come before, the heavy weight on my chest, the complete panic I can't ease or shake.

I drop my purse and bag just inside the door not caring when stuff spills out. Stumbling, I make my way straight to the freezer. Behind some ice cream, I find the bottle of vodka I stashed there when I moved in. I don't even bother with a glass. Gripping the cap tightly in my hand, I tilt my head back and gulp. It burns, but not enough to overshadow the racing of my heart or the blood thundering in my ears. Tears burn behind my eyelids as I clamp them shut and count to ten.

I twist the cap back onto the liquor bottle and make my way down the hall. My foot catches and I trip over nothing. That's all it takes to set loose the tears I've been holding back.

Grabbing some sweatpants from the end of my bed, I slide them on. I swipe at the tears running down my cheeks, but they are quickly replaced as I pull my shirt over my head with jerky movements and dig in my bottom dresser drawer for a tank top. Once I find one, I pull it over my head without much thought.

My eyes stay glued to the photo album that's caught my attention. I shoved it there the last time I had a night similar to this one. I can't bring myself to get rid of it even though I can't

stand to see it. I don't even need to look inside for it to ramp up my heart rate. The soft, black leather cover, the scrolling letters across the front—it all makes me feel things I don't want to.

With trembling fingers, I grab the album from the drawer. In a daze, I make my way back to the living room, stopping only to grab the vodka bottle from the kitchen counter. Tears streak down my cheeks as I sink to the floor. Laying the photo album on the coffee table, I run my fingers over the leather.

When I finally gather the courage, I slide my fingers under the cover and flip it open. This album signifies the first of many wrong turns in my life. Things I'm no longer sure how I feel about. Once upon a time, I wouldn't have hesitated to tell everyone I'd take it back, but now I'm unsure.

My gaze skims over the first page.

My wedding album.

Seeing our smiling faces brings back so many of the angry words we spewed at one another, before we were married and after. Memories of his last deployment flood me. Static fills my ears as I flip through the photos of another life

I freeze as the tips of my fingers brush against something tucked between the next pages.

My eyes close as my tears and breaths come faster.

I don't know if I can look at it.

I don't know what will happen if I do.

It feels soft against my fingers. When I can finally bring myself to open my eyes, I don't look down. I take a minute, but it doesn't lessen the crazy inside my head.

Lifting the picture, I take in the black and gray image. It's worn, barely able to be seen. When it was taken, I couldn't make sense of it. Now, I know all too well what it is.

My baby.

A sob rips from my lips and my stomach lurches. The dull pain that never leaves me flares to life, burning brighter than it has in a long time. I don't know what's worse, the constant ache of knowing I lost my baby or the fiery flame of guilt that comes with knowing it happened the day of Mason's funeral.

I drop the ultrasound photo like it burned me.

A scream bubbles up inside me and I fling the album across the room as I let it loose. I grab whatever I can reach and throw it against the wall as my heart pounds so hard, I hear it and nothing else. I watch as the vase I've thrown shatters, but I don't feel better. I feel nothing.

How did I get here?

So lost. Afraid to feel anything for anyone else. Guilty over losing my baby. Mason's baby.

If I'd left Mason like I'd wanted to so many times, it would be different. If I'd told him 'no' that last night, if we hadn't slept together before he left, I never would've gotten pregnant, but it happened.

I never got the chance to tell him about the baby.

We didn't talk after he left. Our plans were to get a divorce when he got home and we left it at that. By the time I worked up the nerve to set a time to video chat with him, he was dead.

My body shakes with the force of my sobs. Guilt flows uninterrupted through me, filling every nook and cranny of my mind and body.

I can't help it when I grab the edge of my coffee table and flip it, sending the contents flying. Collapsing to the floor, I wrap my arms tightly around my knees and bury my face, giving into the tears flowing steadily down my cheeks.

The sounds coming from me resemble a cat dying, but I can't stop them any more than I can stop my runny nose.

I keep thinking the same thing over and over. What type of person wishes away a baby?

Me.

I did.

I never should have married Mason in the first place.

I never wanted a baby with him. I was selfish and young. When it happened, I was scared. Alone. I knew I'd end up raising him or her alone. Mason and I would have never worked.

Afterward, in the hospital, they told me so many times it wasn't my fault. That these things happen, but I was so scared. So worried. I kept thinking it would be so much easier if I weren't pregnant. Then ... I wasn't.

Nothing changes the guilt I felt about losing a baby I hadn't wanted in the first place. Not time. Not distance.

It seems these days the only thing that makes me feel better is Brady. I'm not blind to the fact that maybe that means something, but I don't know what to do about it.

I know I've been punishing myself for far too long and I have to stop at some point. This is no way to live, bottled up and lonely, but it's the only way I know how to exist.

Struggling for a deep breath, more sobs slip from my trembling lips.

I don't know how to stop punishing myself,

how to let go of my anger and guilt, so I cry.

I cry for Mason.

I cry for our baby.

And I cry for Brady.

I put my fear of hurting Brady and myself into my tears, letting them flow down my cheeks and onto my neck, hoping to set myself free.

I cry and scream until I can't anymore. Until the storm inside me calms and I'm exhausted.

My throat feels raw. My eyes feel like sandpaper covered in glue, but I don't move. I stay in my place on the floor surrounded by the mess I've made.

I have no clue what time it is, but my eyes drift shut as I lean my head back against my couch. Tomorrow.

I'll clean up the mess. Tomorrow.

Britni Hill

7

At eight in the morning, my alarm goes off with the blaring volume of a foghorn. I groan and roll over into the couch. Frowning, I attempt to open my eyes and rub my face, trying to remember why I'm on the floor. One look around my apartment at the shattered glass and overturned coffee table and it all comes rushing back.

Evidence of my miserable breakdown covers the space before me.

I'm stiff and disoriented as I crawl to the spot where I left my purse. I sift through the contents spilled across the floor, searching for my phone. I feel wrecked. Put through the meat grinder and spit back out. My head aches. I know my eyes are horribly swollen. I don't need a mirror to show me how much of a mess I am.

I silence the alarm before scrolling through my contacts to find Miss Kaye's number. I can't go to work. Not today.

I may not leave the house at all.

Ever.

Lucky for me, my voice sounds like I've been swallowing hot coals, so calling in sick is easy enough. Miss Kaye wishes me well, giving me recommendations on how to get rid of a sore throat. I say 'thank you' and swallow the guilt of lying to her, even though I know I won't be any good in the studio today.

Looking around my living room makes me feel ashamed. I expect tears, but they never come. I'm all tapped out. I feel surprisingly cleansed if I look past my achy body, stuffy nose, and shame.

Staying where I am, I fall back, lying flat and stare at the ceiling. Though I'd completely lost it the night before, I did have some good revelations. And now, in the morning light, they're swirling rapidly through my mind.

At some point, I lose myself, staring at the shapes in my ceiling. I know I need to get up and clean the shards of glass from my carpet and right my table, but I don't want to move yet. I have no clue how long I've been lying here, but there's a dull sound interrupting my newly found peace.

Thump. Thump. Thump.

I sit up, frowning.

The sound is coming from my door.

I can't imagine who would be knocking, but they don't seem to be going away.

I struggle to stand and kick the mess of my purse out of the way. Still a little disoriented, I don't bother with the peephole.

The second I wrench the door open, I wish I would've.

Brady stands in before me holding a paper grocery bag in his arms, looking way too handsome. His sandy hair is flopped over his forehead like he forgot to put product in it. It's windblown and I want to reach up and touch it, but it's his eyes that get to me the most. I see nothing but concern when I meet his gaze.

Feeling self-conscious, I run a hand through my messy hair and try to remember what I threw on the night before. I can feel that I'm not wearing a bra and chance a discreet glance down at my sweat pants. They're stained and about two sizes too big.

I sigh and scrub a hand across my crusty feeling face before finally looking up again. Brady's eyes are wide as they roam over me and I cross my arms over my chest. When his stare flicks over my shoulder, I cringe, but it's too late to close the door and keep him from seeing the state of my apartment. He doesn't react, though. He takes a deep breath and gives me that crooked grin he seems to have perfected.

"Does it always smell this delicious up here?" he asks, inhaling deeply.

I nod.

My mouth seems to be broken because it's not making a move.

The bakery downstairs provides me with my very own air freshener for free. Baked goods. It's usually the first thing everyone notices when they come over.

Something in Brady's jaw ticks.

"Miss Kaye came in this morning and said you were sick. I brought a care package. Soup, Lysol, tissues..." he trails off, looking behind me again.

My body locks up, breath halting in my chest as a warm flush spreads throughout me. His expression twists and I know the instant he realizes I'm not actually sick.

His expression tells me he wants to say something, but it's more than obvious he doesn't know what to say. He's watching me with his mouth slightly open, a frown tugging down the corners. My weight shifts from one foot to the other, anticipating whatever he might say, but he

doesn't go on. His jaw snaps closed and he takes another quick glance at the disaster in my apartment before bringing his searching eyes back to mine. I don't budge. With a clenched jaw, I raise my head. He can judge me all he wants. We stand and stare at each other.

That's when I realize I don't see any judgment there. The only thing reflecting back at me is care, concern, and maybe some curiosity.

It's so awkward this standoff we're having, but I don't know what to say.

Seconds tick by. I'm unsure of how long it's been since he knocked on my door or how much time has passed since he figured out I'm more messed up than he knows, but eventually it becomes too much. Neither of us speaking makes me want to crawl out of my skin. When that happens, I instantly need some space from his penetrating gaze, so I step back, resisting the urge to slam the door in his face and lock it behind me.

I should've done it.

Brady takes my distance as an invitation.

He moves inside my apartment before I can protest. By the time I process what's happening, he's already shut the door and made his way to my dining room. He sets the grocery bag on the table keeping his back to me. His broad shoulders are slumped and I can feel an intensity radiating off him I've never felt before.

"I'm not sick," I admit quietly. *Duh.*

Finally, he turns to face me.

"I can see that," he says carefully.

Brady places his hands on his hips, drawing my attention to his trim waist and muscled chest. For the first time, I notice he isn't wearing a Brunette Brew shirt. Instead, he's wearing a black V-neck t-shirt.

"Are you okay, Cora?" he interrupts my perusal and my cheeks heat for more than one reason.

Embarrassment spurs me into motion. Moving across the room, I grab the photo album lying face down and open on the floor. I snatch up the ultrasound photo, and tuck it back inside, hoping he didn't see it. I right the lamp leaning haphazardly against the wall, ignoring the glass scattered across the floor since there's nothing I can do about it. My eyes dart about the leftover mess, and I set the coffee table upright.

I swipe a hand across my face and try to ignore the pounding in my head, the too fast way my heart races.

"Um ... yeah. I'm okay," I say softly.

He's watching me with that quiet intensity

again. I need something to do, so I make my way to the glass and kneel down. Brady crosses the room, crouches down next to me, and helps me gather the biggest of the broken pieces.

I hate seeing him cleaning up my mess. I hate that I don't know what he's thinking.

I watch his face, searching for a reaction of any kind, but his features are blank.

That ever-present lump in my throat is back.

Once we've discarded what we can get with our hands into the trash, I sit on the sofa and watch Brady take my vacuum from the closet and go over the area a few times. It pains me every time I hear a shard of glass clatter through the vacuum. I cringe and close my eyes, unable to watch him continue to clean up after my meltdown. I feel stupid. He's seeing the results of one of my lowest points, something no one should witness, but I don't want him to leave, so I sit, unmoving, watching as he moves about my place like it's his own.

When he's finished, Brady stores the vacuum where he found it in and sits next to me on the couch. His arms come around me, wrapping me up tightly, pulling me into him. He's warm, his arms firm and comforting. I sink into him. I can't help it.

I've needed this, craved this, and I didn't even know it. Maybe I just need human contact, but something tells me I need what this man is offering me. That coming from just anyone, it wouldn't be the same.

It's been so long since I've allowed someone to comfort me, my mind is racing, telling me to push him away. The words form on the tip of my tongue, but they won't come out. It seems I can't deny Brady the chance to try to make me feel better even if I don't want it, even if I don't deserve it. My muscles are tense, my body ready to bolt, but I can't. I just can't. I give in. I bury my head in his shoulder as his hands rub up and down my back. His palms are large, and I'm acutely aware of the thin material of my shirt as his touch glides over me.

"I'm sorry, Cora. If this is my fault, I'm so sorry." His voice is a low murmur, and it takes a second for what he's said to sink it.

Jerking from his embrace, I search his green eyes. There's no way I can let him think any of this is his fault. Brady pulls me back, keeping his arms loose around me instead of hugging me against him. Almost like he needs me close but understands my need to pull away. Placing my hands against his cheeks, I note the way his light scruff feels against my skin. He leans into my touch.

"It's not your fault. God, Brady, it's my fault. There's so much …" I trail off, feeling lost. "There are so many things that happened that I'm still dealing with. And some things I haven't dealt with. Meeting you may have pushed me to think about … things, but none of this is your fault. I promise."

We're close, our faces only inches apart. His eyes search mine, flicking back and forth. He seems to find whatever he's looking for because relief rolls across his face before he leans his forehead against mine.

Tension tightens my body. His forehead pressed against mine is intimate, something I haven't experience with anyone. I don't know how to take such a sweet gesture, but the way his eyes drift shut makes me relax. If this is what he needs, I'll give it to him for now.

"Okay," he whispers. "Why don't you go get dressed?"

He gives my arms a squeeze before setting me back from him and letting me go completely. I hate the loss of his warmth. I've only felt it for a few moments, but it's done something to heal a tiny part of me and I want more.

When I frown at his suggestion, he places a few fingers under my chin, tilting my head so he can look into my eyes. The second our gazes clash, the warmth comes rushing back but this time it's not from being wrapped in his arms.

"Come on. I'm off today and I don't want to leave you alone. So, you're stuck with me." Once again, two parts of me are at war. Anger boils somewhere deep inside me at his words. I don't need a babysitter. I was fine without him. I want to shove him away, tell him to leave, but by the look on his face, I can see he doesn't mean anything by it. His actions are genuine. "There's somewhere I was going to go. I want to take you with me."

I fidget under his gaze. I don't want him to feel sorry for me. That's why I don't tell people about Mason. I hate the pity, and I hate that Brady's seen the result of my breakdown. I want to show him I'm not a total head case, that I can stand on my own.

"You don't have to do that. I'll be fine." I pull his hand away from my chin. "I'm fine."

"I want to, Cora." I love the way he says my name. I shouldn't, but I do. "We're friends, right?" he adds. Once again, there's nothing but sincerity in his warm gaze.

I gulp down my nerves and fears, the negative thoughts clawing around inside me.

Once those things are locked down tight,

the thought of spending the day with him makes my heart go fluttery. Everything inside me trembles with the realization. It makes my decision for me.

"Okay," I whisper, swallowing thickly. This could all go very wrong. I won't let my doubts stop me.

I stand and make my way to my bedroom. My knees feel weak and my breath comes a little too fast. I need to gather myself. I'm not even sure I can keep my anxious feelings at bay.

I start to wonder if I can do this at all—if I can move on, if I can let Brady in, if I can take a little more of what he's offering me.

"Wear something comfortable. Definitely tennis shoes, and bring something warm. Just in case," Brady calls after me.

I pull a worn band tee over my head and find my favorite pair of jeans. Once I'm dressed, I pull a brush through my hair and wander to the bathroom. I'm horrified when I look in the mirror. My skin is blotchy, dark circles rim my blood-shot eyes, and my face is all swollen and puffy. Sighing, I brush my teeth and debate putting on makeup.

At this point, it's safe to say Brady has seen me at my worst, so it doesn't actually matter. With one last glance in the mirror, I sigh. I grab a light hoodie and some shoes before heading back to the living room—back to Brady.

I don't bother packing up my entire purse. I just grab some cash, my phone, and my ID, and tuck them into my pocket. I take a seat next to Brady so I can slip on my shoes. He watches me from the corner of his eye. His attention takes me back to the night before and the way my apartment looked when he showed up. Uncertainty flares up again.

As much as I think I might be ready to start moving forward, maybe Brady would be better off staying away from me. My road has been rocky, and I have no doubt it will continue to stay that way. Can I drag this sweet, innocent man in to my fucked up mess? I open my mouth to tell him to go about his day without me, but he stops me before I can form the words.

"Don't. I can see you thinking. I *want* to spend the day with you. I like your company."

I nod and watch my feet as he stands, but I don't move to follow. I'm glued to my seat, weighed down by all my baggage.

"Ready?" He extends a hand to me.

Am I? Guess we'll find out.

I take his offered hand without hesitation. As he pulls me up, I savor his warmth and the safe feeling that seeps into my skin, my bones, and

quite possibly my soul.

Britni Hill

8

Brady packs me into his SUV and takes off without telling me where we're going. We drive for a while before I really start to wonder, but I still don't ask. I'm content just sitting next to him. I trust him more than I originally thought.

It scares me.

The city fades behind us and we cross the Farley limits into the country. A few winding roads later, and we're surrounded by trees, the fields giving way to woods. An old rock song plays low on the radio and I find myself humming along. It earns me a look from Brady, but he doesn't comment. The corners of his lips curve upward. Brady turns down a path and heads into the woods. It's obvious he's been wherever we're going many times before. This is where I should probably be concerned that he's carting me out into the woods for nefarious reasons.

"Where are you taking me?" I finally ask, my curiosity killing me.

Brady laughs, but he doesn't answer. His eyes stay on the road.

"Just relax, babe." *Babe?*

I like the sound of that little endearment more than I should. It rolls across my skin, making me melt into the seat of his SUV.

"Alright. I trust you." And I do, even if I didn't mean to tell him.

My words have made him happy. His lips split, spreading into a wide smile, showing me rows of perfect white teeth. Brady's smile is something else. It makes my heart soar. He has me feeling lighter than I have in a long time with just the curve of his lips.

A clearing in the trees comes into view. Brady pulls in, puts the SUV in park, and I frown. This is not at all what I was expecting. I stare out the windshield, wondering what we're doing here. I see a small fire pit and picnic table. The sun peeks through random spots in the trees, giving the area a glow but offering some shade at the same time.

"Are we camping?" If we are, I don't know how I feel about that. Aside from being wholly unprepared, I'm not sure I want to spend the night away from home, or with Brady. The thought of

what could happen sends a chill racing up my spine.

Brady peers at me from the corner of his eye.

"I was going to, before I knew you were coming with me. I thought we could just hang out for the day. I mean, we can camp if you want." He shrugs like it's no big deal.

I shrug too, still unsure, then open my door to climb out.

Brady follows my lead and hops from the truck, heading around the back to pop the latch. I follow him to help him unload whatever he has back there, but he just smiles at me and holds out two camping chairs.

"Don't worry about anything else, just take these."

I sling them over my shoulder and huff when one of them slaps my butt.

"Got it?" he teases.

I nod and look up into his eyes.

His stare holds mine captive. His eyes are soft and warm. I could lose myself in them. I know I'm smiling. I've probably got idiot written all over my face, all dreamy and teenage girl-like. A sigh slips from my lips and my cheeks immediately heat. I can't believe I forgot myself. The corners of

Brady's lip tilt upward knowingly, and my cheeks burn brighter.

"You're so small, I wasn't sure you could handle it." He taps the tip of my nose with his finger.

I narrow my eyes.

"Oh, I can handle it," I huff.

There's a twinkle in his eyes and I wonder what he's thinking because this conversation sounds anything but innocent. I turn to move away from him.

"And I'm not that small," I tack on for good measure.

"I didn't say it was a bad thing," he calls after me.

Our banter energizes me and excitement zips through me causing me to grin the entire way to the fire pit where I lay the chairs down and get to work pulling them from the covers. As I place the chairs next to each other, my mind wanders to Brady's flirting and how close I was to flirting back—hell, I may have actually been flirting back. It all felt so ... normal.

Maybe I'm not as broken as I thought.

Maybe my breakdown the night before was good for me.

Brady makes his way over, dropping a blue

cooler on the ground near me before heading back to the car. His walk is slow, unhurried. He's graceful without trying and I can't help raking my eyes over the broad curve of his shoulders and the way his waist tapers into his jeans. Before I can do something to embarrass myself, like sigh loudly or drool on myself, I pry my eyes away.

Needing something to do so I keep my eyes to myself, I pop the cooler open and check out what's inside. Just as I drop the lid and snap it closed, Brady comes back carrying a bundle of wood and a guitar case. I take the wood from him and set it by the fire pit.

"One more trip," Brady says with a wink.

His wink steals the air from my lungs. At this point, I don't know if it's me being so out of practice and the fact that I haven't been attracted to a man in so long, or if it's just Brady and how he makes me feel. Let's face it, I haven't had a man's attention for a long while, so it could be either. Because there's just something about him. I drop down into one of the chairs and watch him as he closes the back hatch and carries a cardboard box my way.

I get up, follow him to the picnic table where he's placing the box, and peer inside to see it's full of snacks. He's packed enough food to feed three people. I study him, wondering if he'd planned to come out here on his own or with someone else—someone not me.

Am I ruining his plans?

Did he only bring me because he thinks I'm a nutcase?

No, I reassure myself. He said he wanted to. He said so himself.

I refuse to let myself get sucked into that doubt and loathing. I've been living there for far too long.

My stomach rumbles and I laugh. It has to be close to lunchtime and I didn't have breakfast, so I'm not surprised by how loud it is. There's no way Brady didn't hear it. It's embarrassing. I grab some chips from the box and watch Brady move things around the campsite the way he wants.

Hopping up onto the seat of the picnic table, I walk from one side to the other, pretending it's a balance beam. When I reach the end, I twirl around without thinking and come face to face with Brady. He stands on the opposite end, a crooked smile on his lips.

"How long have you been dancing?"

His question makes me wistful.

"I started dancing as soon as I could walk. I took every dance lesson Miss Kaye offered until I graduated high school. I always loved it, but I haven't done it in years. Not until I got the job at the studio." I jump down from the bench and make my way to the camping chairs, ignoring his gaze on my back. His attention is unnerving and I really hate to talk about myself.

"You never wanted to be a dancer when you grew up?" he asks, curious.

It's a common question, one that makes sense but always amuses me.

"No," I answer quietly. Brady's brow furrows as he takes the chair next to mine.

"What did you want to be?" he asks, studying my expression.

Good question.

When I was little, I'd dreamed of things I wanted to do. And as I got older, I was still quite the dreamer. I wanted to travel and have adventures. My heart wanted to wander. The moment I met Mason, he snared me with his carefree attitude. I lived and breathed him. He promised me my dreams, but they never happened. Not really. Not the way I thought they would. And after a while with him, I only wanted one thing.

"Free," I whisper. Tears burn the back of my eyes, but they don't fall. "And happy."

Brady leans forward, bracing his arms on his knees. He's quiet for so long, I don't think he's going to say anything else. Then he turns his probing gaze on me.

"Were you … before?" His voice is soft, careful, as if he's afraid to spook me. "Were you free? And Happy?"

I don't even have to think before I answer.

"No," I breathe.

I've never told anyone how unhappy I was. A shuddering breath leaves me.

Brady frowns and it pains me to see it. He reaches for me, taking one of my hands between both of his. Comforting me. Supporting me. He gives me a squeeze then links our fingers together. His palm is warm against mine, and it tingles on contact. The affect he has on me starts on the inside and works its way out, stirring something inside me. I stare at our linked fingers, wondering if I've ever felt this, whatever it is, before. It's a foreign feeling. One I think I'd remember, but it's also oddly familiar.

Mason was exciting and thrilling, but it was different than this. When Brady touches me, it's a slow burn, and the hotter it builds, the more scared I am to give into it.

His thumb strokes my hand, mesmerizing

me with the rhythm of that simple motion. I can't tear my eyes away. I can't fight the thrill radiating up my arm and straight to my chest. He's woven a spell over me. We're having a serious conversation about my dead husband and I'm thinking of everything but that.

"I'm sorry, Cora." I see the regret in his eyes and it brings me right back.

Right back to here and now. Right back to Cora Daniels who lost her husband and so much more.

I give his hand a squeeze and pull mine free from his grasp.

Scrambling for something else to talk about, I look around the campsite. My eyes land on the guitar case and my curiosity peaks again.

"You play the guitar?"

Brady nods. "I'm better with drums, though."

A wicked smile spreads across his perfect lips.

My heart skips a few beats and I feel like I'm in a daze. I pull my knees to my chest and rest my chin on them.

"Were you ever in a band?"

"I was." He eyes me with that same wicked gleam in his gaze. "I even lived in L.A. for a while."

I have to smile. I could totally see him behind a drum set all sweaty. And shirtless. He doesn't strike me as the fame-chasing kind of guy, though. I have a hard time seeing him fleeing to L.A. Maybe that's why he's back here.

"What happened with that?"

"That's a long story," he says, and his tone tells me there's something big there. A story.

I raise my eyebrows and watch him lean back into his chair and gaze up at the sky. My eyes follow his and I let the sun wash over my face.

"How old were you when you moved away?"

I stiffen automatically. So much for steering the conversation away from me. Frustration runs through my veins. I remind myself that this is how normal people get to know each other.

"I thought I told you. Eighteen."

I keep my face tilted upward and close my eyes, hoping he'll let the subject die off. I don't have to answer his questions, I know that, but I won't deny him. Something about Brady makes me want to give in.

A shadow blocks the sun from my face.

Brady says my name and I know he's moved closer. His voice is soft and lulling and my eyes pop open. He's standing in front of my chair, hovering

above me, hands braced on either side. I try to breathe normally, but it's impossible. Everything about him, his looks, his scent, his warmth, throws me off. It makes me feel ... it just makes me feel.

"You can talk to me about it." The softness in his low tone unravels me, undoing me further than ever before. I know I'm going to give in before I've really thought about it.

I don't know what else Brady wants from me, but he wants this. This story. I'll give it to him. Because deep down, I want him to have it.

His eyes dart to my lips as I wet them and my heart beats a jagged rhythm. I run my tongue over them again just to watch his eyes flare once more.

"Can we walk?" I whisper.

Brady backs off instantly, holding out a hand to help me up. He nods before pulling me up. His grip on my hand is comforting, but it's almost too much. He releases me as soon as I stand. Because, once again, he seems to know where my head is.

"You like to walk, don't you?"

"Helps me clear my head," I mumble as we start down one of the trails.

As we walk in silence, I try to gather my thoughts. Brady doesn't push me to speak and I'm so thankful for that. My phone makes a muffled sound from my back pocket. I should ignore it, but I crave the distraction. Waking up the screen reveals a text.

Mel: Lunch today?

I tap out a quick response.

Me: With man candy … can't.

I know I'll get an answering text quickly, so I keep my phone in my hand.

Mel: Oh … so he did ask you out.

I smile.

Me: Not quite. He probably thinks I'm crazy. I'll explain later.

It feels good to know I have someone to open up to if I want.

Mel: You should go for it. You deserve some fun.

My smile droops a little when I read her response.

Go for it.

The words rattle around in my head. The way they sound makes me smile. I chant them in my head, repeating them over and over.

That's what I need to do.

Just go for it and tell Brady about Mason.

****

I take a shaky breath.

"I was really young when we got married. Mason promised me the world. I was dumb." I can't help the resentment that fills my tone.

Brady watches me from the corner of his eye, waiting. His patience is astounding. I swallow thickly. The admission I'm about to make is huge. It's something I've never shared with anyone.

Ever.

"We were young. So young." I shake my head. "We pushed and shoved. It wasn't his fault. It wasn't mine. It was both of us. We thrived off the pain and anger. We used to argue so much. I loved it, seeing the passion in his eyes die. It was even better when I could spark his anger."

I shake my head again as the memories flood me. Hundreds of fights rolling through my mind, all the angry words spat at one another, all the times I waited anxiously for him to lash out so I could do the same.

"We had good times," I shrug, "but there were so many bad times. We ruined each other."

I laugh without humor and avoid looking at Brady.

He's quiet.

Just letting me talk, and that makes this so much easier.

I need to get it all out.

"We weren't happy. We didn't love each other. Not at the end. Maybe we never did. I don't know, but we decided to get a divorce. Problem was, he was deploying the next day. So we agreed we'd wait until he got back. I worried even though I knew I didn't want to be with him. We'd been together for so long … and then, he never came home."

I let out a long sigh, surprised by the fact that I'm not crying. It's been an emotional few days, weeks, months … maybe years, so I expected there to be tears. A sense of pride fills me for getting the story out, for even telling it.

I brace myself for Brady's reaction, but he doesn't seem to have one. For some reason, that stings, even though the last thing I want is his pity or for him to look down on me. My relationship with Mason makes me sound so callous. So cold. Who would want that in their life?

"I think that's why it's so hard for me. When he left, I-I didn't miss him. I should have missed him."

The tears are there now, threatening to fall, but I blink them back. These words are true. It makes it hard for me to move on when I feel like I did wrong by him. But there's so much more to it. I did wrong by Mason. I did wrong by my baby. And I

did wrong by me.

"You feel guilty." A statement instead of a question, something he obviously doesn't need an answer for, but I find myself nodding anyway.

I release a wobbly breath.

I'm guilty for so many things.

Things I still can't tell him.

Brady pulls me to a stop with a firm but gentle grip on my arm. He turns me so I'm facing him and places his big hands on my shoulders. I keep my eyes on the ground.

"Look at me, Cora," he demands gently. When I don't look up, his voice becomes more firm. "Cora."

I instantly comply, the command in his voice giving me no other choice.

Pulling my eyes from the ground between our feet, I meet his gaze. He towers over me. Leaning in, he catches my stare with his and cups my chin, so gently.

"You don't need to feel guilty. Especially not for him dying. It wasn't your fault. You feel what you feel, and that's not wrong."

A tearless sob slips from me. If only he knew. But I also know he's right. It's not my fault that Mason died, it wasn't my fault our relationship was ending.

"I know," I whisper with a sniffle. "That's why I came here. I couldn't escape the guilt in South Carolina, but I thought coming here and starting over would help. And it has."

Brady moves his hand from my chin to my cheek and holds my gaze. There's so much compassion coming from him, so much warmth in his gaze, a shudder rolls down my spine. I know he feels it because his grip on my shoulder tightens.

"You deserve to be happy."

He's so close, his words so soft and soothing, a balm against all my broken pieces. All I can do is lean into his touch and stare at his lips.

Brady pulls me closer, just a little.

"What do you want, Cora?"

He licks his lips as his eyes search my face. My body sways and I'm thankful for his arms holding me in place.

"I don't know." I keep my voice quiet, afraid if I speak too loudly, it'll disturb the energy flowing between us. It's fierce and strained, but I wouldn't wish it away. I'm feeling something for the first time in so long, and it feels so, so good.

The feel of his thumbs brushing my cheeks is almost too much.

What do I want?

It's on the tip of my tongue to ask for a kiss,

but I can't bring myself to say the words. The flare of Brady's eyes tells me he's thinking the same thing. My gaze is pinned on his lips.

He leans down a little more, his warm breath washing over my mouth, making me feel light headed. One of his strong hands cups the back of my neck.

I'm frozen.

Afraid of how I'll react if he does put his lips on mine, but anticipating the feel of them at the same time.

"When you know, tell me, and I'll make it happen."

He abruptly lets me go and I have to catch myself, my knees feeling weak.

His lips turn up at the corners and I know my cheeks are red because I feel the burn.

We start to move forward again and I take a deep, cleansing breath, but it does nothing to slow the thrumming of my heart, the ache in the pit of my stomach, or the weakness in my legs.

"You hungry?" Brady asks when we near the campsite.

I look over at him. He looks completely unaffected, but the husky tone of his question tells me otherwise.

Still unable to string together words, I nod

and sit at the table while he busies himself with making sandwiches. I watch him work with one question rattling around in my head.

What do I want?

9

I've tossed and turned for two nights, unable to get Brady off my mind. We didn't camp that day in the woods, but we stayed late into the night, talking about music and movies, and he played his guitar. We ate and laughed and I can't remember the last time I had so much fun or felt so relaxed. When Brady dropped me at my apartment, he walked me to my door, hugged me tight, and flashed that crooked grin of his.

I've started waking up to texts from him every morning and I'm hoping today won't be any different. A glance at the clock tells me it's nine, so I decide to roll out of bed. I've had two days off since the day I called in. I feel bad about having so much time away and even more so for calling in.

Maybe I should head to the studio and pick up some of Miss Kaye's classes, or just lend a hand. I feel good, relaxed, far better than I have in a long time. As soon as the thought crosses my mind, I dismiss it.

Heading to the dance studio would only be a way to assuage my guilt over calling in, and I'm thinking I needed this time away from everything. It's ridiculous since I did nothing and avoided everyone for so long, but sometimes you just need a mental health day—or two or three.

Pulling my phone from the charger, I wander into my kitchen and hit brew on the coffeemaker before grabbing a box of cereal. I'm about to swing around and open the fridge for some milk when the sound of my phone buzzing against the counter draws my attention.

Giddiness instantly fills me. It's comical how quick and wide I smile because I'm sure I know who it is, or at least I hope I know who it is.

Hope. Something so easily taken for granted. Something I haven't felt in a long while. Something I seem to grow more of each time I see Brady.

My cheeks even hurt from all the smiling I've been doing recently.

I snag my phone from the counter. A few quick swipes show me that right now, my hopes are real.

Brady: Good morning beautiful.

My stomach flip-flops and my smile widens.

Me: Morning!

I groan the second I hit send. An exclamation point? I'm incredibly bad at this. That wasn't flirty. It was overly excited. And lame.

While I'm busy grumbling to myself and trying to come up with better ways to flirt via text, my phone chimes again.

Brady: How did you sleep?

I won't admit that thoughts of him kept me up all night. I want to, I want to be that girl, but I'm just not. I type something non-committal instead.

Me: Fine.

Was that too non-committal?

Probably.

Damn.

I'm waiting for a response and as the seconds tick by, I start to feel dumb. I lay my phone down and snatch it back up, intending to ask him how he slept, to add something to my nothing of a message, but I shake my head instead and drop my phone back on the counter. Ignoring my private embarrassment, I take my cereal to the couch.

After two bites, my phone buzzes. I tell myself I'm going to ignore it. Scooping some more cereal into my mouth, I chew, but can't keep my eyes from wandering to the spot where my phone sits. My foot taps impatiently on the couch cushion and I squirm, trying to get comfortable.

Another bite, and I can't take it anymore. I set my bowl next to my coffee cup on the table in front of me and scramble to the kitchen.

Brady: Do you have plans tonight?

I snort. I haven't had plans in well over a year.

Me: No.

I chew my lip as I wait, unfamiliar feelings swimming inside me. My heart beats faster as I wait for him to say more.

Brady: Have dinner with me?

The rapid pounding of my heart stutters before it takes off again. Butterflies swarm my stomach. Nerves, anticipation, excitement—all three fight for top billing.

Before I can stop myself, I type out a 'yes' and hit send.

Brady: Be ready at 7. I'll pick you up.

In a daze, I make my way back to the couch. I sit, feeling stiff … unsure.

Am I really doing this?

I am.

Smiling, I dump my cereal, pull my cleaning supplies from beneath the sink, and go to work on my kitchen. When everything gleams, I head to the

bathroom. I concentrate hard on what I'm doing. It helps keep my mind from wandering. Cleaning has always been a way for me to get out of my head. After Mason died and I lost the baby, my hands were raw from how many chemicals my skin came in contact with. I didn't stop, though. I just bought gloves.

This time, I'm so far in the zone, my mind begins to wander. And where does it go?

Brady.

Questions bombard me.

Is it a date? Do I even remember how to date? Do I want to date? Is he going to kiss me?

If it is a date, it will be my first since I was seventeen.

Seven years. Wasted.

I hate to think about those years as wasted because I'm not sure that's true. What I felt for Mason had been wild and crazy, but somehow tame in comparison to what I've been feeling lately. Whatever it was we had wasn't healthy, but I'm starting to see that maybe that doesn't mean it wasn't real. No matter how toxic our relationship had been, we loved each other at one point. So it was real. It just wasn't right.

Right?

My stomach churns, a sour taste filling my

mouth.

A lump forms in my throat. By the time seven rolls around, I'm sure I'll be a buzzing ball of nerves if I don't get a grip.

Giving up on scrubbing, I put everything back in its place and sit on my bed. My open closet draws my stare. I haven't been shopping in who knows how long. Other than buying new dance clothes, I haven't had a reason to buy dresses or anything else. If I had more time, I'd drag myself to the mall, but I'm feeling too jittery to even attempt that. There has to be something in there I can wear.

Something cute.

I run a hand through my auburn hair and sigh. I'm not sure I even remember how to dress for a date. I haven't looked in a fashion magazine in ages. Another heavy sigh slips from me.

Before I tackle something to wear, I'll shower.

I strip down and head into the bathroom.

All the things I usually rush through consume me. I scrub my skin until its pink and use my favorite body wash. When I step out of the shower, I rub lotion into my skin and dry my hair meticulously. My stomach rumbles and I know it's past lunchtime, but I don't think I can handle eating.

My nerves are getting the best of me. I start to wonder if saying yes was the right move, but I can't seem to actually regret it. I find myself staring longingly into my closet again, which isn't getting me anywhere.

I need a friend.

A girl's advice about this whole situation.

The guy.

The date.

The clothes.

I smile when I realize I know just the person for the job.

****

After eating something that came from my freezer and went straight in the microwave, I sit and wait. I flip through the channels, but nothing catches my attention. Mostly because I'm not actually looking at what's on the screen. I'm lost inside my head. So lost that I jump when there's a knock on the door. Melanie smiles on the other side when I yank it open.

I step back, eagerly letting her in.

"It smells delicious in here," Melanie comments as I shut the door behind her. I laugh. Every time.

"You can thank the bakery below for my

never-ending air freshener."

My whole body relaxes. Just having my old friend here makes me think I can do this.

Melanie whirls around, taking me in from head to toe. I'm still in my robe. A mischievous look tips up the corners of her lips.

"So, *he* finally asked you on a date?" She looks all too pleased with this revelation.

A groan slips out from between my lips.

"I'm not sure it's a date," I protest, but I'm not fooling anyone.

It's totally a date. A date with Brady. Hot, sexy Brady. Sweet Brady.

My cheeks heat and I damn my fair skin as it's happening.

"By the way you're blushing, I think it's a date."

With a hand on her hip, Melanie pins me with her gaze. I squirm.

"Well, maybe it's a date, but I don't know. He never said," I mumble and look away.

"Cora..." Her voice is sharp, no bullshit, drawing my attention back to her.

"Okay fine, it's a date," I huff.

I don't know why I bothered trying to say it wasn't.

Denial.

That's why. I like to live there, in my safe place, all alone.

"How do you feel about that?" She eyes me wearily.

I can't say I blame her. This is a hard situation. One she just recently watched me breakdown over.

I scrub a hand over my face, mentally cataloguing.

How do I feel?

Most days I can't make sense of my emotions. They're all over the place—especially since Brady came into my life. For so long, I thought there was a way I was expected to feel, or better yet, a way I wasn't supposed to feel. And now? So many feelings and needs and wants rush through me. One stands out among the others, screaming loudly at me. It's probably my least favorite. I want to hold it close, keep Melanie out— keep it for myself and no one else. But that's not what moving on is about, so I give in. I set it free.

"Scared," I admit quietly.

Melanie nods.

"It's okay to be scared."

I sigh. Deep down, I know it's okay, that all these confusing things in my head are acceptable, but they make my heart beat too fast and fog my thoughts. They consume me, and that's not acceptable. What I thought I'd do for the rest of my life and what I'm allowing to happen are colliding inside me.

"When is he coming to get you?" she asks.

"Seven." I look at my feet.

Melanie's eyebrow raise and she laughs a little while she watches me.

"You know it's only two, right?" I fully expect her to tease me, but her voice is soft, warm, and friendly. Just what I need, even though know how ridiculous I'm being.

"I'm nervous," I shriek at her.

Melanie makes her way toward me. She's careful as she does, as if she's afraid to spook me. Once she's close enough, she wraps an arm around my shoulders. I can't help but lean into her as she leads me down the hall and into my room. I needed her. Way before today.

"I've missed you," I whisper, on the verge of tears.

"You just need my help with your man candy," Melanie teases, lightening the mood. I hear the tremor in her voice, though.

"You missed me, too," I say.

"I did."

I knew it.

With her hands on my shoulders, she pushes me down on my bed before walking into my open closet. She starts flipping through the hangers while she tells me about something her fiancé did the other day. It's like no time has passed between us.

I zone out again and start chewing on a ragged cuticle. It stings, but that doesn't stop me from pulling on the skin. Melanie comes out of the closet, her arms full of shirts and dresses. Pulling my hand from my mouth, she gives me a stern look and sets the clothes next to me on the bed.

"So, you like this guy?"

Yes. "I think so."

Melanie gives me a look. She knows I'm full of it.

"He makes me feel …" I trail off, searching for the right words, but they evade me. Nothing can fully describe it, not in the right way. And that's when it hits me. I shrug. "That's it. He makes me feel."

As soon as the words leave my mouth, I feel dumb. I catch a flash of Melanie's knowing grin before I flop back onto the bed.

"I've never felt like this." I give her a meaningful look, hoping she understands what I'm trying to say. "I barely know him."

"Sometimes you don't need to know someone. That's what attraction is—an instant connection. Sometimes it grows and sometimes it dies. It's up to you to find out. All you have to do is make a decision."

When I finally work up the nerve to meet my friend's gaze again, she's giving me a look I don't think I like. I test out her words, rolling them around in my mind. Maybe she's right.

I'd been thinking something similar earlier when I realized what I felt for Mason had been so different from what I feel for Brady. Some deep, buried part of me knows I've never felt this before because it's never been right with anyone else.

I need to stop stressing over this and all the things about it I can't control. I need to see where it goes—end of story. The same part of me that recognizes how I feel about Brady, the one that's buried so deep, knows I'll regret it if I don't let myself explore this.

I turn down everything Melanie suggests I wear. Eventually she drags a teal sundress from the mess left in my closet. It's cute and flowy. I've never worn it. It was an impulse buy from what now seems like ages ago. I finger the soft material as Melanie holds it up in front of me and smiles widely.

My own lips split into a grin. I know just the thing to wear with this dress. Inside the closet, I find what I'm looking for easily.

"With this?"

I pull out a black, cropped leather jacket.

"And this?" Melanie adds, holding up a wide black belt.

I nod and place my outfit for the evening on the bed. Only one thing is missing.

"Shoes?"

"That's easy. Since you don't know what you are doing, go with flats, but I wouldn't do sandals. It might get chilly tonight." Melanie kneels down and starts digging in the bottom of my closet. "I saw some black flats in here." Her voice is muffled as she dives into my mess of footwear.

A squeal sounds inside my closet and I assume she's found them.

She turns, triumphantly holding them up.

"Okay, try it on. Then we'll talk makeup and hair."

I groan and she shoos me away with a flick of her hand. I start shedding my clothes, replacing them with what we've picked out.

Once I'm ready, I look myself over, a smile curving my lips. I love this outfit. When I spin away from the mirror so Mel can look me over, she nods her approval and gives a little clap.

"Nailed it!"

We laugh. It feels so good to have some girl time, I feel myself getting a little weepy and blink it away.

"Now, I wait," I pull my bottom lip into my mouth and then frown, "until seven."

Melanie dissolves into a fit of giggles on my bed. I scowl down at her. This is going to be the longest day. Ever.

16

Just before seven, there's a quick rap on my door. I let out a sharp breath and smooth my dress as I hop up from the couch. My lungs burn and I wonder if I've breathed a full breath since we made this date.

I don't know what to expect and my nerves are through the roof, but when I open the door, my eyes land on Brady and an eerie sense of peace fills me. My tension melts away with the rightness of the moment. I'm completely calm for the first time since the last time I saw him.

"Hey," I breathe in the most embarrassing way.

"Hey." I was hoping he hadn't noticed my breathy greeting, and I'm disappointed when a cocky, knowing smirk twists his lips. "It smells so good in here. I can't get over it," he says as he steps inside and wraps me in a hug like it's the most normal thing to do, like we do it all the time. He buries his face in the hair on top of my head as he draws in a deep breath. "You might smell better, though."

Goosebumps cover my arms and my lips split at the huskiness in his voice, the feel of his warm breath washing over my ear. The rasp in his voice tells me this isn't one-sided. It's nice to know I affect him, too. We pull apart and my legs tremble beneath me, making me unsteady on my feet.

Whether it's his closeness or his words, I'm unsure.

As he pulls back, he looks deep into my eyes, searching for something, which sends my heart and mind racing.

I'm putty in his hands and we haven't even left yet. If I survive this date without ending up in a gooey puddle on the ground, I'll be amazed.

"Ready?"

I nod and grab my purse.

Brady smiles down at me and leans in to place a hand low on my back, the contact making me shiver. Now that he doesn't have me wrapped up in his strong arms, I can't help but look him over.

From the corner of my eye, of course.

He's wearing jeans and a pale green button-

down shirt that brings out the color of his eyes. His sleeves rolled to his elbows show me his forearms and I have to bite back a sigh.

Are forearms that sexy?

He's too good looking for his own good— wait, for my own good.

It's not fair.

Really not fair.

He stays close as we make our way down the stairs outside my apartment to the curb where he parked.

Brady opens the passenger side door for me and I slide inside, careful to keep my legs together and my dress down around my thighs. No need to be flashing the goodies on my first date in seven years. It's been so long since I've wanted a man's eyes on me, I have to admit, it's making me a bit uncomfortable. Maybe I'm being overly cautious.

Brady takes his time making sure I'm safely in the car. The corner of his mouth quirks up as he runs his eyes over my exposed legs. The green depths heat and I tilt my head down, hoping he can't see the smile curving my lips.

He throws me a wink and closes the door softly before jogging around the front of the car. Once he's buckled himself into the driver's seat, he pulls away from the curb.

"Hungry?" He smiles over at me.

"Yes, starving. Where are we going?"

Brady looks back to the road and I feel robbed without his gaze on me, which is dumb since he kind of has to watch the road to drive.

"You like Mexican?"

"I do," I answer, hoping there's gum in my purse.

I start to worry about what I'll order and whether I should drink or not. I remind myself this is supposed to be fun and to go with the flow, to relax.

And quesadillas are usually safe.

Brady talks about the coffee shop and his mom while he drives. I'm surprised to learn he helps her run it. That he helped her open it when he moved back from L.A. And because he did so much and put some of his own money into the business, she gave him partial ownership. I'm impressed.

I find myself smiling widely the entire time we're in the car. I know I made the right decision because I feel like a real person again.

A guilt-free person.

On a real date.

****

I slurp the last of my margarita down and

slide my empty plate to the side. Two hours have flown by and I find myself astonished. I don't want the night to end. Spending time with Brady has become a top priority. I hope he's not going to take me home after this.

Maybe be has something else planned.
Can I convince him to do something else?
I should have sipped my drink.
Slowly.

Brady watches me as he pays the bill by sliding cash into the booklet the server left behind. He ushers me out of the restaurant with a hand placed gently between my shoulder blades, his fingers brushing the naked skin above the top of my dress. That touch, the feel of his warm skin on mine, it's the only thing I can focus on. It quickly becomes my whole world. My heart races and my lungs pump. Making sure I put one foot in front of the other without stumbling and making a fool of myself becomes hard work.

We make it to Brady's SUV without me making a fool of myself. His hand slides slowly down my back, following the path of my spine while he reaches out to open my door for me. Always the gentleman, he waits until I'm in to close it and winks at me through the window before smiling and jogging around to his side of the car.

The glint in his eyes is a bit mischievous.

He twists the key in the ignition and looks over to me with raised eyebrows. "One more stop."

Not taking me home then.

I smile wide, then narrow my eyes at him.

"Are you going to tell me what it is?"

He seems to be big on surprises, which is something I've had enough of in my lifetime. But I know when I ask the question he's not going to answer me. I think he enjoys seeing me squirm.

"No." He laughs when I scowl at him. "Just trust me, babe."

There's that word again. Babe.

I swoon and try to hide my smile. I do a good job. I think.

It's not long before Brady's driving us just past the Farley city limits. He turns down a gravel drive. My curiosity is piqued. We pull up to a darkened house with a small barn and a good amount of land.

I swallow thickly before throwing him a questioning look. I don't have a clue what we could be doing out here. I don't think this is Brady's house, but I could be wrong.

"What happened to trusting me?" he asks with a chuckle as he unbuckles his seat belt and climbs from the vehicle.

I do the same and follow him around the car.

I watch, unsure, as he grabs a stack of blankets and a small cooler from the back. My nerves amp up as I look around. We're seriously in the middle of nowhere.

I'm not sure I'm ready for whatever Brady has in mind, but deep down, I know he won't push me for anything I don't want. Swallowing my anxiety, I follow him up to the house.

"It's my cousin's house." He pauses, as if he doesn't want to say anymore. His words are careful when he does speak again. "She's deployed."

I wait for the usual feelings to come.

Dread. Guilt. Horror.

And they do, but they're dull and don't pack the normal punch.

It's a good feeling.

"And?"

"Just hold on. I've got to grab something."

Brady takes a flashlight and jogs around the side of the house, taking my only source of light with him. Once he's rounded the corner, it's pitch black. I try my hardest to fight the urge to look over my shoulder. Now that I'm all alone, the darkness is eerie. I chew the inside of my cheek and step closer to the house. A few minutes pass before Brady emerges, bringing back the light. He's holding something up triumphantly and I squint into the dark, trying to make it out.

A key.

"A key? Okay ..." I'm still in the dark about what we're doing here, but I really hope we aren't breaking and entering.

"What did I say?" He looks at me. "Trust me," he finishes.

"Babe," I mutter sarcastically.

Apparently, my voice wasn't as low as I thought. Brady laughs, the warm sound curling my toes. I flush from my hair to the tips of my feet.

Thank God it's dark out.

He gestures me up onto the porch.

"Now what?" I ask once I'm standing by the front door.

"We're going in."

"I kind of figured that out, but why?"

He gathers up the cooler and blankets before joining me.

"Well, we either go in or climb a ladder. And you're wearing that dress ..." his voice drops, deepening as his eyes roam over my legs again, "so I figured the best way to go up, is to go in."

The smirk he gives me is a bit naughty and a

lot hot, so I'm guessing he'd be totally fine with the ladder. I must be looking at him like he's crazy because he laughs again.

"Fine. There's a meteor shower tonight. My cousin has the perfect place to watch it."

The center of my chest feels tight and tingly.

Is this guy for real?

Watching a meteor shower is one of the sweetest date ideas. Ever. A girl could definitely get used to things like sweet dates and sexy guys checking her out.

Brady unlocks the door and switches off his flashlight as he reaches inside. It's clear he's done this before. When the light just inside the door comes on, I step inside behind him, my eyes roaming over the interior.

The house is beautiful.

Old, but restored. It has a twist of modern flair without losing its historic charm. I want a full tour, but Brady leads me quickly up stairs that creak beneath our feet. We take a second set and come to a closed door at the top. Brady twists a key already sitting in the lock and swings it open. I peer through the open door and it takes my breath away, leaving me in awe.

"My cousin restored the entire house when

she moved in. She added this." His voice holds a soft reverence, telling me what stands before us affects him in the same way it does me.

He takes my hand and pulls me onto the rooftop patio complete with its own garden. His touch lingers, his fingers lightly caressing my palm and holding on for longer than necessary. I give him a shy smile and he beams back at me. I want to tighten my grip, hold onto him and not let go. Just as the thought filters through my mind, our fingers lose touch.

Flipping another switch turns on soft twinkle lights that allow us to see but do nothing to detract from our open view of the country sky. Brady busies himself, spreading out one of the blankets while I look up, taking in all the stars shining bright in the clear sky. Once he's satisfied, Brady holds his hand out to me, drawing me to him and toward the blanket spread out for us. We settle in side by side and Brady covers my legs with another blanket before reaching into the cooler.

"Water or beer?" he asks without looking at me.

"Beer." I haven't been much of a drinker since Mason died, fearing the emotions that may come leaking out of me if I lowered my inhibitions. But I'm having a good time with Brady, and I know

I'm safe, so I'm throwing caution to the wind.

Brady pops the caps off two beers and hands me one. The bottle is wet and cold, making me shiver. Brady shifts, scooting closer until his side brushes mine. I shiver again. This time for a reason other than the cold bottle I'm gripping tightly in my hand.

"Okay, if you watch in this direction," he points to the right, "we should be able to see it."

Sweeping my gaze across the starlit sky, I take a sip of my beer. It really is amazing up here. So clear, the stars twinkle above us, and you can see everything for miles.

It's perfect.

"Do you do this a lot?"

Brady shrugs. "Not really. When I was a kid."

"It's beautiful," I murmur.

From the corner of my eye, I see Brady nodding. When I turn to look at him, he's gazing back at me. It's so wonderfully cheesy, I can't do anything but smile.

"What?" he asks.

"Nothing." I take another sip of my beer and lay back against the blanket. Brady sinks down next to me, his arm brushing mine.

When the first meteor streaks across the

blackened sky, I sigh, following its bright burning tail until it disappears, slowly extinguishing, until poof, it's nothing but a memory.

This moment … this moment is the perfect one. This whole night, it's all so perfect. I'm absolutely, one hundred percent in love with it and the way I feel right now.

Brady shifts, rolling to his side, bringing his mouth right to my ear. My pulse thunders, throbbing in my neck. My chest heaves as his breath treks across the skin of my neck. I feel the brush of his soft lips and my eyes drift shut as goosebumps pebble along my arms.

"Don't forget to make a wish," he whispers before drawing back and propping himself up on his elbows. There's a rush of cool air as his warmth leaves me, making me want to drag him back so I can press myself against him.

Stars begin to fall, drawing my attention. They streak across the sky here and there as I search the recesses of my mind for my wish. I give Brady a sidelong glance before letting my head fall fully to the side, running my eyes over him.

What do you wish for when you've lost everything?

I run my tongue across suddenly dry lips, scanning his profile.

My eyes clamp shut and I send a silent prayer up toward the stars. Tears burn my eyes and I lurch up into a sitting position. Brady sits too, turning to face me. His eyes roam my face, the corners of his lips curling upward. He tucks the blanket around my legs in a sweet gesture of comfort.

Since Mason died, I've often wondered how long it takes to move on. How long it takes before you don't feel wrong about it. Is it the same for every person? What amount of time is too short? What will people think when I do? If I do?

When I look at Brady, those things don't matter anymore, but I'm not sure what that means, even though it feels good. So good.

I lean forward, closer to him. Brady's eyes track the movement, his expression serious but his lips tilt upward. Something hot slides through me when his eyes flick down to my mouth. I move even closer. Our lips meet, mine touching his first. The thrill that shoots through me short-circuits my brain. I freeze, my mouth pressed to his.

All I can think about is how soft and warm his perfect lips are under mine while I remain unmoving, pressed against him, stealing his breath, his warmth.

A chuckle slips through, vibrating against

me, and he pulls back a little. His eyes search my face. For what, I don't know, but they scan my features intently.

"What do you want, Cora?" he mutters huskily, caressing me with his words.

That question again.

His tongue snakes out, dragging across his lips. As he does this, it brushes against my mouth and my stomach dips, muscles clenching. Heat like nothing I've ever felt curls through me, wrapping around my limbs. It penetrates me deep, all the way to my core. Lust fires in my veins, scorching my blood, but even that deep, hot desire is filled with the need for more. I want his kiss, desperately. I also want his kind sweetness just as much. His warm smiles and his laughs, the safety I feel when he's around—if I can have it all, I should surely take it.

I know the words that will seal my fate.

The words that will get me what I want.

I brace myself. Once I say them, I know there will be no turning back. I'm opening myself up to all the things I've fought since Brady and I met, as well all the things I thought I lost when Mason died, and maybe even some things I never knew existed.

I take a second, basking in this moment. It's

peaceful, calm, unlike the hurricane usually swirling inside me. I smile at Brady and take a deep breath.

"Kiss me," I demand, a little breathlessly.

As soon as the words fall from my lips, he moves in, pressing close to me, just like he said he would. I asked, and he's making it happen. Only, he seems to be a lot better at this kissing thing than I am—a hell of a lot better.

Brady presses his lips to mine, their softness cushions mine. My mind instantly goes blank as too many sensations rush over me. I can't keep up.

His hand circles the wrist I'm using to prop myself up and grasps gently, lowering me to my back. His other hand wraps around the side of my neck, just below my ear. Fingers plunge into my hair, his palm wide and warm. His thumb extends, making its way across the front of my neck and rubbing against my racing pulse. There no hiding how into this I am. The proof is thumping rapidly beneath his thumb. If he didn't know before, he certainly does now.

Brady takes my bottom lip between his and sucks softly, causing me to shudder. The sensations he's igniting launch me into motion.

I'm no longer unmoving.

I press myself into his body, crushing his lips with mine.

Hard.

He nips at me before sweeping his tongue across my mouth. Gasping, I open for him. His tongue swoops in, sending chills across my shoulders and down my arms as fire burns through my muscles. The feel of his tongue rasping against mine turns me on like nothing before. It's a straight shot of warmth to a place I thought was dead.

Breaking away, Brady puts a small amount of space between us, but I wrap my free hand around his neck, drag him back, and swoop my tongue into his mouth, taking over. A small groan comes from between his lips slipping into my mouth. I swallow it down and revel in the reaction I'm drawing from him.

It's mine.

All mine.

I won't give it back and I won't share it.

When I finally let him go, we're both panting, chests pressed together. He's hard against my thigh and I'm in desperate need of dry panties. Licking my swollen lips, I couldn't be happier.

11

Closing down the dance studio has become second nature to me. I can run through the list of duties on autopilot, making the end of the day a snap. Especially since I've become preoccupied with the man that works across the street lately.

As I run a dust mop over the floor, my eyes drift to the window where I have the perfect view of Brunette Brew. The urge to make my way across the street when I'm done is strong, but I'm unsure of whether such an action would be welcome. I waffle, trying to decide. I know Brady is working. I want to say hi, to see his handsome face and feel his strong arms around me, but I don't want to look too stalkerish.

It's been two weeks since our first date.

I've seen Brady a handful of times since then.

He still shows up as I'm locking up and takes

me on walks. We talk and learn little things about each other. We've been to a movie and to dinner again. Is an impromptu drop by too much? Too soon?

We haven't talked about where we stand with one another. We haven't defined our relationship—if that's what it is. And while we've held hands and he's always finding reasons to brush against me or kiss me, I don't want to push too far.

When I look down to see I've been cleaning the same spot on the floor for the last few minutes, I groan. With my thoughts already in the café, I decide I'm done for the day.

I change in the office, pulling a dress over my head and slipping on flipflops. Tucking my dance clothes in my bag, I zip it up and leave the office, still unsure of what I'm doing. Distracted, I flip light switches as I make my way back to the front door. With my purse and bag over my shoulder, I dig around to find my keys and move to pull the door open. My lips instantly curl upward when I come face-to-face with the man on my mind.

Brady stands just inside the door, a few bags dangling from his hands. My mood is instantly lighter, happier. The sight of him sends a shiver

down my spine. I try to hide my reaction, not wanting to seem too eager, but I fail miserably. It's okay, though, because he's giving me a smile of his own—one that tells me he's just as happy to see me.

I step closer without even meaning to.

"Happy birthday, Cora." Brady leans down to brush my cheek with his lips and electric tingles zip across my skin, lighting me up like fireflies on a warm night.

Inhaling sharply, I can't hide my surprise.

I mentioned my birthday in passing, but we didn't make plans. My birthday isn't something I normally make a big deal out of, it's just another day. The fact that Brady took the time to remember and surprise me is incredibly sweet and thoughtful. I'm still getting used to it. The way he is. I always feel like a priority. He makes me feel special, without even trying.

I'm speechless for a moment, running my gaze over him, taking him in.

"Thank you," I say as what I'm seeing really clicks.

He's wet.

Drenched from head to toe.

"You're all wet." *Obviously.*

I frown and look out the window behind

him to see rain pouring from the sky. It must've started when I was changing. How I didn't notice is beyond me. I blame Brady. Damn distractingly handsome man.

"Yeah." He runs a hand through his rain-darkened hair. Drops of water roll down his neck and cling to the skin above his collarbone.

I lick my lips the way I want to lick the moisture from him.

I try to focus and stop my thoughts from landing right in the gutter, but I can't seem to help it around him. The more time we spend together, the more he affects me.

It scares me, but at the same time, I like it.

"I had a picnic planned, but that's ruined," he says, drawing my attention away from those little beads of moisture I'm quickly becoming jealous of. He gives me as shrug and a carefree smile, like his plans being ruined doesn't matter to him at all. He so good at letting things go, moving on. His carefree attitude is one of the sexiest things about him.

I still can't believe he's here. Or that he's planned something when we hadn't talked about it. He asked me about my plans, but I brushed it off.

My eyes dart over his shoulder again. The

rain isn't letting up. I bite my lip, silently cursing Mother Nature. I hate that his picnic is ruined. It doesn't mean that our entire night has to be called off. I'm going to make the best of this moment.

Reaching out, I take the bags from him and set them on the floor. He unbuttons his gray plaid shirt and wipes his hand across his neck. I start looking through the bags to see what he brought me, trying to come up with a solution. We could always go to my place, but that means going outside. And that's something I don't want to do in the pouring rain.

"We can just have a picnic here," I say with a laugh. It's actually pretty perfect.

My laughter dies on my lips as I look up just in time to see Brady pull off his shirt and hang it over the back of a chair. He's left in jeans and a slightly damp white t-shirt that clings to his chest and arms.

What a chest. And those arms. He's so leanly muscled. Carved and sinewy. No bulk, but you can still tell he's strong.

My mouth goes dry at the sight and a surge of desire pumps through me—hard. A feeling that had become foreign to me until Brady walked into my life. He's awakened something long forgotten and now I can't seem to calm myself down. I'm a giant ball of hormones whenever he's near, aching and heated.

He raises his head and meets my gaze, a knowing smile curving his lips. His own eyes heat as he watches me watch him. He clears his throat before making his way toward me with determined steps. I can feel the redness creeping into my cheeks and I want to look away, but I can't break his gaze. I hate that I wear his effect so plainly on my skin.

My heart thunders.

He steps closer, leaning down to scoop up the bags by my feet and gives the end of my nose a tap.

He flashes me a cocky smirk as he straightens and I let out a *whoosh* of a breath.

"Okay, dance studio picnic it is."

Catching me by surprise, yet again, he swoops in and plants his lips on my temple. Such a soft, sweet gesture. A rush of something unknown squeezes at my chest, making it hard to breathe, but not in a bad way.

We spread the blanket he brought out in the middle of the wooden floor and Brady drops his phone in the dock by the piano. He scrolls through until he finds what he's looking for and makes his way back, kicking off his shoes. Soft music flows around us as he settles himself next to me.

The happiness flowing through me has me a little on edge. I shake it off and try to bring myself back to the here and now. I'm tired of waiting for the other shoe to drop.

Bags rustle.

"So, what did you bring me?" I pull my legs up and tuck them beneath me as he starts to unpack the goodies.

"Well," he says, setting two plastic cups between us, "I brought turkey sandwiches, because I know how you love my turkey sandwiches, beer— the kind you like—grapes, cheese, some chips, and a surprise." He raises an eyebrow and gives me a look that says he's knows I'm going to ask about the surprise. It's a silent challenge.

As he talks, he spreads the food out before us. Except the surprise. Of course.

I lift my chin defiantly, trying my hardest to hold in the words.

I can't take it.

"What's my surprise?" I lean forward, grabbing the edge of the bag.

He swats my hand playfully and sticks the bag behind him.

"It's a surprise, like I said." He gives me a smug grin as he hands me a sandwich wrapped in plastic.

I unwrap it and pull the bread away to see what's on it before taking a bite.

"No onion, but with tomato and mayo," he says, grinning. He learned about my hatred for onions when we were in the woods a few weeks ago.

He remembered.

My heart swells.

I'm the damn Grinch around him, my heart growing all the time.

Brady pours beer into the cups between us and nudges one closer to me. I chew and watch as he unwraps his own food. I don't have one ounce of regret that I've taken this chance with him. Believe me, I've looked. I've searched the dark crevices of my heart and mind, looking for something to tell me I shouldn't be doing this, and I found nothing.

"Thank you, this is really nice," I say, feeling a little overwhelmed by his gesture. It happens often when he does and says nice thing. It makes me feel vulnerable and it's hard not to retreat into myself. But I want to make sure he knows I appreciate it, in case I forget to say so later.

Brady doesn't respond. He just looks back at me, his eyes soft. He busies himself with his own

food and I study him while I can. While I'm free of his intense gaze on me. A warm rush of gratitude for his patience flows through me. He could've walked away, he could push me, but he didn't, and he doesn't.

I don't know many men like him.

I didn't think they existed.

On my hands and knees, careful of the food spread between us, I move closer to him. He looks up, meeting my gaze as I lean in. Surprise flares in his eyes as I brush his lips with mine. His hand lands on the back of my neck, tugging me closer as he tilts his head and deepens the kiss. It goes from sweet and soft to needy and blazing in seconds. His tongue snakes its way across my mouth before he plunges it inside. He reaches deep, grazing my own, and I gasp.

The sound seems to snap Brady to his senses and he drops his hand before pulling back a little. Heavy breaths wash over my lips. His eyes are darker than I've ever seen them. He leans back in and gives me one last heated kiss but pulls away before we can get too lost.

Confusion twists my lips and they turn down with his rejection.

"Sorry," he rasps.

He's breathing heavily. I'm breathing

heavily. I don't understand what just happened, I just know I feel bereft and alone without him touching me.

I scoot away from him, settling myself onto the blanket.

Sorry?

Cold seeps into my bones.

I finish eating with stiff movements, hating the doubts plaguing my mind. Rejection isn't a feeling I've prepared myself for and I don't know what to do. Everything he says and does makes me think he wants me, but the second things get heated between us, he pulls away. Am I reading the signs wrong?

Silence stretches between us and for the first time since we've met, it's uncomfortable. Done with my food, I pick at my chipping nail polish and keep my head down so he can't see my face. Brady clears his throat. I hear it, but it doesn't really register as I focus on a stubborn corner. Warm, strong fingers grasp my chin and tilt my head up.

"Cora," Brady's voice is soft, pleading, and I lift my eyes slowly, "you okay?"

There's not a single hint of the rejection I'm feeling in his green depths.

I nod.

I don't know what to say.

I'm not about to let my insecurities loose on him. He's had enough of that since he stumbled upon me. His eyes search my face and his mouth turns down slightly, a crease forming between his eyebrows. The music in the background changes to something slow and soft. Brady gives me a tender look.

"Dance with me?" He stands, holding out his hand for me.

"Here?" I scrunch my face up, unsure.

Brady gestures around the room.

"This is a dance studio. That's what it's for."

He gives me a boyish grin, the one that never fails to make me smile.

This time when he reaches down, I take his hand and let him pull me up without hesitation.

I don't know how this will work since he's so much taller than I am, but he quickly proves it doesn't matter. With a gentle tug, Brady pulls me close, my hands landing on his hard chest. His large palm spans my waist, his fingers gripping my hip.

Brady pulls me closer, until we're chest to chest, and starts to sway. I can't tear my eyes away from his. Trapped in a sea of green, his manly smell engulfs me. It's warm, rich, and spicy. A shaky breath leaves my lips. I feel warm and safe and the furthest from lonely I've felt since Mason died.

   The way his hands grip me tightly is making me dizzy. The hard press of his body against mine tells me all I need to know about the way he feels. In his arms, my doubt seems far away, ridiculous even.

   Leaning in close, Brady runs his nose along my jaw, starting at my ear and making his way down. He inhales against my skin and my own breath hitches. Warmth races from my cheeks, down my chest, through my stomach, and straight to my core. I tremble against him. He hasn't even kissed me, he's barely touched me, and I'm completely worked up.

   With a ragged breath, I turn my face into his, feeling the brush of his stubble. Our noses rub together and even that feels good. My skin feels like an electrical mine field and every time he rubs against me, something detonates and crackles through me. I find his mouth with mine, seeking the kiss I'm tired of waiting for him to give me.

   Our lips meet.

   We press closer together.

   I go up on the tips of my toes and push my tongue inside his mouth, earning a low groan from him. The sound makes me weak-kneed. Without Brady's strong arms banded around me, I'd have hit the floor already.

The second my lips touch his again, everything begins to spiral out of control. Brady sucks in a sharp breath and I push myself against him, fighting to get closer, even though there's no space between our bodies. Our tongues tangle desperately and Brady's big hands smooth up and down my waist, the tips of his strong fingers digging in.

My hands roam over his chest before moving lower to bump over the hard ridges of muscle that make up his abs. I can feel everything beneath his clothes and I want to see it with my eyes. My fingers find the hem of his shirt and I slide them underneath. His stomach sucks inward as his muscles jump beneath my touch. He groans, angling me backward. His grip and control over my body as he holds me suspended sends my blood racing.

His skin is hot and smooth and I can't get enough. I want to touch him everywhere, all at once. Brady breaks the kiss and drags his lips to my neck. His tongue sweeps across my pulse point before I yank his shirt over his head.

His fingers glide beneath the thin straps of my dress. Slowly, he slips them off my shoulders, the tips of his fingers raising goosebumps as he pushes the fabric down. Warm lips press to my collarbone as Brady frees my arms and lets my dress fall to my waist.

He pulls back, running his hungry eyes over my bare skin. His gaze on me, hot and needy, like a touch.

A soft caress.

One I want more of.

He's not moving and I need him to. I need something to take the edge off the desire coursing through me, so I do the only thing I can think of. A low sound tears from his throat as I palm his hard dick through his jeans.

"I'm trying really hard not to push you," he whispers against my skin as he pulls me back to him. His hands roam down and grab my ass, fisting handfuls of my dress.

I moan.

His erection presses against my stomach.

My whole body flushes.

He rocks his hips.

I look up into electric eyes. They hold so much hot lust and want in their depths, I could combust from his look alone, yet he's holding back. For me. Because he wants to make sure I'm ready. This moment seals the deal for me.

I'm ready.

I want this.

With him.

I crush my mouth against his and fumble with his belt and the button on his jeans, my hands shaking. His teeth sink into my bare shoulder as he buries his head there. Brady lets loose a low growl and pulls me into the hard line of his body. His strong hands push my dress off my hips, leaving me in nothing but my lacy, black boyshorts. As soon as my dress hits the floor, Brady grasps my waist again, hands hot against my bare flesh. His tongue swoops inside my mouth and I think I might black out.

White dots dust my vision.

I stutter out a breath.

Pleasure like I've never known works through me. I'm panting as I push Brady's jeans down. He's wearing tight, black boxer briefs that do nothing to hide the outline of his hard cock.

Letting me go abruptly, he walks back toward the piano bench. He runs a hand down his face as his eyes rake over me.

His chest heaves with the effort of his breathing. I can tell he's trying to get himself together. To find some control.

I'm frozen in place as he stares.

"I don't want you to regret this," he grits

out. "I said I wouldn't push you. So, if you want me, you're going to have to come get me."

A thrill zings through me. His words mean so much.

They reach something deep inside me.

He's once again giving me an out, but this time, I don't need one.

I make my way toward him, my steps sure.

My hips sway. I feel sexier than I ever have before. And I know I've never seen anything as sexy as Brady sitting there in nothing but his underwear waiting for me to seduce him. His tongue flicks out and runs over his lips as I move closer.

I step between his spread legs and his gorgeous eyes look up at me as his warm fingers hook into the waistband of my panties. He doesn't pull them down. Instead, his eyes roam over my body, lingering on the tattoos normally hidden beneath my clothes. I search his face, looking for something to tell me what he thinks of them.

His fingers flutter over the riot of black birds that start at my right hip and break apart, flowing up and over my ribcage. My eyes drift shut and I swallow thickly as he moves his other hand to gently caress the image of Mason's dog tags on my other side. Brady leans in and presses his lips to the coiled chain. The touch is so light and tender, filled

with so much emotion, I can't breathe.

Tears prick my eyes. This man is kissing my dead husband's mark on my body as if it's nothing.

For the first time in a long time, maybe ever, I feel like a lucky girl.

Carefully, I climb onto his lap, my legs on either side of his thighs. His hips thrust upward, wrenching a whimper from me. I lower my mouth to his, kissing him hungrily.

"I want you," I pant into his mouth.

He murmurs something that sounds like an agreement, but isn't really words. Standing, I boldly slip my boyshorts off. Brady watches them fall to the ground, his eyes glowing brighter as they stay glued to the scrap of lace on the floor before slowly skimming up my legs.

The air is cool against my naked skin, but the look in Brady's eyes sets me on fire.

Lowering myself to my knees in front of him, I tug at his black boxer briefs. Brady watches me through downcast lashes, lifting his hips to let me pull them off. I suck in a sharp breath as his hard length bobs free. Licking my lips, I move closer and sink my teeth into his thigh.

A sharp breath hisses through his lips.

Gripping the hair at the nape of my neck, he tangles his fingers there and tugs my head back so I have to look him in the eye. He pins me with a hard, sexy look that has me panting and climbing up to straddle him.

Forget foreplay. Who needs that when sex oozes from his gaze?

My legs slide over his as I slowly lower myself onto his lap. I try to fight against the urge to grind down against him, but I can't stop myself. I roll my hips against his length, feeling all of him. I'm so wet, his cock slides through easily, hitting the perfect spot. I repeat the movement, rocking harder, and this time, he meets the motion with a thrust of his own.

Our lips meet in a desperately deep, heated kiss. Brady leans back and lands on the piano keys, filling the room with disjointed tones.

I giggle. He curses.

His lips are back on mine within a few breaths, stealing my thoughts and filling my brain with nothing but him.

His touch.

His scent.

His kiss.

Him. Him. Him.

His mouth moves over my neck and my chest before his tongue snakes over my nipple and his lips follow suit, sucking. His mouth is warm and the pressure sends tingles straight between my thighs. My hips rock uncontrollably and a whimper wrenches from between my lips as he opens his mouth wider, drawing more skin, sucking harder. He can't seem to get enough, and that's okay. Because however much he wants, I want more.

All I want is him.

Inside me, stretching me.

Filling me.

Making me lose myself.

"Condom," Brady mutters roughly against the skin of my breast, his deep voice vibrating against me, but he doesn't take his mouth from me.

Instead, he slides his lips against the sensitive skin between my breasts and to my other nipple. Meeting my gaze, he runs his tongue over it slowly.

He said something. I know it. But I can't take my eyes off of him and my mind is too muddled to know what words just came out of his mouth.

I pant and clutch his shoulders, trying to clear the pleasure-induced fog I'm living in.

It finally sinks in.

"What? Where?" I ask, my chest heaving.

I moan when Brady gives a sharp tug on my

nipple. He watches me as he oh-so-slowly drags his tongue up to my collarbone. The sound that comes barreling out of my throat is pretty embarrassing, but his mouth on my skin feels way too good.

It's been too long since I've been touched this way.

His arms loosen and he kisses me quickly once more before releasing me fully.

"My pants," he responds and my lips turn down a bit because he's lost me.

Oh, right. Condom. In his pants.

Giving myself a little shake, I take a deep breath.

I stand on shaking legs, anticipation coursing through me at a rapid pace. Snagging his pants, I drag them to him. He gives me a cocky grin as he digs a hand into his pocket, searching. Arousal flares in the depths as I watch him.

He tears the condom open quickly and I watch in fascination as he rolls it down the length of his hard, thick cock. Something unknown settles into the pit of my stomach as I stand before him—nerves, guilt ... I can't name it.

I feel exposed and cold without the heat of Brady's body. Fear of what we're about to do lances through me.

Thickness swells in my throat.

I gulp.

Before I can question what I'm doing, his hands are back on my waist. I love it, the feel of his large hands spanning my curves, the way his touch takes all my fears away. It's instant. The second his skin touches mine, I remember why I'm doing this and forget all my doubts.

Our eyes lock and Brady's hands start to move, slowly. They glide down my sides, skimming over my hips, touching every inch of skin they pass with reverence. His eyes follow the path his fingers take, his gaze hot and hooded. One hand stops, fingers gripping my ass, while the other continues on its path, until he's sliding his fingers around the back of my knee. He tugs lightly and I take his lead, letting him pull me so I'm straddling him again. My thigh moves over his grazing softly, the friction rushing through me. I whimper in anticipation.

Brady kisses me deeply. When he backs away, I lean in for more, desperate for his taste. The small sample he just gave me wasn't enough. I need more. I need him to consume me, or I need to consume him. I don't know which is truer. All I know is I've never been as needy as I am right now.

I need him.

Every part of him.

On me.

In me.

All around me.

My tongue slips out, running over my lips.

"Take it, if you want it," he grunts as he pulls me down and thrusts his hips against me, as if to accentuate his point.

I take a deep breath, steeling my nerves.

I smile down at him, hoping it's sexy, but I don't know if it is. Reaching between us, I wrap my hand around his cock and stroke him slowly. His tip hits my clit, causing me to suck in a breath before lining him up and slowly sliding down. As I sink deeper into Brady's lap, my eyes roll back.

I pause, breathless, unable to process the sensations rolling though me at the feel of Brady stretching me from the inside out.

"Brady," I gasp, needing to be grounded.

This is so intense. It's so much more than I thought it would be. His name is a desperate plea for something, but I don't know what.

Thick arms wrap around me, bringing me closer. His warm breath washes over my chin as he leans in. The movement pushes him deeper and my muscles clench, causing him to groan and shift beneath me.

So many things cross my mind, but one

thing sticks out, I've never felt something this amazing before. Not just him inside me, or maybe it is the feeling of him, but not just physically. I haven't felt anything like this for anyone else. *Ever*. Guilt over Mason surges for a second.

If I'd felt even half of this with my husband, my life would have been very different, but then I wouldn't be here. With Brady. And the truth is, Mason's gone, and there's nowhere I'd rather be. Whatever I'm feeling is big. And I like it.

I want to keep it.

More, more, more, my head, and heart, and body demand.

Soft lips flutter over my neck and a shudder barrels through me. I roll my hips and wrap my arms around Brady's neck. I slide up and down, moving faster and faster. Brady's grip tightens. Soon, we're both moving, pushing and pulling, my moans echoing and mixing with his deeper grunts.

My body is on fire, muscles tight. I'm slipping further and further away from myself and into something that feels so, so good. My eyes snap open to find Brady's closed, his full lips parted. He's gorgeous and sexy. He must sense my gaze, his eyes flick open and meet mine. With a rough hand on my chin, he pulls my face to his and nips my bottom lip with his teeth.

Heat flashes through me, spreading like wildfire. Brady's body tenses, his grip tightens, and that's all I need. My inner walls contract, pure bliss shoots through me. I arch backward as my orgasm takes over. My rocking hips falter, but Brady's grip keeps me moving, wringing every last cry and spasm from me. My name falls from his lips in a hoarse whisper and he thrusts into me a few more times.

I lean into him, panting. Our chests brush as he pulls me closer and nuzzles the side of my face. A laugh slips from my lips. I can't help it. I've never felt so free and satisfied in my life.

"You're always laughing at me," Brady mumbles against my shoulder.

Pulling away, I laugh again. He smiles back at me. "I'm not laughing at you. I promise."

"I'd hope not. It's been a while, but I didn't think I was that rusty."

"Not at all," I reassure him. Now, I'm wondering how long it has been but I won't ask. I'm enjoying my blissed-out state too much.

I drop a kiss on his reddened lips and he groans, tightening his hold on me. His lips curve against my mouth.

After a few minutes, Brady lifts me from his lap. I pull on my boyshorts before settling onto the blanket with my dress in my hands. He pulls his underwear back on and joins me, giving me a light kiss on the forehead.

"Can I have my surprise now?"

"That was it," he says, straight-faced. For a second, I don't get it, and then I laugh, because really ... that's cheesy. He smiles and hands me his shirt. "Put this on first, you're distracting me."

I pull his shirt over my head and making sure to breathe in his rich scent. Brady opens a box to reveal two cupcakes. He even pulls a candle out and sticks it in one. He's thought of everything. This has been the best birthday I've had in a while.

I make a wish and peel the paper away. As I take a bite, Brady looks around the studio.

"Do you think anyone saw us?"

I follow his gaze to the window.

Ah, yes, that.

Like I'd get naked and down and dirty and let everyone in this town watch.

"Mesh blinds. We can see out, but they can't see in."

I waggle my brows and stuff the rest of my cupcake in my mouth.

"Good to know," he says, voice low, a sexy smirk playing across his lips.

Britni Hill

12

As I pull onto my parents' street, I'm still grinning too widely. It's been a whole day and whenever I think of Brady, I can't help but smile. Which is a lot. Seriously, a lot.

It's all Brady's fault.

He made my birthday more than memorable. It was perfect.

We eventually pushed our makeshift picnic to the side and used the blanket to cuddle up on the studio floor, our hands laced together, and talked until four in the morning. The rain still hadn't let up, so he drove me home and insisted on walking me to the door where he dropped a smoldering kiss on my lips and gave me a heated look. His sandy hair was mussed from my hands and he was missing his shirt because I was still wearing it. I'd been so close to asking him to stay, but I hadn't.

I couldn't.

Something churns in the back of my mind, telling me it's too fast, too soon, too much. Eventually, I'm going to have to deal with that voice, my doubts.

My guilt.

Right now, I'm just enjoying him. My phone lights up in the cup holder and I have a feeling it's Brady.

He's been texting me all day and these little messages from him are quickly becoming my favorite thing.

I turn my car into my parents' driveway and park before reaching over to check the message. I'm cheesing hardcore and kind of surprised I remember to put the car in park before grabbing my phone. I'm so excited to see what he's said to me, it's a little embarrassing. Good thing no one is around to see me.

Brady: Spend the day with me tomorrow? I have an idea …

Reading his words brings the flutter in my chest to life again.

Who am I kidding? It never went away, it just thunders with a quickness now.

Taking a deep breath, I forced myself to relax.

I debate calling to cancel this birthday dinner with my parents, but I'm already in the driveway and chances are they heard me pull in. The anticipation of seeing Brady tomorrow will likely drive me crazy, but I tell myself it's something to pass the time between now and then. Plus, they're my parents.

I type a quick 'yes' and tuck my phone into my purse. I'm curious about this idea of his, but I don't have time to ask. Plus, I've already learned that Brady loves to surprise me, so I doubt he'd tell me even if I did.

With a deep breath, I let myself into my childhood home, passing my dad in the recliner in the living room. He doesn't even bother to look up from the TV even though the front door closes with a clap behind me. I try to ignore the sting of his rejection

I keep moving through the house, not stopping to say a hello of my own.

Mom is in the kitchen pulling something from the oven when I finally find her. The smell of home-cooked food makes my stomach rumble. It's the one thing I miss about living here. My apartment never has fresh made meals in it. Who wants to cook for one?

"Hi, Mom," I say, tossing my purse and keys

onto the counter. My mom spins around, greeting me with a smile.

"Hi, baby. Happy birthday." She makes her way around the counter and drops a warm kiss on my cheek.

"Thanks, Mom." I wrap an arm around her slender shoulders and give her a squeeze.

"Did you say hi to your dad?"

I can see the look she's giving me from the corner of my eye and I hate it. It's the mom look. The one I can feel in my soul. It's awful. It makes me feel ten again.

My mother has always had the uncanny ability to read me. It's almost like she can see every thought I've ever had. So, of course, I avoid looking at her now. I don't want to give anything away. Instead, I stare at the granite countertop without responding.

"Cora Elizabeth!" It's not loud, but her tone says it all.

Damn.

"No, I didn't say hi to him. He ignored the fact that I even came into the house," I admit, hating the childish tone to my voice, but it hurts so much.

"What am I going to do with you two?" my mom sighs.

I shrug and grab a stack of plates, napkins, and silverware. "I'll set the table."

This is my ploy to get her to forgive me. To change the subject.

As I place the plates and silverware on the table just so, I try hard to ignore the guilt that pings me. Maybe ignoring my dad wasn't the right thing to do, but I don't know how to approach him. It's been so long since we've really talked. When I moved home, Mom welcomed me with open arms. My father, however, couldn't seem to be around me.

Still can't.

I sigh and brush the hair from my face as I line up the last fork. Lifting my eyes from the table, I jump when I spot my dad lingering in the doorway. It's as if my thoughts have summoned him. His gaze flicks over me and I try to give him a smile, but it feels all wrong. I let it drop and my lips firm into a thin line.

"Dinner ready?" he asks without meeting my gaze. His jaw is tight and I can't help but roll my eyes.

I can't figure out what I did to make him so disappointed in me, but that's all I see when I look at him. Disappointment.

After I left with Mason, we didn't talk much.

He doesn't know about the baby or that Mason and I were going to get a divorce. Not that anyone knows those things, but it just reiterates the truth. He knows nothing about me.

Biting back the questions that want to spew forth, I watch him as he steps into the room. "I think so."

My dad moves closer and I don't know what to do. I feel trapped. I want to retreat and join my mom in the kitchen, but I also wonder where this is going. I do want to talk to my dad, I just don't know how. So I linger in the room, waiting.

I let my arms dangle awkwardly by my sides before crossing them over my chest. I open my mouth to say something, to make small talk maybe, but I don't have a clue what to bring up, so I close my mouth and say nothing instead.

"Happy birthday." His voice is gruff, like the words ripped directly from his throat.

He clears his throat just as my mom comes barreling into the room, carrying a steaming dish. She takes one look at us, her head swinging back and forth as she observes the tension, and shakes her head.

"Thank you," I finally manage to say.

I try to meet his eyes, willing him just once to allow me to see what he's thinking, but his gaze

is downcast, most likely staring at his bare feet because he hates to wear socks.

My mom busies herself with the food on the table, but we both ignore her. I wait for something more from him, but it never comes.

My heart sinks.

I feel cold.

"Well, sit down," my mom says in an exasperated tone. She drags a chair from beneath the table and plops down in it.

I stifle a groan. This dinner is going to be worse than pulling teeth. What I wouldn't give to have Brady by my side. I've started to rely on him and his calming presence, which is as surprising as it is scary.

I follow my mom's lead and sit. As soon as I've lowered myself into my seat, a giant bowl of salad is promptly shoved under my nose. And that's how it goes for the rest of dinner. We pass dishes between us in silence, the clanking of spoons and dishes the only sound filling the room. My jaw clenches as the uncomfortable silence grows. It's suffocating, bearing down on my chest. My foot starts to tap the floor beneath the table restlessly.

"So," my mom breaks the silence, "Ginger heard that you've been running around with a boy lately."

My dad is the one to sigh this time. My head snaps up and I shoot him a dirty look that he, of course, doesn't see, because he's starting at his plate. Why I thought he'd be looking at me, I don't know. Clearly, I'm delusional.

With pursed lips, I turn my attention to my mom.

I don't really know what to say.

Was that a question?

No.

She's being nosy, and next time I see Aunt Ginger, I'm going to strangle her. That thought makes me smile. Wide.

"He's not a boy," slips from my mouth, and I pretty much want to smash my face into the mashed potatoes on my plate.

"Well, you know what I mean." She's talking to me like I'm being ridiculous and I can't help but roll my eyes and bite down on the inside of my cheek.

I take a deep breath and decide to go with it.

Seems to be a theme lately.

Just. Go. With. It.

"I've been seeing someone, yes." I stall, coming up blank. That's all I've got.

Brady and I haven't defined our relationship. He's been letting me lead and I'm sorely out of practice when it comes to all this relationship stuff.

My mom looks like she wants to say something I'm probably not going to like, but she snaps her mouth shut and watches me carefully. She's considering her words as she studies me. I can't stand it. This concerned look is the same as the mom look. I start to squirm in my seat. I'm five again and she's trying to figure out what I've done wrong.

"You're okay?" she finally asks.

I freeze, every muscle in my body going stiff. I don't want to talk about this. I know she's just concerned, so I count to ten, slowly, in my head and take a deep breath. And another.

I nod in answer.

I don't know if I trust myself to speak. She's still watching me, concern filling her brown gaze. I decide to throw her a bone and be honest at the same time.

"He's good to me, Mom," I start. "He's patient and he makes me talk. We talk about— Mason." The lump in my throat is back, causing me to gulp when I swallow. My voice comes out so low, I'm not sure my parents actually heard what

I've said—that I said Mason's name.

I chance a look up and see a smile flash across my dad's face, which puzzles me. My mom still looks uncertain, but she also looks a little relieved. She reaches over to where I'm sitting and gives my hand a squeeze. When the corners of her mouth tilt up a bit, I relax. The water in her eyes is a little alarming, but I think she's happy for me.

Maybe.

"It's nice, right, Naomi?" My dad's deep voice breaks into our moment. My heart leaps and does a few quick pliés at his comment. To say I'm taken back by his sentiment is a huge understatement.

"Of course it is," she answers, and gives my dad a warm, watery smile.

I think we're both a little stunned because we move on after that and finish dinner with idle chitchat. Every now and then, I glance up to see my dad watching me with an expression I can't name. All I know is it's different from the trepidation I normally see when he looks at me. It gives me hope, even if every time I meet his gaze he looks away.

I wish I knew what it meant, though. For so long, I've wondered if my dad was mad at me for running away with Mason. I left home young and in a rush and I don't think my parents understood. But now, I don't know. I can't make sense of the way he's treated me since I moved back to Farley.

After we clear the table, my mom brings out a huge strawberry cheesecake. I refuse to let her sing *Happy Birthday* to me. I hate it. She pouts a bit, but she's used to it. I stopped letting them sing to me on my twelfth birthday.

After all the dread I felt about coming here for dinner, I'm full and oddly content as I gather my things to leave. My dad gives my arm a squeeze and retreats to the living room. I hear the TV power on and my mom's eyes linger on the doorway my dad just went through.

She gives me a grin with tears in her eyes again and I don't know what to say. All of her ping-ponging emotions this evening have drained me. I've never seen her so all over the place. I gather my things and say goodbyes carefully. Mom sends me on my way with a tight hug and a plate full of cheesecake.

Once I'm buckled into the driver's seat of my car, I finally check my phone, hoping for something from Brady.

I'm not let down.

My chest squeezes as I swipe across the screen.

Brady: I'll see you bright and early. 8 am.

Brady: Let me know when you're home safe.

13

I hit snooze.

Oh my god!

I hit snooze!

Shocked awake by panic, I jump out of bed, my heart racing.

Brady's going to be here any minute. I'm not dressed and my hair looks like birds could be nesting in it. I sprint for the bathroom. Fumbling my toothbrush, I finally manage to get a grip on it and swipe some toothpaste across the bristles.

I furiously brush my teeth with one hand while running the fingers of my other through my tangled, auburn locks. I don't have a clue what to wear, and I don't have time to figure it out before Brady's knocking on my door. I pad quickly through my apartment, my brain still fuzzy with sleep. I can't believe I'm not ready. I don't want Brady seeing me like this, but it's too late for all that.

With my hand on the doorknob, I take a deep breath.

Electric excitement rushes through me when I swing the door open.

Brady's eyes roam over me from head to toe. His gaze feels like a caress and it warms me all over, but it doesn't make me forget what I'm wearing or that I'm entirely unprepared.

"I didn't wake up." I gesture to my sleep clothes in apology.

Holding out a brown paper cup, he smiles down at me.

"Coffee?"

"Yes," I hiss excitedly and grab the cup. "Thank you."

Savoring the robust liquid, I take off for my room to get dressed.

"How was dinner at your parents?" Brady calls after me.

I shove my yoga pants down my legs, using one foot to fling them off and across the room. Turning toward my closet, I jump when I see Brady standing behind me. My heart pounds as I give a shaky laugh, pressing a hand to my chest.

"It was dinner," I answer evasively. I don't want to talk about my dysfunctional relationship with my parents, but even if I did, it would be hard

to do with the way his eyes linger on my bare legs.

Brady clears his throat. "I'm going to wait out here."

His wide shoulders are stiff as he turns to make his way out of my bedroom. A smile curves my lips. It's a good feeling, knowing I affect him the way I do. Because he definitely affects me. Bending to grab the maxi skirt I plan to wear, I get a firm smack on my ass. I squeal and look over my shoulder at a smirking Brady. Warmth pools in my stomach and my face heats. I rub a hand over my stinging cheek and raise a questioning eyebrow at him. I hadn't even heard him come back into the room.

He shrugs.

"You have a sexy ass." He pats said ass with a smug smile and finally leaves my room.

Mascara, perfume, brush my hair. I curse myself for sleeping in, but this is as good as it's going to get right now. It'll have to do. I take one more look in the mirror before I make my way to the living room where Brady's sprawled out on my couch.

A do-it-yourself show plays on the TV screen.

Something strange washes over me at the sight before me. He's obviously comfortable in my place and it's so perfect that he is. It amazes me how much I've changed in the weeks since Brady and I have grown closer. It feels good, and I want more of it.

"Where are we going today?" I ask, even though I know he's not going to give me an answer.

Brady looks up at the sound of my voice. I bite my lower lip when his eyes slide over me, taking in my purple maxi skirt and tight, white, ribbed tank. Once he's done with his perusal, a lopsided grin tugs his lips as he stands.

"Nowhere. Anywhere," he says with laughter in his eyes.

Um …

At my confusion, Brady's grin widens.

"Okay, Riddler, tell me. Please?"

Amusement brightens his handsome features before a cocky look flashes across his face. He grabs my purse from the counter and holds it out.

"Ready?" He's obviously not going to answer me.

I sigh.

I pout.

None of it's working.

His surprises are so frustrating, but I really am beginning to love them, so I nod and follow him to my door. Taking the steps two at a time, he leads me down to the street, stops next to a shiny black car, and opens the door. It's an older model and obviously well taken care of, but I've never seen him drive it.

"Where's your car?"

"This is my car," he says in a *duh* kind of way. It's clear he finds my curiosity entertaining.

"Okay," I huff. "Your other car?" I specify.

Cocking a hip, I rest my hand on it then pin him with an exasperated stare.

Brady reaches out, tucks a hand into the front of my skirt, and drags me forward. He catches me with an arm around my waist and presses me up against him. There's nothing but hot, hard male body in front of me. It's the nicest thing ever.

My breath catches in my throat and that pesky muscle in my chest races toward an unseen finish line. He smells of soap and cologne and … man. It makes my knees weak and I'm thankful for his tight grip on me. Falling would be beyond embarrassing.

Tenderly, Brady presses his lips to my cheek before dragging his nose along my skin in a light caress until he reaches my ear. His warm breath coasts over my sensitive skin and I shiver despite the spring air.

"It's in my garage," he breathes before letting go and gesturing for me to get in the car. "This car is the perfect road trip car, which is what we are doing today."

Happiness leaps inside me and that slick thing that's been wiggling around in my chest warms a little more. I climb inside the car and inhale the scent of lemons and leather upholstery as he makes his way to the driver's side.

I know nothing about cars, but I can appreciate that this one is pretty, inside and out. I take it all in and realize this car is older than I first thought. My awe of its beauty makes my only comment about its age. It slips from me without thought, earning me a look from the man next to me.

"Hey now!"

I giggle. I can't help it. His exasperation is cute.

Brady runs a hand along the dashboard lovingly.

"Yeah, she's old, but that's not a bad thing." I don't say anything, because I don't know what to say. It's cute how intense he is about this car. After a few seconds of me just staring at him, he laughs. "You don't have a clue what kind of car this is, do you?"

"Nope." I pop the 'p' and laugh. "Tell me about this road trip."

"First things first, this is a 1968 Chevy Corvair. It was my first car. My dad and I rebuilt it together. Second, we're going to start driving and stop and do whatever we want. No plan. No particular direction. Then, eventually, we'll turn around and come home."

Be still my heart.

This man. He listens to everything I say. He remembers all the important things. He's trying to make my dreams come true. The soft, gooey feelings for him inside me are growing by the second. I'm so happy.

I want to bounce around in the seat and clap, but I rein it in and smile instead.

"Road trips always make me feel free," he adds, glancing over at me. The look in his eyes is soft, aching. Almost too much. I want to hide, but he holds me there with him. My throat burns and I blink back emotion. From the moment he said it, I knew he was trying to give me the freedom I'd always wanted in his own way.

I can't tear my eyes from his. Swallowing thickly, I scoot across the bench seat and take his scruffy cheeks in my hands. The hair on his face is a little darker than the sandy tone on his head and the day old stubble he's rocking is quickly growing on me. Either way, he's sexy. And mine. I lean in and kiss him softly. Taking his bottom lip in between mine, I stroke it lightly before pulling away.

"Thank you," I whisper as I scoot back toward the window.

Brady reaches out, catching me before I make it across the seat, and drags me back. Once our thighs are brushing, he lets go, drapes a long arm over the back of the seat, and tosses me a wicked grin.

"You were too far away," he explains, his mouth against my hair.

He kisses the side of my head and turns the key in the ignition.

Swoon.

The car comes to life with a low, sexy rumble.

Brady hooks his phone to the dash and hits play.

Rock music flows around us as he pulls away from the curb with me tucked into his side, his arm back around my shoulders.

It's perfect.

19

We grab a greasy, diner breakfast that I love, then Brady drives us to the edge of town and stops. I immediately recognize the area from the night we were at his cousin's house for the meteor shower. With an arm wrapped around my shoulders, he looks my way and quirks a brow.

"Which way?" he asks.

I peer left and then right, not really knowing what we'll find in either direction. It's amazing how much I've forgotten about the area since I moved away. It doesn't matter, though. This day will be great, no matter what.

I tilt my head back and forth in indecision.

Brady watches me with an amused grin.

"Left," I blurt.

Brady doesn't hesitate.

Jerking the wheel, he steers us down the country road.

The windows are down and I'm pressed against Brady with my feet propped on the dash. My favorite songs come from the speakers and float around us before getting lost in the wind, and my cheeks start to ache from the constant smile parking itself on my face. It's been a long while since I felt this light and free.

I slide to the opposite side of the car and duck my head out the window to feel the sun and wind on my face. When I settle back into my seat, I slip off my flip flops and kick my legs up on the door, making sure to keep my skirt covering enough of my legs so I'm not flashing anyone we pass.

The song changes and as the singer croons about his next girl being nothing like his last, Brady reaches out and twines our fingers together. I glance over to find him looking at me. Something I can't name lurks in his eyes before they flick back to the road in front of us. I can't be sure, but I think Brady's been hurt.

A small town creeps onto the horizon. It might be the smallest town I've ever seen.

Brady pulls into the gas station and I spot an ice cream shop across the street. Who doesn't love a hand-dipped sugar cone on a warm day?

Bouncing up and down on the balls of my

feet while Brady pumps the gas, I give him a pleading look.

"Want to get ice cream?" I ask.

He laughs and I can't stop staring at the upward curve of his lips.

"I think the question is do you want to get ice cream?"

I take a step closer and smile up at him, doing my best to entice him.

"Yes!" I'm like a kid on Christmas, lips curving upward while I give him my best puppy dog eyes. It used to work on my dad when I was a kid.

"Then we'll get ice cream."

Brady screws the gas cap back on and takes my hand, lacing our fingers together. A small gesture, yes, but in my world, it's huge. It's still a little foreign for me to have his big palm pressed against mine, but I love it. We cross the street and as we get closer, I can see this shop is the real deal type of ice cream shop. It's cute, and small. I know everything will be amazing.

With a hand on my back, Brady pulls the door open. Every small touch is the most amazing thing to me. It's been so long since I've let someone handle me the way he does. I've never had a man be doting and caring, letting me know with little touches here and there that I mean something. Sometimes when Brady touches me, it feels like I mean everything.

The girl behind the counter smiles at us.

"What can I get you folks?"

Brady peers over her head at the menu while I look into vats of sugary goodness behind the counter.

"Can I get one scoop of mint chip in a sugar cone?"

"Of course," she answers enthusiastically. The smile hasn't left her face and I'm jealous of her perkiness.

She gets to work on my cone and before long, I'm holding it in my hand while Brady orders his butter pecan scoops. Brady pays and we head to the door.

"Have a good day!" Perky Counter Girl calls behind us.

Her smiling voice makes me smile too. "You, too."

****

Hand in hand, we stroll down the sidewalk of this picturesque little town. I'm taking it all in. It's charming, but I don't know if I could live here.

Ice cream drips down my cone, landing on my thumb, and I swipe if away with my tongue instead of letting Brady's hand go. I can feel his eyes on me, but I can't look at him. If I do, I know I'll be blushing less than a second after.

I don't understand why it happens with him, it just does. He gets me all hot and bothered with just a look. So I avoid his eyes and search for something to say.

"This town has about four streets, did you notice that?"

The small town square and one-of-a-kind restaurants amaze me.

"Not a small town girl, huh?"

I shrug. "Never thought about it. I always thought Farley was small, but this … this is so small."

Brady inhales sharply and I look over at him. His jaw is tense, his brow furrowed. I instantly wonder what I've said or done to cause this change in him. I keep my eyes on him for a second before he puts me out of my misery.

"Are you going to move away again?" Trepidation weaves its way through his tone.

Am I?

"No. I don't plan on it," I say with a frown.

When I moved back to Farley, it had been out of desperation, a need to get away from the memories, the guilt. I was running from so many things. I hadn't thought about whether I'd stay or move on. I haven't thought about it since I've been back.

My eyes drift over Brady's tall, lean form, snagging on the way his shirt hugs his chest and arms. The feel of his palm against mine is warm and soothing. I smile. I don't think I'll be leaving.

"Good." He gazes into my eyes and his hand flexes around mine, giving me a little squeeze.

I worry that he'll press the issue and I don't think I can have that conversation. I don't even know what that conversation would be, but I'm not ready for it. So when we walk a ways and he doesn't say anything else, I'm relieved.

It's getting unseasonably warm for April and I love it. The sun warms my shoulders as I pop the end of my cone into my mouth and crunch down on it.

"Ready to head out?" Brady asks as he wipes his mouth with a napkin. The action draws my gaze to his firm lips. The entire day I've felt like a live wire, one touch is all it would take to set me off. I know what it's like to be with him, so every touch, every brush, every look, is almost too much. I want to kiss him.

I nod absently to answer his question.

Then I decide to be brave.

To give in to what my body and mind both

want.

My eyes lock with his, impossible green sparkling in the sunlight. His lips curve as he watches me stretch up on my toes and lean in. Brady ducks his head when he sees my intention and meets my mouth with his. The warm, softness of his kiss is still a sweet shock. Mason's mouth was always hard and usually angry on mine. But this … this is all the things I never knew I was missing.

Brady wraps a hand around my hip, securing me to him. His tongue slides along my lower lip, making me shiver. I started this kiss, but he's completely taken it over, making it wholly his, molding and manipulating my mouth with smooth caresses. His kiss slows. He gives me another sweet peck before pulling away and resting his forehead against mine.

"Let's go." His voice is low, strung tight with something that tugs the desire coiled inside me.

We make our way to his car in comfortable silence, hands joined between us. He opens the passenger side door for me and I climb in. His hand slides down my hip and around the curve of my ass with the lightest touch, and I laugh, looking over my shoulder so he knows he wasn't sneaky enough. His grin is unapologetic.

As we move away from the town square,

things become more sparse. The streets fade into country roads and we pass a sign reading Hollow Oaks High School. I can't imagine attending a school so small.

I lean back in the seat, rest my head against the soft leather, and breathe in deeply. I'm content. Calm. My brain is quiet, which is rare. It makes me incredibly thankful I met the man sitting next to me.

****

Just after we pass the high school, I start seeing signs for a campground and Bear Paw Lake. I don't say anything, happy to be along for whatever adventure Brady takes me on, but I think it might be fun to stop there. My gaze wanders to the passing scenery as I lay my head back against the seat.

The side of the road boasts another set of signs and excitement bubbles up inside me. I can't keep quiet anymore. I really want to check out the lake. My lips curve upward as I look in Brady's direction.

"Let's go to the lake." I bounce in my seat a little and flash him my best puppy dog eyes.

He looks over, an amused smile curving his lips as he raises one eyebrow in question.

"Yeah?"

"Yes." I draw out the 's' and twine my fingers in a pleading manner.

"Whatever you want."

"Yay!" I give a little clap.

I huff a little. I've never been overly bubbly. Not that it's a bad thing, but the happiness I'm feeling is so great it's spilling over, and I don't know if that's a good thing or a bad thing. After the way the last few years have gone for me, I feel like it could all come crashing down at any second.

I'm losing my mind, bouncing from one side to the other inside my head.

Laughter bubbles up from deep inside, but I hold it in. The last thing I want is for Brady to think I'm a complete lunatic. He already has enough reasons to run from me and never look back. Hysterical laughter over nothing doesn't seem like something I should add to the list.

With no more questions asked, Brady begins following the signs and taking the turns that will lead us to the lake. Forcing my embarrassment down, I breathe in the fresh air coming from the open window.

The time I've spent with Brady so far has been more than I ever thought it would or could be. We're learning about each other slowly, moving at our own pace. I find comfort in the fact that he seems to know when to push and when to take a step back. We don't have to fill every silence with small talk. I thoroughly enjoy our walks and our dates.

Not so long ago, I hadn't been able to see a romantic future for myself. At all. There are still things I don't know how I will handle, things I don't think I'll ever be able to do, but I find myself wondering more and more what will become of this thing between Brady and I, what will become of us.

Brady runs a finger over my cheek, drawing my attention.

"What are you thinking about?" His eyes are concerned as he smiles softly at me.

"You. Me. Us," I answer honestly.

"Ah." He nods in understanding, his eyes flicking quickly over my face.

I search his gaze once more, but it gives nothing away. Usually his eyes tell me what I want to know. It worries me that that I can't read him.

Maybe there isn't an "us".

Before I can set off too far down that track, I stop myself because I don't really think that's true. I take a deep breath and make the decision to take this conversation further. There's no reason to play games. I can't afford to have my heart crushed

any more.

"Does that scare you?" I pin him with my stare and wait, watching for some sort of reaction, some indication that he doesn't want this with me.

Brady leans forward a little, sliding to the side and turning so his back is against the door. With his arm draped across the steering wheel, he's the perfect picture of lazy ease when most guys would've jumped from the car. Or so I've heard.

"Nah, I kinda figured you liked me," he drawls and flashes an arrogant smile.

He's being evasive and I don't know what to make of that. I want to think it's for my sake and not because he doesn't see a future between us. He's not usually the type to skirt around an issue. If he is, there has to be a reason.

"Yeah, okay, you got me." I hold my hands up in surrender and laugh, deciding to let it go for now. I don't want to ruin our day.

He smirks in my direction and motions me closer. I scoot over and he leans in, pressing his lips to my temple before turning back to the road.

The road in front of us turns into a dirt path and the lake comes into view. I sit forward, scanning the area. It looks fairly large. A few homes litter the shore, but there are more empty lots than anything. Places I'm guessing people camp or set up RVs and campers. Several wooden docks jut out over the water, some with boats, others without. Brady steers the car toward an isolated patch of land empty of boats or houses.

"This good?" he asks as he slows the car.

I nod and smile.

As soon as the car rolls to a stop, I'm out the door and making my way to the water. A glance over my shoulder tells me Brady is following, his steps a light jog, eating up the space between us. I whirl around, give him a flirty smile, and grasp the hem of my shirt.

"Swim with me," I say, whipping my shirt over my head, still moving backward. His eyes widen in shock, surprise, or desire—I'm not sure which. Once I hit the dock, I drop my skirt, slipping my shoes from my feet at the same time.

Turning to face Brady, I'm surprised to find him already down to his tight, navy blue boxer briefs. He's making his way toward me with determination. A shiver slides down my body, and it has nothing to do with the temperature and everything to do with the heat in his gaze.

The way his muscles ripple as he moves closer quickly grabs my attention. I'm hypnotized, unable to look away. The sun hits his hair just right

making his sandy brown hair shine with golden hues. I have a second to notice his mischievous smile before he hoists me in the air and tosses me over his shoulder. I squeal at the sudden movement. His big body shifts beneath me and he launches us off the end of the dock with my laughter echoing around us.

Cold water engulfs us, shocking my system and making my teeth chatter. I cling to Brady, seeking some semblance of warmth. We surface and I pull myself closer.

"It's so cold," I state the obvious and wrap my legs around his waist at the same time he wraps me up in his arms.

"Yep. I didn't think it would be this bad, but we haven't had enough heat to warm the water yet." His hands dip down to cup my behind, pulling me tighter against him. "Can't say I'm complaining, though."

His eyes spark with happiness and I get lost in them—in him. Again. Drops of water roll down his neck and onto his chest, landing where we're pressed flush against one another. Brady kisses the corner of my mouth softly, sweetly, and nuzzles my cheek. The tightness in my chest is making it hard to breath. Something warm uncurls lazily in my stomach.

"We should probably get out," Brady says after a moment.

Reluctantly, I unwind myself from him and swim to the ladder hanging from the side of the dock. The sun feels great on my too cold skin as I stand and drip. I stretch out on the dock, letting the rays warm me and hoping it will dry my bra and panties a bit. Brady settles himself next to me and my eyes drift closed. Warm fingers skim over my neck and across my cheek, soft and lingering, barely a caress before they slide back down to my shoulder, his lips following his movement. His fingers continue on sending goose bumps across my skin. A gratified sound slips from my lips and I don't need to look at him to see the cocky smirk he's wearing.

Brady chuckles softly.

"Tell me about your band, about L.A.," I whisper, afraid to disturb the quiet intimacy between us.

Brady's fingers falter for a moment and I peer at him through one cracked eye. He's on his side propped up on an elbow and I search his face, just like earlier, it tells me nothing. My eyes narrow. Easing himself down so he's on his back too, he laces our fingers together and places our linked hands between us.

"I moved out there when I was nineteen. We thought we were going to make it big. We were good, but we weren't that good. We got some gigs, decent ones, but we were young and it just wasn't going to happen for us." He laughs fondly, lost in his memories. "There were four of us. I still talk to them every now and then."

"Did you like it in California?"

Living and working in a city as vast as Los Angeles blows my mind even though I feel the same about small towns. I can't imagine either way. I'm a somewhere-in-the-middle kind of girl.

"Yes and no." He pauses and I can hear him swallow. "I was kind of wild when I was younger. I did a lot of things there that I wouldn't have done here. Partied too hard and too often." He breathes out loudly. "I-I made some decisions that molded who I am today," he trails off. A feeling of premonition wiggles over me, nagging, but I can't place it, so I ignore it and wait for him to go on. "I wouldn't take them back. I'm glad for the experiences I had." Absolute conviction rings through the low tone of his voice.

Mason comes to mind as Brady's words sink in. Lately, that's the same way I've started to think of him. I don't regret him or our relationship. My time after Mason is the same as Brady's time after

L.A. I like knowing that I'm not the only one who messed up when they were young. I like that I can recognize now that the things that happened in the past have shaped me into who I am today. And while there are some things I would definitely change, I wouldn't take everything back.

"I know that feeling," I say softly.

My outlook has changed so much recently. When I think about my miscarriage, I don't feel the usual catastrophic need to doom myself for my actions. No panic rises uncontrollably inside me. I feel sad and still guilty, but I don't feel like I'm about to explode and come apart in a billion tiny pieces.

I guess that's progress.

I roll to my side and face Brady. I don't miss the thoughtful look on his face just before he turns his head toward me. He opens his mouth and frowns, but doesn't say anything. That knowing feeling is rubbing against the inside of my brain again. I'm lost as to what it means. It's possible I'm letting my own emotions lead me to think Brady has something he wants to tell but isn't. Completely unsure of how to handle it, I say nothing. Again.

"Thank you for today."

Brady shifts onto his side and brushes

against me, sending chills across my bared skin.

"Anything for my girl," he says with a smile and a wink.

It's incredibly cheesy, but he just called me his girl with an added wink, which is too sexy. My heart beats fast and my fingers tingle. Leaning in, I brush my lips against his cheek.

As I pull away, he catches me with a hand around the nape of my neck, holds me in place, and lowers his mouth to mine. His touch is gentle, but strong, letting me know he means business. His fingers coax me closer as his tongue works the seam of my lips. I open for him and he tilts his head, deepening the kiss, stroking inside my mouth with just enough force that I feel it in other places. I moan and he pulls away, smiling, before dropping one more kiss on my lips. My breathing is ragged and his eyes are glazed, but we just stare at each other.

"Ready to head out?"

He brushes a few loose strands of hair behind my ear.

"Sure."

****

We've turned around, heading back in the direction of Farley, but we're taking different roads. I watch the fields fly by without recognition.

A white wax covered bag full of burgers and fries sits between us. I'm sipping homemade root beer. It's delicious and the perfect ending to this day. I offer Brady a drink, holding out the cup. His lips wrap around the straw and the brown liquid moves upward.

On the right, a field full of wild flowers stretches as far as I can see.

"Look, it's so pretty. I've always wanted to run through wild flowers," I say, keeping my eyes on the field. A laugh escapes me. It's such a simple, childish thing. One I've always thought looked so carefree. "That's kind of dumb, right?"

"No, it's not," he assures me. "You want to stop? It'll be a good place to eat."

I smile over at him and nod.

"Okay."

Carefully, he pulls the car to the side of the road and into the field. I expected him to stop on the shoulder, but no, he keeps going, astonishing me. I'm worried he's going to mess up his car somehow, but he doesn't seem bothered at all. He eases us slowly onto the expanse of land, feeling out the terrain. Once we're a good ways into the field, he stops the car and throws it into park.

Grabbing our food, Brady climbs from the car and walks around to the hood where he helps

me climb up. We stare out over the field of brightly colored flowers and eat. It surprises me when Brady starts to name some of the different flowers. I don't have a clue what any of them are. Just another thing about his to add that's endearing. Once the food is gone, I gather the trash and stash it in the car so it won't blow away. Taking Brady's hand, I tug him from the hood and give him a serious look.

I press myself against him and rise up on my toes.

When my lips brush against his ear, I whisper, "You're it."

Stepping back, I flash my own knowing smirk and take off running.

I run and run with the wind in my hair and my arms spread wide, the flowers brushing against me. With the breeze and my smile and the floral scent in the air, I'm in love with this moment. I can hear Brady behind me, but when I look over my shoulder, I don't see him.

Laughing, I turn back and run to find him. When I do, he's lying on the ground, smiling up at me. I grab his arm and try to pull him, but he doesn't budge. His eyes flash a second before he pulls me down with him. As I fall, he wraps me in his strong arms and rolls us. He hovers over me and we stare at one another. It's nice and tingly and all the things falling for someone is supposed to be. His head dips and I know he's going to kiss me, and while it won't be the first time, it might be the best time. It seems every kiss with him is better than the last.

His mouth seeks mine out. Warm and firm, soft and sweet, it's all those things and more. Something brushes against my wrist. I think it's his fingertips until I realize his arms are banded tightly around me.

I shriek, flinging my arm, and hopefully the bug, wildly around. Brady lets me go. His rich laugh booms around us and I jump up. My skin crawls and I shake my arms out, doing a little dance. Brady stands too, still laughing, and I swat at him before marching away.

"Back to the car then?" He can't hide the amusement in his tone even though he tries.

When we reach Brady's car, I turn to face him, placing a hand on his chest. All it takes is one look and something hot and needy thrums between us. His large hands grip my hips and lift me onto the hood before sliding down my sides. He finds the edge of my skirt and lifts. Draping it over my thighs, his fingers graze my skin.

"So soft," he mutters as his eyes carve a

path over my legs.

Brady pushes his way into the space between my thighs, spreading them further. Strong fingers wrap just above my knees and his mouth comes down on mine. The emotion I feel from him is … wow. He's pouring everything into this kiss. Breathing suddenly becomes optional. Surely, I can survive on his kisses.

Molten warmth washes over me. Starting in my chest, it flows like liquid through my stomach and all the way to the tips of my toes. He starts slowly brushing his lips against mine. Taking my bottom lip between his, he sucks softly, sending pulses of desire straight between my legs. He licks into my mouth, meeting my tongue with his. A hand works its way under my skirt, cupping my butt, and he rolls his hips. A muffled sound slips from my lips.

My hands slide up his back, my fingers digging into strong muscles. Brady moves lower, pressing kisses along my collarbone. When he reaches the top curve of my breast, he inhales deeply and tugs the top of my tank aside. I feel the warmth of his tongue first, then his oh-so-soft lips before he's on the move again. He lifts my shirt and presses a kiss to my stomach before licking over my navel. My hands are in his hair now, grasping desperately because I think I know where he's going. I suddenly feel exposed out in the open, but I really, really want him to keep doing what he's doing.

His nose grazes my inner thigh as he pushes my skirt even higher. Spring air flows over me in a soft caress. I lift my head, taking in the sight of him between my legs. Warm breath washes over my center and even with the lace barrier between us, it burns me up. A shuddery sigh leaves me. Gripping my hips, he draws me closer. Burying his face between my thighs, he tugs my panties aside and then his mouth is on me.

One long swipe of his tongue and my hips roll, pushing against his mouth. His tongue swirls around, and I moan. He just started, and already, I can't think. I reach out, but the hood of the car doesn't offer me anything to hold, so I grip his head. My fingers flex and Brady groans, sending vibrations straight through my core.

"Fuck," I whisper as Brady slides a finger inside me. His tongue never stops flicking over that perfect spot. I'm a goner, lost to the sensations he wrings from my body. I come, moaning his name and squeezing my thighs against him.

Brady pulls back, flashing a wide smile. It's self-assured and satisfied. He wipes a hand across his mouth, which is somewhat crass and should be gross, but instead, it turns me on all over again. He rests his chin on my thigh and watches me as I come down from my Brady-induced high. When I feel like I can finally think again, I notice the sun is setting, turning the sky a pretty blend of oranges.

Brady leans over me, a hand planted on either side of my hips.

"We missed the sunset."

"I'm totally fine with that."

He runs his eyes over me.

"Mmm … me too." His voice is deep, husky, buzzing with passion. He looks back up, meeting my gaze. "You ready to head home?"

I run my hands up his chest and over his shoulders. He's firm and strong and I wish I was touching skin instead of his t-shirt.

"Will you stay with me tonight?"

Brady nods and smiles before kissing me. He helps me from the hood of his car and opens the passenger side for me to climb inside. I slide over as he makes his way around to the driver's side.

Nestled against him, I let my eyes drift shut.

"You're pretty great," I say quietly. I'm bare, open, vulnerable—words falling from my lips without thought. Honesty at its best with no walls to hold me back.

"I know," he whispers, and I laugh lightly.

I feel myself sinking into sleep and I can't seem to drag myself back, but just before I'm fully under, I hear him.

Barely, but I do.

"You're amazing, Cora Leigh."

15

The sun shines between the slats of my blinds. My alarm hasn't gone off, but I'm wide-awake—not something that happens often. I groan, close my eyes, and snuggle closer to the warmth behind me. A large palm rests on my stomach beneath my shirt, its weight heavy against my heated skin. Brady shifts closer, sliding his hand upward, stopping when he's cupping my breast.

Warm lips trail over my shoulder until they meet the strap of my tank top. His nose nudges beneath the fabric, pushing it aside so he can place his lips there, too. A happy sigh leaves me and my cheeks warm as soon as I hear myself. I wonder if the hot blush of my reaction to Brady and his kisses will ever go away.

His lips move on, pressing against my neck softly. I shiver when they brush the nape of my neck and up to my hairline. I'm not sure what it is about having someone's lips touch the parts of you that are rarely touched at all, but it's divine.

Brady in my bed feels right and intimate in a way I've never been with another person. My heart pounds at the thought. I'm moving on. I'm falling for him. I find myself waiting—waiting for that awful guilty feeling that's been poking at me for so long now. It rears its ugly head less and less, but still shows itself sometimes. Telling me I shouldn't be doing this, that I'll never really be ready, that I'm forgetting all the things I've lost, that I'm doing a great injustice by not mourning the way I should. But...

"Good morning," Brady says, his voice husky and sleep-ridden. It succeeds in drawing me from my thoughts.

He pulls my hips back and into him, groaning into my ear. We're flush against one another, pressed together from shoulder to thigh, my back to his front. The feel of his body and the sensations pulsing through me wrench a quiet whimper from my lips.

"Morning." I clear my throat in an attempt to get rid of the creaky, broken sound.

Brady's hand slides from between my breasts, his fingers slipping over the hard nub of my nipple. Heat shoots through my veins. My muscles tense and I inhale raggedly. His mouth presses against my shoulder as his fingers slide down and into the band of my shorts. They stop there, even though I want them to dip further.

"I have to go to work," he mutters against my neck seconds before his tongue snakes out and drags roughly across the skin bared to him. Warm breath coasts over the damp area, sending sparks through me.

"Me too." Disappointed doesn't even begin to describe the sound of my words.

Strong arms tighten around me as Brady buries his nose against me and breathes me in deeply.

I wiggle against him, trying to turn in his arms. I want to look into his eyes, and the perfect slant of his cheekbones, the curve of his lips.

"Nope." He holds me firmly in place against his hard body. "If you turn around and I see those gorgeous eyes of yours, I won't be leaving this bed."

I pout, even though he can't see me.

He releases me after dropping his lips to my cheek, and before I can turn to face him, he's standing at the edge of the bed.

I flip the comforter back over me and pull it over my head, burrowing back into my pillow. The bathroom door clicks shut and I launch myself from the bed to study my reflection in the mirror above my dresser.

It's not as bad as I expected, but definitely not what I want Brady to remember as the day goes on.

Rubbing a hand over my face, I catch a few flakes of mascara from under my eyes and then try my best to comb through my hair with my fingers. Satisfied, I make my way to the kitchen to start some coffee. Brady strolls down the hall a few moments later, pulling his shirt over his head. He rubs a hand over his flat stomach, drawing my gaze. I might be drooling.

He kisses my cheek as he passes through the kitchen on his way to the couch. The smile he gives me is open and warm. I keep watching him like the weirdo I am as he moves through my apartment. His phone chimes and he quickly checks it. His lips purse into a thin line, all warmth and softness gone from his expression, but he doesn't respond to whatever it is. If I wasn't a creepy stalker girl, I wouldn't have even noticed. Unfortunately, I did. Now the air in the room feels different. If he knows I'm watching, he doesn't let on. He just bends down and slips on his shoes.

I want to ask what's wrong, but I don't.

I want to ask when I'll see him again, but I don't.

The magic of yesterday and his reassuring words are gone and I find myself back in that unsure place where I've been living.

I don't know what his schedule is like.

Or if he wants to see me soon.

I'm working up the nerve to ask when he speaks.

"I've got some stuff going on this weekend, so I won't be around."

His eyes stay trained on his feet as he stands. There's something in his tone, but I can't place it. Uneasiness fills me. Everything is off now.

"Alright."

Finally, his gaze meets mine.

"You working on Monday?"

I can't shake the feeling that he's keeping something from me. It might be insecurity. It might be my own nagging thoughts. I don't know. What I do know is that text changed his demeanor. I turn away, pouring some coffee, trying to shake off the tension I feel.

Still not looking at him, I shake my head to answer his question.

"You should come by the shop around eight. We can have dinner."

Abandoning the coffee mug, I make my way toward him.

"Sure. Sounds good." I smile, still feeling off, but chalk it up to my own guilty conscience.

His hands find my hips and he steps into me. All my doubts seem to vanish with the touch of his hands. His kiss is heated, leaving me flushed and breathing heavily. He gives me that knowing grin, amusement dancing across his face.

"Have a good day. I'll text you later." His hand is on the doorknob when he pauses and gives me a little smile. It's lacking his normal swagger.

My heart sinks.

"Bye," I say quietly.

I close the door behind him and lean my forehead against it while I turn the lock.

Something icky and dark has settled in my stomach. I swallow down its bitter taste.

I need to get a grip. If Brady and I keep going the way we are, I need to tell him about the baby. I'm just not ready. but when I am, I can only hope that whatever he's holding back will come out, too.

I finish my coffee and find that I have to rush through my morning routine. I've spent too much time feeling down and worrying about the past catching up with me.

As I pass Brunette Brew on my way to work, I tell myself not to look inside, but as I step into the dance studio, I can't stop myself. I just want one little glimpse of him. Before I know it, my eyes are scanning the windows across the street.

When I don't find him, I abandon my post and force myself to head inside. I'm a lovesick fool.

My phone chimes just as I drop my purse on the desk in the office.

Brady: It's going to be a long weekend. xoxo

My heart soars, but at the same time, I can't shake the feeling that it's all going to come crashing down.

Britni Hill

16

It's Monday. I'm unloading groceries and counting down the hours until I see Brady. My phone rings as I'm stretching to slide a box of cereal into the cabinet. Without looking, I pull it from my back pocket and swipe a finger across the screen.

"Hello?"

"Cora, I need a favor." Miss Kaye's smoker's rasp comes through.

"Sure. What's up?" I ask, hoping whatever she wants from me doesn't interfere with my plans with Brady, but she's done so much for me, I can't deny her.

"Patti is sick and she's going to the emergency room, so I need someone to cover the three and four year old class later. It's at four thirty. I've got all the others covered."

My heart skips a beat as I listen to her. Once

her words sink in, it takes off in a surprisingly quick gallop. My throat tightens. My ears burn. I don't know if I can do *this*. Anything else and I wouldn't hesitate to say yes but this ...

I've avoided children at almost all costs since my miscarriage. The guilt I feel when I see them is too much. It's an undeniable aching feeling I can't stand to live with. I freeze up around them.

Something rustles on the other end.

"Cora? Are you still there?"

I gulp.

Can I do this?

I clamp my eyes shut and steady myself.

I think back to the last time I saw a child. It wasn't so bad. Not the same as it was the first time.

Maybe I need to do this.

Maybe this is what moving forward is all about.

My sweating palms tell me this might be a disaster, but I want to try. I want to move on. I want to let go of my need to punish myself—my guilt. I see how unhealthy it is.

I'm getting better ... I think.

But even if I'm not, I can't bring myself to say no.

"I'll be there," I say firmly, and hang up.

Bracing my hands on the counter, I bend forward.

Deep breath in. Deep breath out.

In through my nose. Out through my mouth.

The swirling emotion in my stomach riots against my attempts to calm myself, jabbing at my insides with steely knifes of pain.

I sink down, counting slowly from one to ten. Over and over again.

A deep, dark pit cracks and opens wide inside me, but I won't let myself fall. I feel its pull, but refuse to give in. I'm stronger than this, and for the first time in a long time, I feel like I can conquer this.

I stay like that, crouched on the kitchen tile of my apartment, counting softly to myself. It takes a while and maybe I should feel embarrassed, but it feels good to talk myself down. The panic was close, but it never dug its sharp claws into me. I kept it at bay.

When I feel centered enough, I stand and stretch my stiff muscles.

I change into dance clothes and pull on a soft cotton skirt. Throwing some things into a bag so I don't have to come home before I meet Brady, I head out. I'm going to be early, but if I'm doing this, I might as well do it all the way. Face my demons, head on.

****

The kids filter in slowly and my heart pounds. Some of the parents' stay, settling in the seats provided. My hands shake as I watch the kids laugh together. This is simple. I can do this. It's a basic tap class. Teaching them rhythm and finding the beat in a song, along with a few simple shuffle steps.

Easy.

Deep breath.

I gather the little ones in a circle and hand them all drumsticks.

They smile and giggle and tears sting my eyes. My heart beats so fast and hard, I'm sure everyone can see the movement through the material of my leotard. I shake it off and tell myself I'm okay as I make my way to the iPod dock to select a song.

I'm a liar, though.

A dirty, dirty liar.

I'm not okay now, but I will be. It's a promise I've made myself.

Brady's presence in the back of my mind as I show the kids how to tap the floor to the beat helps keep me going. He gives me a sense of calm.

His lack of judgment has given me a confidence I didn't know I needed. With that, I have the ability to see that I can let go.

I make it through the class with a ragged sense of peace and my heart in my throat.

As I close things out, one little girl with blonde curls lunges forward and wraps her arms around my legs. I almost lose it. Tears burn my eyelids. My heart cracks, but I manage to pat her on her back and keep it together until she lets go.

After everyone files out, I sag against the door and allow myself a moment to collect my thoughts, and maybe a little bit of my sanity.

I'm exhausted.

I change out of my dance clothes and touch up my makeup, taking my time while trying to clear my head before I'm supposed to meet Brady.

When I'm ready, I feel much better. Teaching little ones no longer seems so daunting.

****

Brady's standing behind the counter when I enter Brunette Brew. His back is to me, but my heart flutters all the same. My eyes roam over the inside of the coffee shop. It isn't very busy. Brady's mom is in her usual spot, glued to her phone, and suddenly, my nerves take flight.

Does she know about me?

What will she think?

She doesn't look up as I move toward the counter, so I feel a bit safer.

Brady's attention is so focused on the machine he's messing with, he doesn't notice me. His brows are furrowed, his lips pursed as he concentrates. It's cute how focused he is, so I watch him for a moment with amusement. After a while, I clear my throat. Brady whirls around at the sound, a smile on his face. That smile drops its polite professionalism when he sees me. His eyes darken and his mouth turns up with a lopsided boyish grin.

"Hey." His hand finds mine on the counter and he pushes his fingers between mine.

"Your mom is really into her phone," I say, leaning forward to be closer to him.

Brady barks out a laugh.

"I got her an iPhone for Christmas. Big mistake." His voice raises and he cups his hands around his mouth in the direction of his mom. "Now, I do all the work and she plays games."

"Shut your mouth, Brady Maxwell," his mom calls good-naturedly from behind me.

Their playful teasing is cute.

"You want your usual?" I nod and Brady busies himself with pouring my coffee. "You're early."

I nod again. Apparently, I've gone mute.

"I picked up a class for one of the girls since she's sick. I just got done."

Brady sets a cup on the counter in front of me. I look down and realize he's made me something that's not my usual. He raises an eyebrow and I smile. A throat clears behind me, and I startle. Just like always whenever I'm around him, I forget we aren't the only two people who exist.

"I'll be over there. Out of the way." I gesture over my shoulder.

Brady nods.

I grab my coffee and head to a table in the corner. As I walk, I take a sip of Brady's concoction. My lips pucker at its sweetness, but it's not too bad. Brady's mom keeps looking at me, sneaking glances, which tells me she more than likely knows who I am.

After a while, the few people hanging around start to leave and Brady's mom vacates her place by the fireplace, disappearing into the back. I stretch and stand, heading for the restroom. When I enter the hall where the bathrooms are, hushed voices greet me. I look around for the source and find a door leading into the kitchen at the end of the hall by the fire exit.

I pause.

I don't mean to eavesdrop, but I can't help it. Brady's voice, along with his mom's, drift through the door, catching my attention.

"You need to tell her, Brady." It's a whisper, but it's fierce.

"I know, Mom." I hear a frustrated sigh. "I didn't mean to keep it from her. It's—it's complicated."

It's pretty clear I'm the *her* in this situation. Then again, that would be jumping to conclusions, and I don't want to do that. There could be another *her*. Maybe they aren't talking about me at all. His mom answers in a hushed voice I can't make out.

"She's been through too much. She's lost too much." Brady's tone is still loud and clear.

Scratch that theory. I'm sure they're talking about me.

I hear the struggle in Brady's voice, but I don't stick around to hear anymore. The unshakable feeling I've had that Brady's holding back from me is all too real right now. I want to be upset, but I can't even do that because I've done the same thing to him. I can, however, be upset about the fact that he's keeping things from me because he thinks I'm too fragile—too broken, to

handle whatever it is.

I stare at myself in the mirror, frustrated and unsure of what to do. The only thing I can come up with is telling Brady my secrets, letting him in on what I've kept to myself. I just need to make sure I'm ready to do that—that once I put it out there, I can handle what he might think or say. I press a hand to my forehead and take a deep breath.

When I step out of the restroom, I find Brady leaning up against the wall, waiting.

A startled, "Hey," slips from my lips.

I can't meet his gaze because my mind keeps replaying the conversation I overheard. His shoes move forward, his hands grasp my hips, and I raise my gaze to his.

He walks me backward, pressing me into the wall next to the door I just came through. It's on the tip of my tongue to tell him what I heard, to ask him what he's keeping from me, but I clamp my lips shut. Now isn't the time.

The scent of his cologne surrounds me just like his body does. His lips brush against mine. I search his eyes and I see nothing but sincerity— nothing but desire and caring. His mouth touches mine again and as usual my brain short-circuits.

"Hey," he mumbles against my mouth

before pressing his long, lean body against me. His tongue slowly strokes against my bottom lip with a slow drag. I inhale sharply and a shiver rides down my spine.

I give in, accepting his kiss by angling my head to deepen it while winding my arms around his neck. My fingertips skim over his broad shoulders. I love the firm feeling of his hard body. He's pressed against me, holding me where he wants me, gripping me tightly. It's not long before I'm breathless and flushed. Brady pulls back, but he doesn't seem too eager to let me go. He drops another kiss, and then another, on my lips before dipping his mouth to my neck. Stepping back, he eases me to my feet. His big hands still grip my waist even as he puts some space between our bodies.

"Hi," I say stupidly when I can breathe again.

Brady chuckles and flashes my favorite grin. He steps away, giving me a heated look before he pivots and heads into the kitchen.

As he disappears through the swinging door, I stay where I am, trying to slow my breathing. When I finally make my way from the hall, I notice Brady's mom switching off the open sign and twisting the lock on the door.

Her smile widens when she sees me. She's petite and pretty, with blonde hair and a warm smile. Butterflies take flight as she makes her way toward me. I don't have a clue how I'm supposed to act. I freeze in the middle of the room, but she isn't fazed at all by my wide-eyed expression. When she reaches me, she wraps her arms around me and kisses me on the cheek with warm lips.

"Hi, honey. I'm Brenda." She squeezes me once more before stepping back. "Brady talks about you a lot."

That warms me a bit, taking the edge off my nervousness.

"It's very nice to meet you." I force a smile. Even though this woman is incredibly welcoming, I'm still rattled and feeling out of place.

"Now, I told Brady to go ahead and close up, that way you two can enjoy the evening." She pats my shoulder. "I'm heading home."

"Okay…"

I wish I could punch myself in the face right now. I mean, seriously. I'm failing majorly at engaging in conversation. My thoughts are all over the place and I can't help but wonder what this woman thinks of me. If she thinks I'm weak and fragile the way her son does.

No, that's not right.

Deep down, I know Brady doesn't think I'm weak. But now I'm thinking about the words I heard them say to one another and what Brady could be keeping from me. And what he's told his family about me.

"Alright, honey. I hope to see you again soon." Brenda smiles again and I curse myself for not saying anything else, but my muteness persists.

I nod and wave.

"Bye," I finally manage to call as she heads for the back.

The amount of relief I feel when she slips behind the counter and disappears is palpable. My breaths come easier and my heart rate slows to something bearable. Now, it's just me and my thoughts, alone together.

Just like old times.

That might actually be worse than hanging out with Brady's mom.

I'm feeling an odd sense of remorse. Brady told his mom I've been through so much, but he doesn't even know all of it. I'm worrying about his secrets when I should be worrying about my own. We're just getting to know each other, so it's fair that I don't know all of him. I lower myself into a chair, trying to sort through my thoughts.

Fear creeps over me.

The way I lived my life after losing the baby and Mason made sense to me before. Now, I don't know if the way I felt was real or based on insecurity and guilt.

Before Brady, I didn't think my fears and emotions were spawned from my own sense of guilt or a need to punish myself. Without a doubt, I thought they were reality. No, I knew they were.

Brady startles me when he comes from the back carrying two glasses in one hand and two unopened beers in his other. Light brows pull together when he sees me. I feel stiff, unable to move as I watch him. I try to smooth out my features, but my skin feels too tight. I know the tension is written all over me. I can't hide it so I chew my thumbnail, instead.

I thought.

Brady sets the bottles and glasses on the table in front of me, his expression worried. Wrapping his long fingers around my wrist, he tugs my thumb from my mouth, but doesn't let go.

I raise my gaze to his.

"You okay, babe?"

I'm momentarily caught up in his intense gaze, in the meaningful look he's giving me. A look that says I can tell him anything. That I can trust him.

I want to. I think I can. But …

"Yeah, I'm good," I lie.

Brady's eyes narrow.

He sees right through me.

I busy myself rearranging the things on the table.

I wait, but he doesn't say anything else.

After a few seconds tick by in silence, I look up.

"I'm gonna grab the food." He finally lets me go.

Brady saunters away and I take a deep breath, resolving to tell him about the baby soon. I love and hate his concern at the same time.

17

I've been a jumpy, guilt-feeling, suspicious mess for a week now. The more I think about what I'm keeping from Brady the more I want to know what he's keeping from me. As a result, I'm tense and awkward. I'm hiding it horribly. Every time I see Brady his eyes tell me he knows something is up. But still, I don't speak up.

Warm fingers wrap around my own, threading our hands together and drawing my gaze from the sidewalk. The crazy inside my head doesn't diminish what I feel every time he touches me. Electric tingles work their way up my arm, zapping my poor heart back into the now.

I smile up at Brady.

"You tired?"

I wince. I can't help it. Tonight is supposed to be fun. We aren't even to the bar yet and he's noticed something is off.

"A little," I mumble. "I'll be fine once we get there. The fresh air feels nice."

I look up again and he's watching me. His eyes flick from mine to my lips and then roam all over my face. He's taking it all in, studying me. His hand pumps against mine, squeezing a little tighter, but his furrowed brow tells me he's not buying it.

I hate this.

We're meeting Melanie and her fiancé for dinner and drinks. I'm excited to finally meet the man who put a ring on her finger, so I plaster on a smile and give Brady's hand a squeeze as we reach the restaurant. It's a seafood place that wasn't here before, so I'm not familiar with it. He opens the door for me and I see Mel immediately. She's smiling widely and waving. The man next to her is not what I expected. He looks polished and … calm. I wave back and tug Brady in the direction of their table.

Mel stands and embraces me when I'm close enough.

"Hi." She's all warm cheer and happiness. It loosens some of the tension coiled tight inside me.

When she steps back and releases me, I link my fingers with Brady's and tug him forward.

"This is Brady. Brady this is Melanie." I gesture between the two of them.

Melanie's focus lands on Brady and her smile stretches wide. The attention doesn't faze him. He grins back with ease and steps forward, placing a hand on the small of my back.

"Hi, Melanie. Nice to finally meet you."

I watch Mel's face carefully as Brady extends his hand. She's running her eyes all over him, not leaving a single part of him untouched by her gaze. She catches my stare, fans herself, and winks at me.

I lean into Brady's side with a smile.

He laughs as she finally takes his hand and gives it a shake.

"Hi, Brady." She gestures behind her where her fiancé stands, waiting patiently. "This is Lance."

I extend my hand but he pulls me into a brief warm embrace.

"I've heard a lot about you," he says. "I'm happy you're back." He turns to Mel and smiles down at her. "My girl needed her friend."

I smile back, and watch as he and Brady shake hands and exchange a few words. Melanie still stares at Brady in an almost comical way. Lance slings an arm across her shoulders, watching her with an amused smile.

"Come on, love. You're staring." His tone is light, playful, telling me he isn't the least bit offended by his fiancé's behavior. She swats at him and tosses Brady an apologetic look.

I look around, feeling myself relax.

I feel much better now that Brady and I aren't alone. It's easier to act normal when I'm not the only one his penetrating stare is focused on. That's awful, and I know it. I need to come clean. I can't imagine how it will feel to get this weight off my shoulders.

Brady holds my chair out for me, waiting until I'm seated to take his own chair. I smile up at him. The look in his eyes makes it all click together. I can't risk losing him—I don't want to lose him.

Conversation flows easily between everyone. Everyone but me, that is. I'm stuck in my own head. I take a sip of wine and look over at Brady as he chats about the coffee shop and their plans to expand over the summer.

I'm so preoccupied I'm barely keeping up.

The curve of his jaw lures me in. The soft, low thrum of his voice as he speaks so passionately about his job draws me in more. He's so laidback and easy going. I love the way he makes me feel— hell, it's enough that he makes me feel at all. He deserves better than my secrets, but I'm selfish. The least I can give him is the truth.

Watching him makes it all click into place.

He looks over and gives me a soft smile before his hand lands on my knee, rubbing softly.

My decision is made.

I'm telling him.

I'm going to let Brady all the way in.

****

We move on from the dinner and head to Gimlet. It's a new bar in town. It's nice and they have live music. The wine with dinner loosened me up, and my decision to tell Brady about my miscarriage lifted a giant weight off my shoulders. I'm having a great time.

Lance is wonderful, and he's perfect for Melanie. She's beaming.

I feel happy.

Until I see a familiar face across the bar.

He gives me a crooked grin and heads toward our table. I swallow thickly. Allen Brandt was Mason's closest friend when he was in high school. They weren't close after Mason left, and didn't talk once after we were married. Allen only talked to those who could do something for him. Once Mason joined the Marines and moved on, he wasn't useful to Allen, but that won't stop him from coming over and saying something.

A chair scrapes across the floor.

Melanie's perfectly glossed lips twist in

disgust when she sees him. Lance stops talking mid-sentence and looks him over. He's greasy and unkempt, his clothes ragged and worn. His eyes haven't left me.

Brady went to the bar for drinks a few minutes ago and I pray he makes it back soon.

Allen drums his fingers on the tabletop and gives Lance a nod.

"Melanie." He turns back to me. "Been a while, Cora." He looks over my shoulder, searching for something before his eyes pin me in my place.

"Hi, Allen." I don't know what else to say, and I can't seem to make myself be rude.

"Where's that pain in the ass husband of yours?"

My jaw tenses painfully.

Melanie opens her mouth to speak up, but I stop her with a hand in the air. Just as I start to tell Allen, four drinks land on the table and a warm hand squeezes my shoulder.

Allen's eyes dart to Brady's hand on my shoulder and something in them sparks. He's an asshole and he likes nothing more than starting shit. You'd think he'd have grown out of it, but from the look in his eye, it's beyond obvious he hasn't.

"Who's this?" he says, looking directly at

me.

I purse my lips.

"This is my—this is …" I frown and huff out a breath.

I don't know how to introduce Brady. I'm flustered because I don't want to talk about Mason. Helplessly, I look up a Brady, and he gives me an amused and indulgent smile, but he doesn't offer any help.

Fuck.

Melanie's grinning from ear to ear. Lance looks like the cat that ate the fucking canary.

Clearly, everyone is enjoying this at my expense.

"This is Brady." There, that works.

Brady's hand shoots out over my shoulder.

"Her boyfriend," he adds, trying to shake Allen's hand.

Boyfriend.

Wait … he just said …

My boyfriend.

Brady is my boyfriend.

My lips curve upward.

I'm feeling a little bouncy and I have to force myself to sit still. I don't even care that we haven't talked about it. That he's just declaring it. But where was he when I stuttered and stumbled over my words?

****

My back slams into the wall by the door to my apartment. Brady's warm body presses against the length of mine. My fingers run over the short hair along the nape of his neck. The smell of his cologne and laundry detergent fills my nose. It's sexy and sends hot desire coursing through me. My mind has been on overload since he called himself my boyfriend. Telling him my dirty secrets is long lost in the racing beat of my heart as he kisses me with hunger.

I take what he's offering and up the ante, pulling him against me, groping at his arms and chest. His tongue plunges inside my mouth with fervor. I moan and grip his neck tighter. When he pulls again, he tugs my bottom lip into his mouth and sucks gently. Rays of heat shoot through me. I open my eyes just in time to catch the fluttering of his lashes and the perfect self-satisfied smile curving his lips.

Panting, I turn in his arms and face the door. I dig my keys out as his hands roam my hips and sides. Every touch, every skim of his fingertips, sends me higher. I'm squirming inside my skin. By the time I find my keys, I've pressed myself back against him so there's no space left between us. I

can feel how hard he is and that only amps up my thrumming libido.

Strong, sure fingers ghost down my arms and grasp my hands. Brady pulls my arms up and presses my palms against the door. He leans his weight against me and runs his hands down to my stomach. With his hands spread wide, he pulls me into him, rolls his hips, and groans. Without warning, his heat and touch is gone. I'm leaning against the door, panting. My keys are in his hands and he's unlocking my door. I struggle to breath. I've never felt as wanted as I do right now. He looks down at me as he turns the lock. His grin is easy, but his eyes are serious.

I'm so mesmerized by him, I haven't moved yet. From behind me, he wraps an arm around me, running a hand up my neck to grasp my chin. With ease, he pulls me against him and dips his head for another heated kiss. This one no less desperate than the last, but still oh-so-sweet. His mouth leaves mine as my door swings open. Brady walks us forward, closing the door and twisting the lock without letting me go.

The hand holding my chin slides down between my breasts and along my stomach. His other hand joins in and he raises my shirt up and over my head. I suck in a breath and lean my head back against him as he unbuttons my jeans, guiding me closer to my bedroom the entire time. Anticipation jumps up my throat. His fingers tuck beneath the waistband of my jeans and spread wide before they curve around and push my pants to the floor.

Both hands palm my ass and squeeze.

I giggle and pull away. His large hands reach for me, but I swat them away. I want him naked too, and I can't wait. I love this caveman side of him. He seems to running on instinct and primal need alone. I can feel the tension coiling tighter as he holds himself back. The look he's giving me is pure sex, but I want to touch him, too. I want all the raw, pure manliness he's exuding bared before me.

I reach out for him.

His eyes are dark and hold so much emotion. He runs a gentle hand across my cheek and takes my face in both of his. I work a hand under his shirt and push it up. He leans down, helping me so I can pull the material over his head. I run greedy hands over all the newly bared skin before me.

Brady groans and pulls my mouth to his. My toes barely touch the floor as he starts moving forward again. I palm the hardness of his cock

through denim and cotton and his footsteps falter.

We haven't spoken a word since his lips landed on mine at the foot of the stairs, but we don't need to. Every touch, every lingering kiss, every bite and nibble says everything we need to. We're beyond words.

My legs hit the mattress and I go down, but stop him from pushing me back. Working the buckle of his belt, I pull it from the loops with a snap. I toss it aside, get to work on his jeans, and lick my lips when he's left in nothing but a pair of navy boxer briefs. Something similar to a growl comes from Brady's chest and I look up.

He brushes hair away from my face, tucking it behind my ear, and suddenly, I want him in my mouth. I want his taste on my tongue. Gripping the elastic of his briefs, I give them a tug. My face must give my intentions away.

"No," Brady barks roughly, and pulls my hands away from him.

He pushes me down onto the bed and covers my body with his. My bra is gone before I even realize what's happening. Brady licks the underside of my breast and my whole body goes taut. Who knew that spot would illicit such a response?

"I'm an impatient, selfish man, and I want

inside you too much to wait," he says around a mouthful of blushing skin.

His words do me in. I'm a goner.

I become frenzied, trying to reach as much of him as I can while trying to pull him into me at the same time. He refuses to let me have my way, though. He slows us, holding his perfect body away from mine.

Soft kisses rain down my torso. He looks up just as he grazes the top of my lacey green panties. I have the fleeting thought that they match his eyes before he pulls them down my legs, leaving me bare. His hands wrap around my calves and travel up to my knees. They skim my inner thighs and push my legs further apart. I'm spread wide and his gaze is pinned on the warm, wet place he's exposed, the place begging for him to fill it.

"Don't move," he orders gruffly.

He stands from the bed in all his naked glory, finds his pants, pulls a condom out, and tears into the wrapper with his teeth. I watch with rapt attention as he rolls it down his long, hard cock and makes his way back to me. I don't think I've ever seen a more perfect man.

The curve of his biceps, the hard planes of his chest, the light dusting of hair leading to my new favorite appendage—all of it is just ... perfect.

Perfect on him. Perfect for me. I know he's flawed, we all are, but those things don't matter.

He climbs his way toward me, grinning. I haven't budged. His hands caress my sides as he lowers himself onto me. With a smile, I wrap my legs around him and can't resist rolling my hips against his. He hits the perfect spot and I moan. I'm only torturing myself more, but I do it again as he kisses up my neck.

I grip his shoulders as he shifts his weight. The movement lines us up perfectly and I suck in a ragged breath as he pushes inside. He pulls out, and his eyes clamp shut as he thrusts forward again. He sinks deep. He can't go any further and it's the best feeling. He opens his eyes and our gazes clash while he remains unmoving.

Lifting my head, I brush my lips against his and rock beneath him, silently begging him to give me his worst. I need to feel him unleash all the things he's held back for fear of me running or breaking. I suck his bottom lip into my mouth and bite down lightly.

My tight grip must let him know I want more. I would ask, but I can't seem to form the words—I can barely think. I don't know what's happening, but I'm lost and speechless as he thrusts into me. I've never felt this connection to someone, this kind of need, this absolute want to have someone take me over in every way.

Brady moves faster, harder, his movements becoming more determined. My moans and whimpers are echoed by his grunts. He's moving me where he wants me, adjusting to get just the right angle, and before long, I'm crying out. It's almost embarrassing, but I'm so out of it, I don't give a shit who hears.

I dig my heels into the back of his thighs and my body starts to clench. All my muscles spasm and my back arches. Brady leans up on his knees, pulling me with him and into his lap. We never lose our connection and I don't think his hips lose rhythm. With his arms wrapped tightly around me and his lips plastered to mine, he drives into me from below. I can't breathe. I can't think. I can only feel. And all I feel is Brady. Everywhere.

He grips me tighter, and I know he's coming, too. We're both panting, our skin slick with sweat as he lowers me to my back. We're a pile of tangled limbs and naked flesh and I think this might be my favorite moment of my life.

18

I've been staring at Brady's door for too long. I need to knock, but I can't seem to make myself do it. It's the first time I've been to his house. We're going to a spring carnival and I'm spending the night here. It's been a week since Brady called himself my boyfriend. We've grown closer and I'm falling hard. Every day he does or says something to show me how great he is.

But this, staying at his house, seems huge to me. I'm nervous. Clutching my little overnight bag tightly, I raise my hand and blow out a breath. I don't knock, though. An invisible force field is stopping my hand from meeting his front door.

I huff.

I'm mentally scolding myself when Brady swings the door open. He grins down at me, amusement dancing in his eyes. My cheeks warm.

I run my eyes over him as he leans a

shoulder against the doorframe. He's wearing a plain black t-shirt and jeans that hang just right. His smile makes my heart beat faster.

"Were you gonna knock or just stay out here?" he teases lightly.

I meet his gaze.

"I'm nervous," I blurt.

Brady leans down, kissing me softly, and takes my bag. He links our fingers and pulls me into his house.

It's warm and masculine with a large flat screen TV hanging in the living room.

"Don't be nervous, babe."

Standing in his entryway, he let's go of my hand as he walks down a short hallway, but I don't move to follow him.

"I'm putting your bag in my room."

"Okay," I call back and make my way to the couch and flop down.

I don't know why I was so worked up about coming here. I think I thought I'd be uncomfortable. I'm not, though. In fact, it feels like home. This house reflects Brady's warmth perfectly. I see touches of him everywhere.

He emerges from a room at the end of the hall and heads back toward me, his long legs eating up the distance easily. Once he reaches the couch, I expect him to sit next to me, but he surprises me by leaning down with a palm on either side of my hips. He's not touching me at all, but his nearness is just as good as any caress.

Brady leans in close and my heart races.

"Hi," he says in a low voice.

His fingers brush my cheek as he slides his hand around the back of my neck.

"Hi," I breathe.

His fingers push into my hair, his thumb stroking my cheek. Warm, minty air brushes over my mouth and I shift on the couch, trying to get closer. The start of a smile curves his perfect lips, but before it can fully form, he's kissing me.

His lips are warm and soft as they press against mine—hard. He melts into me, pressing his tongue into my mouth. With every second that ticks by, I'm getting more and more lost in him. He gives me one more soft kiss before pulling back and running his eyes over me.

I pout.

Brady chuckles and kisses my forehead.

"You ready to go?"

Grabbing my hands, he pulls me from the couch.

"Are you getting me cotton candy?"

"Of course."

"And a corn dog?"

He laughs.

"Yes."

"And roasted corn dripping in butter? And maybe some fried Oreos?"

I grin and look up at him as he leads me toward the front door.

"Where are you putting all of this food?" Brady pokes me in the stomach.

Laughing, I shove him lightly.

"Don't judge me! I've seen you eat a whole large pizza by yourself."

Brady opens my door and as I climb in, his rich, deep laughter fills my ears just before his hand lands on my ass. I squeal.

The driver's side door opens and closes.

"Are you going to ride the Ferris wheel with me?" Brady asks as he starts the car and backs down his driveway.

"Uh, no." I don't even need to think about that.

"Uh … why?"

"I don't ride rickety old carnival rides." Brady's eyebrows rise as he looks over at me.

"You just eat the greasy carnival food?"

"Right." I point at him. "Food, good. Rides, bad."

Brady leans back in his seat with one hand on the steering wheel and gives me a smug look.

"You'll ride the Ferris wheel with me." He gives me a cocky grin.

****

I'm stuffed full of my favorite carnival foods and Brady is looking into my eyes while we lay in his bed. We're naked and sweaty, our legs tangled together. Brady's fingertips run up my arm and grab a lock of my hair. He runs it between his fingers and I snuggle deeper into the pillow I'm lying on.

"Tell me about Mason." His voice is low, quiet, and while his question throws me off and incites a mixture of sadness and panic inside me, his touch and presence soothe me. I swallow down the knotted emotion in my throat.

"What do you mean?" My voice shakes.

"You were so young, but you're smart. There had to be a reason you married him and ran off."

I flinch a little. I can't help it.

"We were both young and dumb." I shrug.

Brady's lips purse as he brushes my hair back.

"Were you ever happy with him?"

"Maybe. I don't know. Our relationship

was—it was …" I sigh, searching for the right words, "well, it wasn't normal."

My words hold so much pain, I want to take them back instantly. Brady kisses me softly.

"Did he ever hurt you?"

His question doesn't surprise me. He doesn't know much, but what he does know I'm sure didn't paint Mason in the best light. But in truth, it was both of us.

"Not in the way you mean." I pause, knowing what I'm about to tell him may make him think differently of me. "He hurt me, yes, but not physically. And it wasn't just him. We hurt each other."

Brady frowns.

I go on before I lose my nerve.

"It wasn't his fault. It was our fault. He pushed and I shoved back. I took pleasure in watching the passion in his eyes die with my words. It was even better when I could make him mad. When I could really spark his anger. We fed off each other." Tears sting my eyes and my voice cracks.

Brady studies me silently and pulls me closer, tucking me into his chest.

"It was so bad, Brady." I sniff. "We loved each other, but it was so wrong."

"Babe," he whispers, cupping my head. He kisses my hair and I let his warmth and his caring nature wash over me. "That doesn't mean it wasn't real, Cora."

Brady tilts my head back and looks into my eyes.

Through watery pools, I take in his handsome face and laugh.

He looks confused and concerned as I wipe my eyes.

"How do you always know the right thing to say?"

He shrugs.

"I really don't. I just say what I'm thinking."

I settle back into his arms with my cheek pressed to his bare chest and let my eyes drift shut.

****

I'm hot. Way too hot. I try to move, but Brady's arm is pinning me to the bed. I blink my eyes open and wait for my vision to clear. Brady is still dead to the world, and lucky for me, he's a deep sleeper, so I lift his arm and slide out of bed. I need a bathroom and coffee.

Right now.

I stop in Brady's bathroom, splash water on my face, then go searching for a coffeemaker. I find it and a plastic bag of what I'm assuming is

Brunette Brew's special blend of dark roast. While I wait, I decide to explore the rest of Brady's house. I should probably wait for him, but it's not like I'm going to go snooping through drawers, I'm just going to look around.

I peek into the first door on the right and it's an office of sorts. There's a drum set, a desk littered with other equipment I'm not sure about, and a computer. Shelves filled with CDs and vinyl records take up a whole wall. Brady has one hell of a musical library and I know his phone is stocked too. I wander into the room and run a finger over the albums before heading back to the door.

I'm most curious about the closed door across the hall from Brady's room. The hair on the back of my neck prickles as I leave the office and head down the hall. I hesitate once my hand is on the doorknob. Whatever I'm feeling doesn't make any sense, so I ignore it and twist the knob.

The door swings open and my heart sinks. It falls straight to the floor before it starts beating fast enough to win a race against the speed of light. My throat closes and I suddenly can't breathe. I don't know what I'm seeing, but I know it's bad. It's something I can't handle. The walls are brown and navy blue. A twin bed sits in the middle of one wall covered in a baseball comforter. Toy trucks litter one corner of the room.

My brain finally catches up to the scene before me and my sweaty palm slips from the doorknob. I shake my head and start to back away from the room. There are so many things wrong with what I'm seeing, I don't even know what to do.

I spin, planning to run—to where, I don't know—and slam into a bare, muscular chest. I dart back like Brady's on fire and his hands land on my shoulders.

"Hey, I should have told you. I know what this looks like, but ..."

I jerk out from beneath his hands and my back meets the wall.

"You have a kid?" I think I had that figured out before he showed up behind me. Now, I'm confused again, or I don't want to believe it—I don't know. What I do know is I'm standing outside a child's room in my boyfriend's house. And I didn't know about any of it. It's bringing up all kinds of feelings I've been pushing down.

Brady leans against the wall behind him, giving me some much needed space. He runs a hand over his messy bed head and blows out a deep breath.

His gaze meets mine, steadily.

"Yes. I do."

It's simple. It's honest. And it's like a stinging slap in the face.

I'm frozen for a second, trapped inside my own body, unable to react.

Fuck me. I can't do this.

My whole body jolts forward stiffly as I step away from the wall.

"Cora?"

I ignore him—hell, I barely hear him. I'm consumed with the overwhelming need to get away—away from him, away from this situation.

"Cora, stop." Brady's voice rises slightly, startling me into obeying.

I turn to face him with tears streaking down my cheeks.

"You should have told me," I grit out. I'm hurt and scared and every guilty feeling I've been chasing away for the past month is coming back. A sour taste fills my mouth, nausea swirls, and I pray I don't get sick.

"You're right," he says. "I should have told you. I meant to, I did."

Brady takes a step forward, but I hold up a hand.

"Don't."

His jaw flexes, but he stays where he is.

"I can't do this." The words are ripped from me and I hate them, but they're true. I can't be with someone who has a kid. I can't live everyday seeing a kid run around when mine never even got to be.

"I'm so sorry, babe. I know I should have told you, but when we met you were so… so—"

"What?" I shout. "Broken! Fragile! Did I deserve to be lied to?"

I spin, grabbing my clothes from the day before.

"What? No." Brady grasps my arm.

"You don't get it!" I wish I wasn't shouting, but I can't seem to stop. My voice has no volume control. "I can't do this, and it's not because you lied."

I pull my arm from his hand and shoulder my bag and purse. Weariness and pain line his face.

"You're not making any sense, Cora."

Brady sounds exhausted and frustrated, but how he feels and what he's probably thinking are nothing compared to how I feel and what's going on inside my head.

"I was pregnant."

I push past Brady, trying not to give in to the dread I feel climbing up my throat. It's sinking its sharp claws in and refusing to stay put. I make it to the living room and I don't hear anything behind me. I don't know what I expected. Why would he try to stop me? I knew once he found out he wouldn't want anything to do with me. I should have told him sooner.

I slam my car door and hastily buckle myself in. My tears won't stop.

Brady has a kid.

Deep breath in.

Brady has a kid.

Deep breath out.

Brady has a kid.

I look up and see him on the porch. He's watching me, but he doesn't come out any further. I don't want him to. I don't want him to have the chance to try to stop me, so I throw my car into reverse and hit the gas. The quicker I get away, the better.

19

I drive aimlessly at first. Tears pour down my cheeks, blurring my vision until I have to pull over. I wipe my eyes and my nose and choke back a few sobs. When I look up, I instantly recognize the neighborhood. I'm three houses down from my parents' house and I don't know if this is a sign or an unconscious decision.

I look in the rearview mirror. I'm a wreck. Crazy bed head is the least of my problems. Smudged eyeliner and mascara ring my bloodshot and swollen eyes. It's all too obvious that I've been crying. I do my best to tame my hair and run my fingers under my eyes, trying to remove the dark smudges. Eventually, I give up. It doesn't really matter.

As I climb from my car, I remember I'm wearing my jeans and Brady's oversized t-shirt. I ran from him so quickly, I didn't do anything other than pull on pants. I sigh and dig some flipflops from my bag.

I don't bother moving my car. With sluggish, dragging feet, I make my way down the street to my parents'. I sniff and try to hold back the tears still stinging my eyes. The house looms over me once I make it to the front yard. I stare upward, unmoving. What am I doing? I'm running on pure autopilot.

My feet hit the porch. I feel oddly numb. I keep waiting for the sweaty palms and the inability to breathe, but it's not happening. My heart beats too fast, but other than that and the burn in my eyes, I don't feel … anything.

"Mom," I call out as I push the front door open.

No answer.

I hear movement in the kitchen and head that way.

"Mom?"

I stop short when I find my dad and not my mother standing in the kitchen. He's still in sweats and a tee, holding a cup of coffee. In my haste, I forgot it was morning. The range of emotions I've already experienced are far more than enough for one day, let alone a few hours.

My dad freezes.

"You're mom's out."

His eyes roam over my face and his gaze fills with concern. He doesn't say anything, but something about the way he's looking at me restarts my tears. This time, I can't hold them in or tone them down. Sobs rip from my throat in messy, wet bursts. I snort and choke in the most unladylike way. I can't even make myself care. My arms hang limply at my sides.

I'm so lost.

As if in slow motion, my dad sets his steaming mug on the counter and approaches me with caution.

"Cora, what's wrong?"

My only answer is a hiccup-sounding cry and more tears.

"Tell me what's wrong. Are you okay?" he asks, his words a little frantic.

The pitch of his deep voice has me looking up at him. His hand lands on my elbow and his warm touch sends me into a spiral of despair. Everything I've been pressing down and ignoring for the last year or so comes rushing up. Add in the caring tone of my father's voice and my mixed emotions about Brady's kid, and you have a shuddering ball of tear-soaked anxiety named Cora.

Yeah, that's me.

A hot fucking mess.

"I'm fine," I mumble.

"Cora, you're not fine."

He pulls me over to the breakfast bar and parks me on a stool. My hands shake as I wipe at my tears. It's pointless, though. As soon as I clear them, they come right back. I sniff and meet my dad's concerned eyes.

I don't know what happens next. I lose all control. I'm mumbling and muttering, telling him things about Mason and losing him. The words spew from my mouth in incoherent spurts, word vomit at its best. With a side of extra crazy that doesn't make any sense.

Before I know it, I've told him how dysfunctional Mason and I were. I bring up the divorce and his deployment, our last night, last fight, and so much more. The words flow out and I can't stop them.

It's almost an out of body experience when I utter the words I've only said to one other person earlier today.

"I was pregnant."

Shock fills my father's features before the lines around his eyes deepen. Devastation and sadness roll over his face when it finally sinks in. I say it anyway, even though it's clear by his expression he's figured it out.

"I lost the baby." It's a whisper, barely audible. I swallow thickly.

Something odd happens then. Something inside me shifts and I feel a giant weight lift from my shoulders.

Dad's arms come around me, wrapping me up tight and holding me close.

"Baby girl," he says into my hair.

A throat clears behind us and I lift my head. Mom rushes over and by one look at her face, I can tell she heard almost every word. She brushes my hair from my face while I cling to my father like a child.

"Honey, why didn't you tell us?" Her voice is low, soothing, everything I miss from my childhood.

I stare at her, but can't come up with anything to say. I just cry, instead, like the pathetic woman I've been since Mason died and I lost the baby. I bury my face in my dad's shirt and let it all out.

****

With lifeless limbs and sore eyes, I climb the stairs to my apartment. My parents let the subject of the miscarriage go. My tears dried. Mom tried to force food down my throat. I never mentioned my morning with Brady. They never asked what sent me running to them, spilling my secrets and opening old wounds.

It was freeing to have someone else help bear the weight of my secret that wasn't a secret anymore. I was glad to have let someone in and sad about how things turned out with Brady. Things with him were over. I couldn't do it. I didn't want to have to face him.

It seems I don't have a choice.

Sitting on the top step just outside my apartment is the most handsome sight I think I've ever seen. He takes my breath away, but it doesn't change anything.

I turned my phone off and don't know if he's tried to find me or contact me, but with the way his hands grip his messy hair, I know he's been here for a while.

He stands as soon as he sees me.

"What are you doing here?" My tone lacks the bite I wish it carried. I'm too tired. Too drained.

I squeeze by him, both craving and loathing the way my body brushes against his. Electricity sizzles through my veins, mixing with despair and hurt. His hand lashes out, grasping my arm tightly. It's not painful, but his grip is firm, stopping me in my tracks.

I keep my back to him, refusing to give him the satisfaction of looking him in the eye. Plus, I don't think I can. I clamp my eyes shut to block out the feel of his fingers on me.

"You don't get to do this," he says over my shoulder, his voice low, his warm breath washing over my ear. It makes me think of the night before, the way it feels when his lips brush against my neck, and I have to force my body not to lean into him.

I jerk my arm from his hold, he lets me go easily, and I slide my key into the lock, needing to get away from him.

"You lied."

Quickly, I open the door to my apartment and try to slip inside, but Brady's too fast. He shoves a foot through the crack in the door, followed by the rest of his body. I huff.

Anger burns through me, prodding me like the end of a red-hot poker. Why can't he just leave?

"Go home, Brady," I grit out.

"No. I didn't lie. I kept it from you. Yes. And it was wrong."

He rubs a hand over his face.

Okay, so he didn't exactly lie. I don't say anything, though. I just fix him with a steely gaze.

"You said it wasn't about that anyway."

My heart stutters. I forgot I threw that out there.

"Please …"

"Cora, you don't get to say what you did and run. I'm not letting you do this."

His words burn through me. I'm done with this conversation.

He's calling me a coward. Not directly, but that's what he means. It's not that I don't know how my actions look, but I just can't accept his words—not right now. Something about him saying it aloud, something about him knowing I'm afraid to let go, to move on, sets me on fire.

My head snaps up. I can feel the redness burning my cheeks. My chest heaves as I step forward.

"You're not letting me?" His eyes widen as I jab a finger into his sternum. I'll admit there's more force behind it than I intended, but it feels good, so I do it again for emphasis. "I'm not running," I shout, stepping into him more. We're toe to toe and I'm fueled by nothing but ire, red-hot and fiery.

All my grief and guilt has switched tracks and morphed into something else altogether. A storm brews inside me and I can't control it, can't tame it—it's begging to be unleashed. I can feel the tight grip on myself slipping and it feels good. Because if I don't let it loose, I'm afraid I'll burst.

When Brady wraps a hand around the back of my neck and tilts my head so I have to look into his eyes, I can't explain why I do what I do. I wrap my fingers in the collar of his shirt, jerk him down, slant my mouth over his, and slide my tongue inside without invitation. Our teeth click together with the pressure and I press harder.

At first, he does nothing, but I don't stop. I push against him, feeling the hard planes of his chest and his tight abs, my body bowing beneath his height.

Then, he's kissing me back, his teeth biting, lips rough. He runs his tongue over my lips and into my mouth. Excitement shoots through me when he groans and curls it around mine. His hands grip my waist, bringing me tighter against him.

Every ounce of what we're both feeling pours into this kiss.

Brady's anger and confusion burns in the way his fingers tighten on my hips. His strong hands carve a path down to my thighs. He stoops over as he slides his hands to the spot just under my ass and hoists me up, slamming my body against him. Without thinking, I wrap my legs around his waist.

Brady tears my shirt over my head and tosses it somewhere behind him. His mouth moves down toward my chest and he nips at my neck. His teeth nip harder than I expect from him and my body jerks. I dig my fingers into his shoulders and his groan is one of almost pain.

Palming my ass in both hands, Brady pushes his hips up into me. He's hard, and I want nothing between us. High on the feeling of his lips and hands roaming over me, I want more.

I slide my legs down, intending to strip him, but the second my feet hit the floor, Brady spins me. He holds onto my hips, pulling me into him, my back to his chest, and at the same time, he propels me forward, his big body pressing against mine.

I stumble a little, my brain fogged with desire and lust and anger and hurt.

Steps away from my dining room table, Brady places a hand in between my shoulder blades and presses. My palms land on the cool stone surface.

"Don't move," Brady orders.

Before I can react, he's reaching around and flicking open the button on my jeans. The zipper lowers loudly in the silence of my apartment. I suck in a shuddering breath at the brush of his fingertips as he tucks them into the waistband of my jeans and pushes them over my hips.

Once they hit my knees, he jerks them the rest the way off and I step out of them. Strong, rough hands run up the back of my legs and curve over my hips. He looms over me, pulling my hips into his. I moan at the feel of his hard length pressing against me teasingly.

I'm wet and aching, but I'm afraid to speak or move. I'm terrified it'll break the lustful spell being driven by so much emotion. I'm afraid I'll come to my senses or Brady will stop touching me.

The thin lace covering my hips stretches with his grip. Brady groans in my ear as he pulls at the fabric. It pops and loosens before it rips and pulls apart, falling away from my body.

Brady's belt jingles behind me and I hear the distinct sound of a wrapper ripping. My blood thunders through my veins as anticipations grows. His hand is back between my shoulder blades and he pushes me down until my chest is flat against the table, my cheek pressed against its coolness. Brady breathes out loudly.

Without a warning or apology, he uses his legs to widen my stance and slams into me. A moan falls from my lips and my fingers slip across the tabletop, grasping for something to hold onto, something to help me work my way through the intrusion. He's hard and thick and I wasn't ready, but it's oh-so-sweet when he pulls out and thrusts back in with the same amount of force, pinning me between him and the table.

It doesn't escape my attention that he's fully dressed behind me, that the only part of him that touches me is his cock as his hands plant themselves next to mine on the table.

He's relentless and unforgiving as he pounds into me.

It's hard and fast.

And I don't want it to stop.

He doesn't slow, but he hitches my hips up higher, leaving me on the tips of my toes. I relish the feel of his hands on me, but then they're back on the table and he's hitting me in just the right spot.

So deep.

I don't want to, but I can't stop myself from clenching around him. I want this to last.

"Fuck," he breathes out harshly.

And that's all it takes. Orgasm bursts through me, a cosmic explosion. Warm and bright, it flows through my body, loosening muscles and leaving me out of control with Brady's name on my lips.

He grunts and presses into me. Once.

Twice. Three times. Just as hard as when he started. He loses rhythm and I know he's close. His primal grunt confirms it.

I'm boneless against the table. When he pulls out, I jerk and moan, but don't move. I can't. I've lost the ability to control my limbs and until my brain reengages, I'm stuck to my table. Brady moves into my kitchen, and when he comes back, his pants are done up and you wouldn't even know we'd just had sex by looking at him. I'm still hunched over my table, naked. Shame bursts through me, clearing the fog in my head. I find his shirt and tug it on.

Brady runs a hand through his hair and looks at me. My heart sinks when I meet his gaze. What I see in his eyes makes me feel cold and vulnerable.

"We need to talk, Cora."

I sigh, I can't help it. He's right. We do need to talk, but I don't want to say the things that need to be said. I firm my jaw and lift my head.

"What do we need to talk about?"

Losing some of my steel, I cross my arms over my chest in a defensive move.

Brady pins me with a look.

"You were pregnant?"

He lets the words hang in the air between

us.

"I was."

He steps toward me and I hold a hand out to stop him, not wanting him closer.

Brady stops, but the look he gives me is pure frustrated helplessness.

"What happened, babe?"

I brace myself.

"I lost it." My voice is quiet and full of every ounce of despair those three words bring me.

He keeps his expression blank and I know it's with effort because his brow furrows. This time when he steps forward, I don't try to stop him. He takes my hand in his, but it doesn't bring me any comfort. I swallow thickly.

"Can you tell me what that has to do with me having a son?"

I flinch. His words give me the courage I need to pull my hand from his. I sink down onto the couch and rest my head in my hands. I jerk when Brady sits next to me.

"I can't," I start. "I just can't. It's too much." I shake my head.

Brady's jaw tightens.

"Babe," he scoots closer and I bolt from the couch, needing to be away from him. "Cora, stop."

He stands, too.

"No, Brady. You stop." He stops moving toward me, but he doesn't sit. "You don't get it."

"You're right, I don't. So, tell me. Make me understand." He gestures to himself, his motions jerky. He's as worked up and agitated as I am.

"I did this. I wished for it." I'm shouting and I can't seem to lower the volume of my voice. Brady frowns. "I hated that I was pregnant. I hated that it was Mason's child." My voice wavers, but I push forward. "I wanted a clean break. No strings. The last thing I wanted was to be tied to Mason for the rest of my life. I didn't want a baby, and now, I don't have one," I spit the last words at him as tears stream down my face.

He reaches out for me, cupping my face gently.

"Cora."

"No, stop." I push him away. "I can't do it, Brady. I need you to leave."

He stares at me, unmoving.

I can't take it. The look he's giving me is a look I never wanted from him—never wanted from anyone. But coming from him, it's even worse than I thought it would be.

"Leave!"

My heart beats out a jagged rhythm and I wait. One beat. Two beats. Three.

He turns on his heel and moves to my door. I expect him to say something, but he doesn't. He doesn't even turn back.

The door closes softly behind him.

Then, I'm left alone. Just like I wanted.

Just like I deserve.

20

Hours later, I'm five episodes into a Netflix binge, watching Gossip Girl. I'm drowning my sorrows in gummy bears and vanilla ice cream when someone bangs on my door. I don't move.

Instead, I scooch down on the couch, ducking my head like whoever's on the other side of my door might see me if I sit up too straight. I shovel another bite into my mouth, hoping they'll go away, but the banging doesn't stop. Reluctantly, I unroll myself from my blanket and trudge to the door.

Melanie's smiling face greets me when unlock and open the door.

"Hey!"

"Hi. What are you doing here?"

I know I sound suspicious, but I am so, whatever. She never turns up without at least texting first.

Her smile drops and she raises the grocery bag in her hand.

"Brady came by the bar and said you needed me. So, here I am. I brought snacks."

My eyes narrow on the bag.

"I'm fine," I say, still staring at the bag she's holding. I wish I could see what's in there, but I don't know if rehashing my sob story is worth finding out.

Dammit. I need x-ray vision.

Determination tightens my friend's features.

"You're not fine. I can see it in your eyes and your hair is all kinds of crazy." She waves a hand around her own head and I frown before rubbing my locks. She's right. I probably look like medusa. I scowl down at the floor until Melanie clears her throat.

Sighing, I open the door so she can step inside and immediately head back to the couch, where I plop myself down. Mel follows me, and I can feel her eyes on me.

"What else did Brady say?" I turn my narrowed my gaze on her. If Brady spilled any of the details of our fight, I might end up in jail. Because I'm going to murder him. Cold-blooded style. Then again, I'd have to see him to do that, so

I'll probably just be really pissed off from the comfort of my apartment.

"Cora," Melanie says, drawing my attention. I look up from my twisted fingers and meet her gaze. "Brady didn't tell me anything."

Relief floods through me.

"He came into the bar looking pretty upset. He was worried about you. He said he thought maybe you could use a friend."

My eyes burn again, but I don't know how I can possibly have any tears left to cry. Is there an infinite supply or what?

Brady amazes me. The awful way I dismissed him, the angry sex, the refusal to let him speak … it all weighs heavily on me. After all that, he went to my best friend because he knew I'd need someone.

Since I met him, he's known when to push and when to back off, when to let me think and when to think for me. He's known what to say and how to make me feel better. Even without knowing me, he has inherently known what I need and when. And he's gone out of his way to give it to me.

And now he's gone.

Because I made him leave.

Because I can't handle my own shit.

Melanie's warm hand covers mine.

"Want to tell me what's going on?"

I lick my dry, cracked lips. It's been a long day—a long, eventful day. Do I want to do this? I'm not sure I can open myself up so soon again.

It felt good to share with my parents today. It was freeing. And even though it wasn't how I planned, and it didn't turn out how I thought or wanted, I'm glad Brady knows the truth. The thing I can't seem to figure out is how I'm feeling about all the Brady stuff.

I was mad and hurt. Then relieved. Then angry again. I've been all over the place since I made him leave.

One look into my oldest friend's eyes and I know I could use her advice.

"God, Mel, I don't even know where to start."

She laughs lightly.

"How about at the beginning?"

Blowing out a deep breath, I rub my face and comb my fingers nervously through my hair. She's right. The beginning is good. My eyes roam to the grocery bag she laid on my coffee table.

"Okay, but first, what snacks did you bring?"

****

Armed with red licorice in one hand and a strawberry margarita in the other hand, I finally feel I can divulge my secrets to Mel. I'm hoping she won't look at me like the monster I think I am. As far as the Brady issue goes, there's no resolving it. I can't handle it, and I won't even pretend I'm a big enough person to deal with it.

I lick my dry lips and open my mouth, but nothing comes out. Why is this so hard?

"Just spit it out, sweetie."

Mel waves her hand between us where we're seated on my couch as if motioning me forward.

One more sip of margarita.

One more delicious bite of licorice.

Here goes nothing. Or everything. I don't even know anymore.

"Okay."

I take a deep breath and rub my hand over my face. Clearing my throat, I wrap my one hand around the other and squeeze. My knuckles turn white, and for a moment, I can't look away. Then Melanie wraps my hands in her warm ones. My grip loosens and I meet her concerned gaze.

"We had a fight. Brady and I."

"And?" she prompts.

My shoulders slump and I blindly search for

my straw while staring over Mel's shoulder.

Icy coolness hits my tongue while I ponder how to say it, what to spill next.

"I called it off with him."

Her brow furrows and she gives my hands a little squeeze.

"Oh, honey, why?"

I swallow against the choking lump gripping my windpipe tighter and tighter by the second.

"He has a kid," I say softly, and with so much longing and despair.

I watch her reaction closely. Her perfectly painted lips purse and confusion settles into her eyes.

"He lied to you? That sucks."

It would be so easy to let her think he's a total asshole who he lied, but I can't do that. No matter what's happened, Brady isn't the issue—I am. I'm the one with issues up to my eyeballs.

"Yes. No. He omitted. Which is kind of lying, but not really," I ramble before taking a breath. "Okay." I hold my hands out in front of me, bracing myself.

I'm going in. All in. Letting it all out.

"He didn't tell me. I stumbled across the kid's room." Something similar to a gasp comes from Mel. She leans in a little, waiting for more.

"God, Mel, it wouldn't have even mattered if he had told me. I'd have run anyway. It's too much." The tears creep back in, burning my eyes. I pull at a loose thread on the hem of my shirt. "I was pregnant."

A shuddering breath leaves me, but it doesn't ease the whirling emotion inside me. I chance a glance at Mel. She flounders for a second, opening and closing her mouth like she wants to say something but doesn't have a clue what it is.

"It's okay." I pat her hand and bring my hands back to my lap.

"Before Mason left for his deployment, we had a huge fight." I shake my head. "I don't even know what it was about. I'm sure it was something pointless and dumb. We used to fight just to fucking fight. It was awful." I laugh without humor. "When we first got together, I told myself our fights were because we were passionate about each other. Maybe that was true for a while. We were both stubborn, we butted heads all the time, but really, I loved making him angry. I got some sort of sick thrill in seeing how far I could push him. That's so horrible." Tears track down my cheeks.

"Oh," Mel croons as she wraps her arms around me.

"Anyway," I wipe my tears away, only to

have them replaced by more, "we decided to get a divorce. We ended up having sex, it was goodbye, one last fuck, whatever you want to call it, but I got pregnant." The words tear from me on a sob.

She hugs me tighter, my oldest friend.

"I never got to tell him." My chest squeezes my heart, my lungs won't take in air. "He never knew," I whisper.

I'm ashamed that I never told him. I hate myself for being selfish.

I sniff.

"I was going to tell him, I really was, but by the time I worked up the nerve, he was gone. And he was never coming back." I shake my head back and forth, reliving those moments after I found out. The lump is back full force and I try to push it down. "The whole time, I kept wishing it away. I didn't want it to be true. I hated it. I hated that it was happening. I wasn't ready for a baby. We were splitting up."

"Cora, I can't imagine what it's like to deal with that, but you can't beat yourself up. It wasn't your fault. Any of it. Okay?"

There they are. The words I knew everyone would want to say to me when they found out. The words I dreaded.

I nod, because that's what I'm supposed to

do. I don't know if I believe that, though.

"I missed his funeral." My words are low, a rasp in the quiet of my apartment. "I woke up that morning in pain. I brushed it off, but it didn't stop. When I started bleeding, I called an ambulance."

My jaw tightens painfully as I hold back the emotion trying to spew forth.

"He was being put in the ground and I was losing his baby."

I pull away from Mel and lean forward, dropping my head in my hands.

"God, that's so awful," I mutter mostly to myself.

Melanie looks likes she wants to say something, I see it written across her face—the usual, I'm sure—but she changes her mind.

"I'm not going to waste my breath saying the things I'm sure you already know deep down. Tell me where Brady fits into this. I get that it's shitty that he didn't tell you, but ..." she trails off and raises an eyebrow in my direction.

I grab my drink from the coffee table and settle back into the couch.

"I can't do it. Even if he had told me about the kid, I can't do it. I just can't. At first, it was hard for me to even see kids. The guilt was ... overwhelming. I've finally gotten to the point where I can see children without wanting to cry, but I don't think I can date someone with a—with a child."

My face twists.

"You also didn't think you could date someone. Period. Remember that?"

I reel back away from her.

She has a point. Maybe.

I don't like it.

"It's not the same. Not at all."

"Isn't it?"

I bite back a sarcastic remark and scowl instead. She's only trying to help.

"Brady is amazing, he's ... great. He always knows what I need and when I need it. Just like sending you here." I give her a sad smile. "I just can't—I'm not ready to be face-to-face with a kid every day. If Brady and I move forward, I'd be a stepmom. I wished my baby away."

Rolling her bottom lip into her mouth, she pins me with a glare. Her expression is full of *don't bullshit me*. I brace myself.

"So, do something about it," she challenges before raising her straw to her lips and draining her drink.

Do something?

Do what?

I meet my friend's stare, wondering what it is I can do. How do I make this better? How do I make myself better?

Britni Hill

21

I twist my key in the lock of the dance studio and turn toward the street. The sun warms my skin and I turn my face upward for a second, absorbing the rays. I've just finished some last minute bookkeeping and have just enough time grab a coffee before I head to a support group meeting.

The day after my tell-all with Mel and my freak out on Brady, I got online and found a list of support groups offered at the hospital. The first one was rough, but it's getting easier each time I go. Knowing I'm not the only one who feels the way I do is surprisingly comforting. And talking to my parents, letting them in, seems to help.

I glance longingly at Brunette Brew. They really do have the best coffee. I miss it. I want tasty coffee. And I want to see Brady. With all the avoiding I've been doing, and the fact that the dance studio is closed for three weeks due to a break before summer session this will be my last chance to stop in, but I don't know if I can do it.

I should keep my distance. I don't know how I would handle it.

Waffling back and forth and cursing my inability to make a decision, I freeze when the door to the coffee shop opens and Brady appears. He looks so good, I could cry. His lean form fills the doorway, showing off how broad his shoulders are. I know his touch and his kiss and I want more, but I can't let myself have it. It's not fair. To him. To me. To anyone involved.

Brady raises his head and smiles widely. For a moment, I think he sees me, but I'm wrong. He sees someone else.

In my very lame and stalker-like observation of him, I got lost and didn't see the sleek black car idling at the curb or the tall blonde making her way toward him. Now that I'm watching, there's no missing the little boy that flings himself forward and wraps his arms around Brady's legs.

"Daddy!" The little voice drifts across the street and it's like a slap in the face. My heart beats faster than it should, the sound almost deafening to my ears.

I thought that this, the distance, would be

better. That I could watch him from afar and it would be fine, but it's not. I'm on the outside, looking in. And I hate it.

I want a closer look at the woman who has a piece of Brady I'll never have. I want a closer look at the boy who I'm pretty sure is the spitting image of his dad.

I'm glued to the sidewalk, staring across the street at them. I can't make sense of the regret and loneliness moving through me.

After all, I'm the one who sent him away. And the reason I did is right across the street. I'm staring at the cause of the end of the best thing I've had in a long time, and my heart aches. It's cracking wide open and there's nothing I can do.

The blonde laughs and rests her hand on Brady's arm. Jealousy flares to life inside me—very irrational jealousy that I can't seem to bat down. I don't have that right. He isn't mine. I dismissed him.

I should be mad at myself—and I am. But not for letting him go. I'm mad because I didn't deal with my shit before now. I'm mad because I let things get all screwed up.

My phone chirps inside my purse and I jump, pulling my eyes from the scene across the street. I run a nervous hand through my hair as I dig around in my purse and silence the alert. I need to get going before I'm late, but my feet don't want to move.

I raise my eyes, needing one last look at Brady. My gaze lands on him, only to find that he's looking back at me, unmoving. The blonde's eyes drift toward me too. I brace myself.

I'm too far away to get a good look, but I can tell she's impeccably dressed and her hair is perfectly coifed. Even from here, I know she's nothing like me. My shoulders stiffen, I hold my head high, and flick my gaze to Brady's. His expression is unreadable.

Spinning on my heel, I head in the direction of my apartment so I can pick up my car. I tell myself the entire way that I'm fine, that things are the way they're supposed to be.

I think I'm lying to myself.

****

My car is warm, too warm. Seeing Brady rattled me and listening to couples and other women tell their stories of loss shook me even more. I can't seem to cool off. I can't catch my breath. Before I know it, I'm parking in the lot behind the studio and letting myself in. I lock the door behind me and make my way to the office where I drop my stuff. Digging through my bag, I ditch my shoes and sundress and pull on some leggings and a top. I don't bother with shoes. I want to feel the wooden floor against my bare toes.

Instinct drives, the need to be free pushing me. I dock my phone and pull up an old playlist. From the center of the room, I face the wall of mirrors and let my eyes drift closed. Taking deep, cleansing breaths, I clear my mind. I focus on the music, the deep thrum of bass, and let it flow over me, into me.

It's been so long since I danced for me, since I danced to be free—long before I was pregnant, long before Mason and I left. I don't know when dancing stopped being a part of me. Even though it was never something I wanted to pursue professionally, it was always a way for me to escape. The same as everything else I left it behind when I followed Mason.

My limbs move, slow and steady, with ease and grace. The music carries me across the floor. I spin, and leap, and dip low. Brady is long forgotten. My miscarriage is no longer a burden on my shoulders. My dead husband isn't a thought. I breathe freely and easily.

My muscles burn and my skin is slick with a shiny sheen of sweat. I love it. The song changes, and so do my moves. No longer soft and slow, I push harder, move faster.

I don't stop until the playlist starts to repeat. My chest heaves and exertion tingles across my skin. I feel good. Exhausted, but better than I've felt in a long time. Lowering myself to the floor, I stretch my legs, loving the pull I feel.

I'm smiling.

I'm moving forward.

And it feels so good.

22

I just had to pick the cart with the wonky wheel. As I make my way through the aisles, there's a horrible crunching sound every few seconds and it's coming from me and the awful cart I'm pushing. Ducking my head, I hope no one sees me.

I sigh and grab a box of cereal from a shelf. It's sugary goodness in a box and I should probably lay off the sweets, but I can't. Being lonely apparently gives me a sweet tooth. It's a good thing I've been locking myself away in the dance studio once a day. I don't know what I'll do next week when the summer session starts. I'm fond of having the place to myself.

I start to move forward, resisting the urge to kick my cart. It's seriously annoying. I give it a frustrated shake as I turn the corner. My eyes drift down the next aisle and my heart drops, it stops beating, my tongue sticks to the roof of my mouth. It's bad enough that I can't stop thinking about him. I can't stop looking across the street at Brunette Brew when I'm at work. I shouldn't want to see him, but I can't stop my eyes from roaming over him.

My gaze drifts across his broad shoulders and sweeps over his handsome face. A whining voice drags me from my perusal.

"But, Daaad…"

My eyes snap to the boy standing by Brady's side. Something flutters in my chest, causing me to gulp back the unidentified emotion. Brady's body starts to turn in my direction and panic bursts free inside me. I lurch forward with my cart, praying he hasn't seen me. I turn quickly and start down the next aisle, trying to rein in the flood of emotion battering at my insides.

Thinking I'm safe, I stop and stare blankly at the many different kinds of rice before me. I don't need rice, but I don't move. I need to get my head straight. The hairs on the back of my neck raise and a prickling sensation crawls over me. The sound of a child's laughter and footsteps draw my attention away from my rice selection. My eyes fall closed instantly. I know who it is without looking. It's *him*.

The footfalls slow and eventually stop. I

know he sees me, so I make myself turn. It's another few seconds before I can make myself look at something other than his feet.

Blue clashes with green when my eyes meet his. We both stand frozen. I smile, but it's weak and feels wooden, stiff. It's fake, and I hate it. Brady takes a step forward, toward me, and his son looks between us, his eyes curious.

Before either of us can speak, ringing sounds from Brady's pocket. His eyes still locked on mine, he answers his phone without checking to see who it is. Feeling like an intruder, I turn back to the rice. I want to abandon my cart and hide in my apartment, but my feet are rooted in place. I can't help but overhear the tension in Brady's rising voice.

"Yeah. She's okay?" He pauses. "Alright." A frustrated sigh leaves him.

I glance at him over my shoulder. I can't help it.

His eyes are on his son, his face lined with stress as he runs a hand over his forehead.

"Let me find a sitter. I'll be there as soon as I can."

He pulls his phone away from his ear and runs a hand through his messy hair. His eyes flick to mine for only a second as he scrolls through the contacts on his phone. That's when I realize I'm still standing there, staring.

"I have to go."

I nod.

He grabs the small hand clutching the bottom of his t-shirt and starts to move away.

"Um, okay ..." I pause. Maybe it's not my place. "Is everything okay?" I have to ask. I can't let him walk away without knowing. I can tell he's upset. The tone of the conversation leads me to believe someone is hurt. The instinct to soothe him is strong. I want to care for him in the way he's cared for me since we met.

"My mom ..." he stops, glancing at the kid by his side. I nod. He doesn't want to say in front of his son. "I have to find someone to watch him."

Words are on the tip of my tongue, but I don't know what I'm thinking. My hands shake by my sides. Fuck it.

"I can watch him."

There they are—those words that were stuck on the tip of my tongue.

They're out there, hanging between us.

And I'm waiting.

A range of emotions flicker across Brady's face before it morphs into something I don't think I could ever describe. Confusion, disbelief, anger, a mix of those and so much more mar his handsome face.

"I don't mind. Really," I assure him.

Brady's head starts to shake.

"Thank you, Cora. I just—I don't think that's a good idea."

His phone beeps. And beeps again.

"We'll be fine."

His gaze meets mine. I nod, urging him to agree.

"It'll be easier. I can just take him. You won't have to drop him off anywhere. So you can go straight to where you need to go."

He's thinking about it. I can tell. I'm nervous, but still hopeful. I don't know where this hope comes from. Or, rather, I don't want to think about it too hard.

I smile down at the boy who looks so much like his dad.

Bending, I put myself at eye level with the little boy and a grin turns up his little lips.

"Hi. I'm Cora." I look up at Brady. "I'm a friend of your dad's."

His smile widens before he buries his face in Brady's leg.

"He's kind of shy."

"So, nothing like you then," I tease, and

smile up at him. The sadness in his gaze sobers me and my smile slips.

This is so weird. I'm trying my hardest not to let it show.

Brady has mercy on me and chuckles a little. He unburies the boy's face.

"Say hi to Cora, Logan."

He giggles and gives me a tiny wave. It's cuteness overload. And his green eyes match his dad's.

"Okay, so I can take him back to my place," I start to say, but Brady opens his mouth.

"Cora," he interrupts, but doesn't say anything else.

"You can trust me. I want to do this for you."

I hope he can hear the truth in my words. I hope he can see that I'm changing, that I'm getting better.

He stares at me for a moment and his perfect lips purse.

"Okay, but you can take him to my place."

Brady pulls his keys from his pocket and starts twisting one off the ring.

"Logan, I have to run an errand. You cool to hang with Cora?"

Little green eyes flick to me and back up to

Brady's face.

"'Kay." He nods enthusiastically.

We both leave our carts and head for the door.

Logan walks between us, gripping Brady's hand tightly.

I watch Brady. Being this close to him brings every feeling I've ever had for him rushing back in. Every day, I remember how he makes me feel and I mourn the loss of us, but now, it's so much clearer how much is missing from my life.

I wonder if he feels the same.

Small, warm fingers wrap around mine, startling me. A quick glance tells me Logan is grinning up at me while he grips my hand. My mouth goes dry.

The picture we must paint.

But it's not real.

"How old are you, Dad?"

"Twenty-eight," Brady answers. "How old are you, Logan?"

Logan laughs.

"Seven!"

I can't help smiling.

We reach Brady's car quickly and he pulls Logan's booster seat from the back.

"Where are you parked?"

I point across the lot and lead the way.

My stomach twists and turns the closer we get to my car. I wipe my sweaty palms against my jeans and take a deep breath.

I hit unlock on my key fob and watch as Brady pulls open my back door. He situates the booster and turns back to me, handing me his house key.

"Thank you, Cora. I will text you when I know more." He pulls his wallet from his back pocket and hands me a wad of cash. "Order pizza. He needs a bath, but don't worry about that. Bed time is at nine. Hopefully, I'll be back before then," he says, the words leaving him in a rush.

I smile and place a hand on his forearm.

"We'll be fine. I promise. If I need anything, I'll call."

"Okay."

He ruffles Logan's hair and helps him climb into my car. Logan buckles himself in and Brady checks to make sure he's secure. Logan rolls his eyes over his dad's head so I know this isn't needed, or probably normal. Brady surprises me when he walks me to the driver's side door and opens it for me.

He's close enough that I can smell his cologne when I slide into the car. I take a deep breath and try to ignore the pitter-patter of my heart as it thumps back to life.

"I've gotta go. Thank you again."

With a pat to the top of the car, Brady calls goodbye to Logan and jogs toward his own car. Adjusting the rearview mirror, I look at the little boy in my back seat. Apprehension fills me, but along with it is something else, something warm, something I can't name.

I back out of the spot and head in the direction of Brady's house, a place I've only been once. A place that hold one of my worst memories.

"Miss Cora?"

"Yeah, buddy?"

"How old are you?"

This kid and ages. I smile.

"Twenty-five."

"Is that older or younger than my dad?"

"Uh, younger," I answer.

I wonder where he's going with this, but what do I know about seven-year-old logic.

He's quiet for a moment.

I'm driving cautiously, more so than usual, and I know it's because of the kid in my back seat.

"Miss Cora?"

"What?"

"Are you my dad's girlfriend?"

My smile falls a little.

"No, buddy. We're just friends."

"Why?"

Of all the questions he decides to ask.

Yeah, why? Good question, Logan.

One I'm not sure I know the answer to anymore.

23

Manly cologne surrounds me, warming me from the inside. I breathe in deeply. Strong arms wrap around me and I nestle closer to the hard body attached to them.

"Brady," I murmur into his shirt.

His hands grip me tighter.

He holds me closer.

I try to pull myself out of the lull of sleep, but I can't. Watching Logan was exhausting, but fun. I'd do it again. I'm just not used to all the playing, and wrestling him into pajamas was a workout.

Brady lowers me and something soft and cushiony pillows my body. A blanket lands on top of me. I snuggle deeper into the Brady smell surrounding me. I swear I feel his lips against my forehead. I sigh.

Grabbing onto his arm, I stop him from

moving away. I manage to crack my eyes open.

"Don't go," I whisper into the darkness of the room. "Please."

Brady looks from my hand on his arm to my eyes. His brow furrows as he lowers himself to the bed next to me. He brushes his fingers across my cheek and tucks some of my hair behind my ear.

"I can't stay, Cora." His voice is low and tugs at the longing deep inside me.

It doesn't escape my notice that he's said my name more times today than the entire time I've known him. I hate it. No more pet names, no babe—just Cora.

Tears sting the back of my eyelids as I watch him watch me.

"I'm so sorry," I whisper, my voice cracking.

The corners of his lips turn down.

A tear slips down my cheek and I hastily swipe it away.

"Don't do this." Brady wipes the rest of the wetness from my skin and it takes everything in me not to move into his touch. "Not now."

"I ..."

"We can talk. Just not now."

I sit up and wipe my eyes.

"You're right. How's your mom?"

Sitting up only brings us closer to each

other, and at this point, I'm not very happy about it. I scoot back a little, trying to gain some space, and bump the headboard behind me.

He runs a hand over his head. Back and forth. Back and forth.

"She fell. Broke her arm. She's okay, though."

He laughs.

"Good."

It's quiet. Too quiet. I want to reach out and touch him, but I don't dare actually do it.

"How was Logan?"

"Great." It sounds so dreamy when it comes out. It's probably obvious that I'm half in love with his kid. "He was really good."

I yawn.

"I should head home."

I look around Brady's bedroom.

"It's late. Just stay here."

"I can sleep on the couch."

Before I can move, Brady's pushing me down into his pillows.

"I've got the couch."

"Brady."

"Cora."

"Fine." I curl up on my side.

"We'll talk in the morning."

Everything inside me jumps and twists and drops again.

Brady makes his way to the door and clutches the knob in his hand.

"Good night."

I swallow thickly. My heart aches. He should be sleeping next to me, but I totally get why he isn't. Regret washes over me, hitting me hard.

"Night."

The door closes with a soft click.

I'm left alone, surrounded by Brady's scent, wrapped up in his blankets, regretting running away from him.

****

The mattress moves and I jolt upright, confused about what woke me. It's still dark and I was dead asleep.

"Miss Cora," Logan whispers. I feel small fingers against my hand.

"What, buddy?"

"I had a bad dream."

Logan crawls closer to me and I wrap my arm around him, pulling him against me.

"You want me to get your dad?"

I don't know if he has nightmares often, or if they have a routine for this kind of thing. I'm just guessing if he's upset, he'll want his dad to soothe him.

"No, can I sleep with you?"

A spark lights within me when I hear those words.

"Okay."

I shift my weight, lie back down, and pull the covers back so Logan can climb under them. When he presses his small body next to me, I'm surprised.

"Let's snuggle," he whispers.

I wrap him up in my arms and press my mouth against hair that still smells of children's shampoo.

"Night, Miss Cora."

My lips curve upward.

"Night, buddy."

****

Hot. Way too hot.

I toss the blankets off my legs and squint into the bright morning light. My arm is numb, but Logan is still knocked out, his head on my chest, so I don't move.

This kid is a mini space heater. I told him the Spiderman onesie he wanted to wear would be too hot, but he insisted. His hair is damp with sweat and sticking up everywhere. He sighs in his sleep and I move him closer to me.

I don't know what it is about snuggling with kids, but it kind of rocks. It makes me ache at the same time. Thinking I could have had this with a child of my own confuses me. I smooth his crazy hair down and smile sadly.

"Did you he wake you?"

Brady's standing in the doorway to his bedroom wearing a pair of basketball shorts and nothing else. My eyes devour his chest and arms.

"No. He came in here last night." I stretch, trying to relieve the numbness in my arm without waking Logan. "He said he had a bad dream."

"Sorry."

"Oh, no, it's fine."

Logan's eyes pop open and he grins up at me.

"Hi, Miss Cora," he says a little too loudly for the hour.

He's wide-awake.

"Good morning."

He's up and bouncing off the bed before I have time to register what's happening.

"Morning, Dad!"

"Morning, bud." Brady ruffles his hair as Logan darts past him.

"Is he always like that in the morning?"

Brady laughs.

"Pretty much. It's like zero to sixty in two point five seconds."

I stand from the bed and stretch before smoothing my jeans. Brady's eyes track my movements. Resting both hands on the doorjamb, he leans into the room.

"Breakfast?"

I really should go, I need to put some space between us, but I also remember him saying we could talk, and I feel I owe him some type of explanation.

"Sure." I shrug.

Brady slaps a hand against the doorframe and pushes off. He smirks at me before he turns and heads down the hallway.

Ducking my head, I smile, then head toward Brady's kitchen.

Britni Hill

29

Cartoon sounds carry from the living room into the kitchen as I stare at Brady's broad back. He's whisking eggs in a bowl and I'm practically burning a hole through his skin with my eyes. I can't seem to look away. I've missed so much about him. I feel the need to soak in every little thing because I don't know if I'll ever get to experience this again.

"Will you tell me about Logan's mom?" I ask quietly.

Brady tosses me a quick glance over his shoulder. His lips quirk up in a sad smile. When he doesn't say anything right away, I start to panic. Maybe I've over-stepped. Things are more comfortable than I imagined they'd be between us and I don't know how to act.

Wiping his hands on a towel, he tosses it so it rests on his shoulder and busies himself with turning the burner on.

I drop my head into my hands.

"What do you want to know?" His tone is hushed and I wonder if it's the subject or the kid in the next room. My eyes flick to his, but his back is to me again.

"Uh ... whatever you want to tell me," I answer just as quietly. "Where did you meet her?"

Brilliant green meets my gaze.

"We met in L.A."

I nod. It all clicks together now.

"All the things you wouldn't take back about L.A. ..."

Brady stirs the eggs and looks me in the eye before his gaze skirts over my shoulder into the living room. His lips curve upward.

"I wouldn't take any of it back."

It hits me then. This kid changed his life. And my child most likely would've changed mine. Instead, I wonder every day what my life would have been like, if I'd have regretted my child. I'll never know. I only know guilt and shame. I'm slowly healing, but it's still there.

"So, how did you two meet?"

A plate settles on the table in front of me.

"She was a model—a wannabe model—and I was in a band. I mentioned I partied a lot. Too

much. Too hard. Kendra and I were casual, but obviously not careful. So, here we are."

Here we are.

I don't say anything, because I don't know what to say. I feel unwarranted jealousy and I don't know why.

He turns back to face me with a smaller plate in hand.

"Logan," he calls.

Little feet pound against the floor. Logan flings himself into the room against my chair and wraps his arms around me. My lips tip upward.

"Dad, can I eat and watch my show?"

Brady looks like he wants to say no, but he seems to think better of it. With a resigned look, he shoos his son into the other room and turns a serious expression on me. I know what's coming. A conversation I don't necessarily want to have, but need.

This is my chance to tell him how sorry I am for how I handled everything. To try to explain. I take a deep breath and shovel a bite of eggs into my mouth. I watch as Brady does the same. I know he's waiting for me—he's always waiting for me to get my shit together.

It just goes to show, he knows exactly what I need nearly all the time. I take a deep breath. So many thoughts roll through my mind. Aside from telling him and my parents I was pregnant, this will be one of the hardest things I've ever said.

Denial. Anger. Depression. Three very dirty words. Three words I never wanted to describe me. Three things that are hard to live—and to move on from.

"I was stuck," I blurt, and slap a hand over my mouth.

Brady looks up, startled, and raises an eyebrow in my direction.

Shit.

That was definitely not how I meant to start this conversation.

"Let me try that again." A nervous laugh puffs out of me.

I close my eyes and breathe through my nose. Letting everything melt away is easier than I thought it would be. In just a few seconds, the only thing filtering through my brain is the sound of whatever kid's show Logan is watching.

I lick dry lips and finally pry my eyes open.

Forcing myself to meet Brady's gaze, I push my plate away.

"I'm so sorry for the way I handled ... telling you. I'm sorry I didn't tell you until I freaked about ..." I gesture to the living room. "You were the first person I told."

It barely squeaks out.

He peers up at me, setting his fork down slowly.

Waiting for him to say something is agonizing.

"I think we both handled that situation poorly."

Sucking my bottom lip into my mouth, I nod. Brady's eyes focus on my lips and pain flares to life in my chest. Ignoring the heat in his gaze and the throb in my chest, I press on.

"I've felt guilty and confused for so long. It was my dirty secret and I just kind of imploded. That's all on me." I swallow thickly. "I was trying to move forward without letting go and that doesn't work."

Brady's eyes roam over my face for a moment before he leans back in his chair.

"As much as I hate how it turned out, I'm actually glad you … imploded. It needed to happen for you to get better."

Time seems to slow down as he reaches out to me. I watch his hand nervously until his fingers graze the back of my own. My eyelids flutter and my lungs freeze as I desperately try to burn this moment into my memory. Knowing I probably won't get to touch him, feel his hands on me again, scares me.

"You're right. It had to happen. Otherwise, I'd still be denying it. But I found a support group, and it's been helping."

"That's great, Cora," he says softly.

Standing, I take my plate to the sink and rinse it before loading it into the dishwasher. I can feel eyes on me, but I don't want look at him right now. Even though I am sorry and I wish I'd handled things differently, it doesn't change the way things are between us.

I dry my hands and lean against the counter.

"I should probably go."

I work up enough nerve to turn around just as Brady stands to bring his own plate over. I go left and he goes right, we laugh, and an awkward dance ensues before we finally get past one another.

Grabbing my purse, I linger in the doorway of the kitchen.

"I hope your mom is okay. And I'm so sorry," I say again, needing to make sure he knows.

"Thanks for helping with Logan."

"Of course. He was great."

The front door looms before us. As we pass

the living room, I detour inside and crouch next to Logan.

"Bye, buddy."

"Miss Cora! I don't want you to leave."

I smile.

"I have to go home, bud. Sorry." I ruffle his hair. "I'll see you again. I just know it."

He wraps his arms around me and I give him a squeeze.

Meeting Brady back at the door, I have to resist the urge to reach out and touch him. He opens the door for me and flashes me a crooked grin.

"See you." I wave and step out onto the porch.

Brady follows me, and when I look back, confused, he points to my car.

"I, uh … have to get the booster seat." He scratches the top of his head.

"Right."

I knew that.

Totally.

Britni Hill

25

Air thick with humidity causes my hair to cling to my already damp skin as I step onto the sidewalk. Summer session has kicked off at the studio and I spend most evenings dancing my ass off before I head home. The exercise helps clear my head. I'm seeing things in a different light and I feel better than I have in a long time. I wish things with Brady hadn't gotten so screwed up. I wish I would've handled my end differently.

I think it had to happen the way it did, though. My mindset didn't allow it to be any different. If it hadn't gone down the way it did, I'd still be stuck in the same place I had been for a long time. I know that. And now I'm moving on.

Two weeks ago, when I explained myself to him, I don't know what I expected. I didn't have a clue how this would be or feel. There's been no word from him. I'm avoiding Brunette Brew. I catch a glimpse of him or Logan coming and going from across the street every now and then, but that's it.

I pull my key from the lock and drop the set into my bag while I dig for my water bottle with the other. I can't find it, so I hold the bag open and dip my head to search some more. I don't hear anyone approach, but when I finally decide I've left my drink inside and lift my head, a pair of green eyes and a boyish smirk greet me.

My lips automatically curve upward. Brady smiles back.

"Hi." It comes out breathy, and my cheeks instantly warm.

His work shirt clings to his arms and chest, light scruff lines his jaw. My fingers tingle with the urge to run over the rough skin.

"Hey." Brady runs a hand through his hair. The action instantly sets me on edge. "Can I walk you home?"

I pull my bottom lip into my mouth and nibble on it while I watch him.

Can he?

Yeah, of course he can.

Why does he want to?

I have no clue.

At my hesitation, the corners of his lips drop and a frown takes the place of the grin his handsome face was wearing. It's not that I don't want him to walk me, because I really do, it's just that I'm a little stunned. Confused. Worried.

I attempt to school my features, but I'm not sure how well it works out. I generally suck at keeping my face from showing every single thing I'm feeling. His smile doesn't return.

"Yes," I rush out, not wanting him to change his mind or take back his offer. I take a deep breath. "I'd like that."

Grabbing my keys, I turn back to the door and look over my shoulder at him.

"I just need to grab my water."

He nods and runs a hand over the back of his neck. Looking up at me from beneath his lashes, he finally smiles again and my heart leaps.

I let myself inside, Brady stays just on the other side of the door, giving me a chance to look over my appearance. It could be worse. Running my fingers through my hair, I scan the room and find my water bottle sitting by the iPod dock.

Chugging half of it down, I wipe my hand across the back of my mouth and take a few deep breaths before making my way to the door. Excited nervousness churns inside me, twisting up my insides the closer I get to Brady.

When I open the door, he looks up from his

phone and smiles. I can't even begin to describe how much I love that he's smiling at me. I lock up quickly, giving the door one last pull before moving away. I'm paranoid that one day I won't get the door locked and I'll come into a destroyed studio. That's the last thing I need, so I always double check, even if it makes me look and feel neurotic.

"Ready?"

Brady's watching me closely and I'm sure he can read my nerves in every move I make. I nod and step in the direction of my apartment.

"How was work?"

Small talk.

Great.

I almost roll my eyes, but manage to contain myself.

"It was good. Summer session is a lot more laid back because there isn't a showcase or anything." His hand brushes mine, shooting tingles up my arm and straight into my chest where it begins to ache. "I stayed late to dance a little," I add shyly.

No one knows about my late night dancing. Maybe Miss Kaye, but not because I've told her. She just seems to know everything.

Emotion dances across Brady's face— surprise, excitement, happiness, and finally, pride.

It makes me uneasy to see him so impressed with me dancing. I'd never told him what it meant to me. Honestly, I hadn't known.

"You look good," he says after a quiet minute. "Happy."

Something flutters inside me.

"Uh ... thanks." I laugh nervously.

I avoid looking at him and bump his arm with mine. I suck in a sharp breath. I still feel *everything* for him and I don't know how to act right now. These little touches, accidental or not, are stirring up something inside me.

I scramble for something to talk about. I don't want this to be weird or end.

"How's Logan doing?"

He chuckles and scratches at his chest.

"He's good." Brady peers over at me, smiling. "He keeps talking about you."

I grin.

"Yeah?" The thought warms me.

"Yeah. He keeps asking if you can watch him again."

I look away.

"I didn't promise him. I know that's not an option," he says in a rush.

I don't like this shift in conversation. I hate that he thinks I wouldn't want to be around Logan.

Then again, the only reason he thinks I wouldn't want to watch his son is because I made him think that. Truthfully, it wasn't as bad as I thought it would be. It was fun. And he's the cutest boy. I'd do anything to help Brady, but I acted full-on crazy when confronted with the idea of having a relationship that involved a child.

We're fast approaching my apartment and I want to clear this up. I like that Brady's coming around. I want him to come around more. I look over at him and have to breathe in deeply. My heart hurts.

"Brady, it's—it's okay," I stutter. "If you ever need someone to watch him, I'd love to. Or maybe I can take him to the park or something. It's really not a big deal."

We stop in front of the bakery and I turn to face him. The wind blows, shifting the stuffy air around us. My hair moves in the breeze, pieces sticking to my face.

Brady licks his lips, a nervous look shadowing his face.

He nods.

"I'll keep that in mind," he says sincerely.

I rock back and forth on my heels.

"Okay, good." I smile. "Well, thanks for walking me home."

He looks over my shoulder at my building and nods, seeming preoccupied.

"I wanted to ... um," he stops and takes a deep breath before reaching out and brushing a few strands of hair from my face. My lungs stop working when his hand moves toward me. The feel of his skin on mine is electric—charged. Those accidental touches while we were walking have nothing on this. This touch ... this touch steals my breath and freezes me in place. "I wanted to talk to you. Would it be okay if I came in for a minute?"

Fear slices through me, painfully reminding me of all the things I've lost. Of how our last conversation in my apartment went. I'm afraid that whatever conversation Brady wants to have will be equally as horrible.

I stare at him blankly for a moment.

I can't tell him no. I swallow thickly.

"Of course. Yeah."

I try to get myself together as I head up the stairs and unlock the door. I'm fully aware of Brady's every step behind me, echoing my own footfalls. Once we're inside, I sit on the couch and Brady follows my lead. I should probably offer him something to drink, but my brain is all over the place and by the time it registers that it's the gracious thing to do, he's already started talking. It seems he's in a hurry to get this over with. The thought causes my stomach to clench.

"I didn't say much when you were at the house." He looks up at me. "I didn't know what to say. I was mad at you. I get it. I get why you didn't tell me. I really do, Cora, but I was angry."

"Brady, I'm so …"

"I know you're sorry. I know that. I just wanted you to know that I'm happy that you've found a support group and that you're feeling better about things. I'm proud of you," he says, cutting me off before I can apologize again.

The corners of his mouth turn up and he meets my gaze.

Tears sting my eyes.

I knew he was mad at me, he had a right to be, but that's not what has my chest burning. It's hearing that he's proud of me and happy for me. If I hadn't been so blinded by guilt and grief, he would've stood by me, supported me.

"Thank you," I say quietly.

"If you ever need a shoulder or to talk, I'm here."

I sniff.

Hearing those words, that he'd be there for me even after the way I ended things, means a lot. Swallowing against the lump in my throat, I give him a wobbly smile and thank him again. The words 'I'm sorry' and 'thank you' can't be said enough to him.

Brady stands and moves closer to me, holding out a hand.

Unsure of what he's doing, I hesitate, but one look up into his gaze and I take his hand. He pulls me up and instantly wraps me in his warm embrace. I bury my head in his chest and breathe in the smell of his detergent and cologne. It's a balm on my already healing wounds.

Britni Hill

26

Like the creeper that I've become, I watch as Brady and Logan head through the Brunette Brew door. Logan sits on Brady's shoulders so he has to duck down to keep the boy from hitting his head as they enter. I smile as the door closes behind them. An ache unlike one I've known before settles in the pit of my stomach. I've felt a lot of pain, loss, and heartache in the last few years, but this is so different. It's the deepest loneliness. Like a part of me is gone, missing—in the distance, but still out of reach.

I gave something to Brady I'd never given to anyone else. I miss him. And Logan captured a piece of my heart just like his father. I'd give anything to spend just a few minutes with them. The direction my thoughts are heading down surprise me. Because it's true. It's not just Brady I want more time with anymore.

"Alright, everyone!" Miss Kaye calls behind me. "Let's do some stretches."

She claps to ensure she has everyone's attention. I peer over my shoulder and watch little bodies scatter and giggle as they find their places before turning back to stare out the window. A warm hand lands on my shoulder, drawing my attention.

"You okay, honey?"

Miss Kaye's smile is as warm as her touch.

"Yeah, I'm good." I give her hand a pat. "I'm going to head out, if you don't need anything else from me."

"I've got it from here. You go on home," she responds instantly. My gaze wanders back to the window. Longing fills me. "You should tell him," she whispers.

Startled, I turn to meet her gaze.

Tell him?

Tell him what?

That I miss him. That I want him. That I need him. That I—that I love him? I don't, do I? Who am I kidding?

I do.

I've known it for a while. I've just been too scared.

I never told Miss Kaye much about Brady,

but she knew we were dating. I have no clue how she read my feelings so easily, but she has. The expression on her face says it all. A soft smile curves the wrinkled lines of her lips as she watches me.

"Maybe you're right," I mutter before a sigh slips out.

When I turn away from the window, Miss Kaye is still watching me. Her all knowing gaze makes me want to squirm. My insides do, but I manage to keep it to that only. I don't know exactly what she's seeing, but I'm sure I don't want her looking at it anymore.

Her words echo through my mind. Maybe she's right. Maybe I should tell him. It's a scary thought. One I want to deny, but doing things my way doesn't seem to work out so well. I can admit I have no clue what I'm doing, but I'm figuring it out.

Slowly.

But I am.

That's what matters.

"I'll see you tomorrow."

Miss Kaye pats my arm and gives a little squeeze.

"Okay, Cora. Have a good evening, sweetheart."

I grab my things from the office and when I

come out, Miss Kaye has the kids warming up. I smile softly as I watch them on the way to the door. Something I never thought I'd be able to do when looking at children. Humid summer air hits me in the face and I immediately dread my walk home. I cross the street and hesitate in front of the coffee shop. My chest feels tight and my eyes burn.

Turning on my heel, I take quick steps away from the door and hope no one's noticed me hovering all stalker-like. I take a few deep breaths, trying to clear my head. The longer Brady and I are apart, the more I miss him. I want to take back the break up, but that's not how real life works. It won't be that simple, and it shouldn't be. I just need a second chance. Time to show him we can try again.

Right?

If I talk to him, tell him how I feel, we can work it out.

If he'll have me.

I blow out a breath and chew my bottom lip. Knowing my luck, I've completely put him off with all my crazy, but I have to try. One thing I've learned through all this is that I'm done letting life pass me by. I'm done not going after things that will make me happy.

And losing the man I'm falling for—*have*

fallen for, isn't an option.

I've made it around the block twice now and I'm quickly coming up on my third time. Every time I pass Brunette Brew, my hand reaches out for the door, but I can't make myself open it. Nerves twist my stomach. My muscles turn to stone, freezing me in place until I turn away. This last time, I don't let my hand reach out. I curl my fingers by my side and keep on walking. With my head lowered in embarrassment, I hope no one has seen me and head toward my apartment.

I need a moment to think, to get my head straight. I'm going to talk to Brady. I just have to regroup. Make a plan. Relax the crazy train barreling through my mind.

Most of all, I need to figure out the best way to say what I need to say to him.

****

My skin feels clammy and flushed as I hold my phone tightly to my ear. It rings once before he answers. A shiver dances down my spine at the sound of his deep voice. I'm a chicken for calling Brady instead of approaching him face-to-face, but I think this is the only way I can actually follow through.

"Hello?" The sound of his voice draws me back, reminding me I didn't respond when he answered because I've been lost in my head.

I take a deep, soothing breath. I've practiced what I will say, but hearing his voice leaves my mind blank and stumbling for words.

"Hey." I sound unsure, breathless. A total mess, as usual.

"Everything okay?" Concern threads his words.

"Uh … yeah. I just wanted to see if maybe you wanted to grab dinner. I know you have Logan, and he can come, or maybe you could get a sitter— either way. I'd just …" The words burst from my mouth in a rushed mumble.

Deep breath.

I clear my throat.

Brady's quiet.

I start to open my mouth, to say more or take it back, I don't know, but I need to fill the silence with something, so why not the sound of my own voice?

"I'd like that," he finally says.

Relief flows through my veins. I sag against my couch.

"Okay," I whisper.

I should probably pick a day, a time, maybe clarify if Logan is coming, but I can't seem to say anything else.

"I'll get a sitter. When were you thinking?"

"Tomorrow?" I blurt.

"Okay, that should be fine. I'll pick you up at seven." He's taken over the making plans part of this, because, as usual, every time this happens, Brady knows when I need him to make decisions and when to let me make them on my own.

"Okay," I manage to say. Brilliant conversationalist I am not.

It's quiet again, and I lay my head in my hand. I need to get it together.

"Cora?"

I swallow thickly. An entire range of emotion screams from within my name when he says it. His deep voice is low, husky.

"Yeah?" I manage to get out.

"I need to know what this means. It can mean whatever you want, but you have to tell me exactly what that is." Desperation tinges his voice. I realize possibly for the first time that maybe being away from me has been hard on Brady too. It's sad that my inability to admit I needed help put us here. While it causes me pain, hearing the need in his words also makes my heart sing.

If he wants this too …

This is my second chance.

It's hard not to blurt the words that have

been swimming around my head for a while now, but that's definitely not the way to do this—to tell him I love him. Because I do. I really do. I manage to hold it in, but I have to answer him.

I have to tell him exactly what I want out of this—out of us.

"It's a date. A second chance." I put it out there with those last three words. It's so much more, but I haven't been a great wordsmith in this conversation thus far, so why change that now?

"Okay, Cora." Still Cora. "But we have to talk."

"Alright." He's right.

"I mean it. We have to talk, because you can't have me until you one day decide you don't want Logan, too. If it's too hard, or—"

"I know. We'll talk."

****

I'm wearing a new dress and heels. My hair is twisted into messy waves. It's growing out and, I've missed the length. I've taken more care with my appearance tonight than I have in a long time, but I want this to be perfect. Mel came over earlier to show her support. She watched me with a small smile as I meticulously applied makeup. All it took was one look into her eyes to know that she approves of this. That she wants me to put myself out there. Just knowing she thinks I'm doing the right thing makes this so much easier.

At five till seven, there's a heavy knock on my door. I stop breathing for a few seconds before I burst into action and make my way to the door while smoothing down my dress and running a hand over my hair. Squaring my shoulders, I grip the knob tightly and twist.

When Brady comes into view, his wide smile makes my knees weak. His sandy hair is its usual mess. His eyes sparkle down at me, and I want to launch myself into his arms. I want to feel his hard chest against mine. I want to feel his strong arms pull me close and hold me tight.
I manage to keep my feet on the ground.

Instead, I just smile up at him and hold the door open.

Brady leans in and presses soft lips to my cheek. He breathes in deeply before he pulls away and I try to hide my smile, but fail miserably. The look on his face when he leans back makes me want to scrap this whole dinner idea.

My face must show him the same thing because he steps closer and runs the back of his fingers over my cheek. His nostrils flare as his thumb slides across my bottom lip. My head tilts back when his hand curves around the back of my neck. Warm, minty air brushes my mouth. Brady's tongue darts out and wets his lips, drawing my gaze.

I feel warm all over, tingly and light-headed, and his next words make me sway against him.

"Tell me you want it, too," he breathes.

He's so close, barely any space remains between us. The heat from his body washes over me, making me tremble.

"I do," I whisper, gripping his shoulders to steady myself. "I do."

His mouth slants over mine firmly before he slows and kisses me softly, a whisper of his lips on mine. He brushes my mouth again and again, causing me to tighten my grip and pull him closer, wordlessly begging for more. His lips curve against mine. He uses his free hand to haul my body against his while his other holds my head right where he wants it. I press myself into lean muscle just as his warm tongue licks into my mouth, flicking against my own.

"I really, really do," I pant when we break for air. Brady doesn't release me, so I keep my hands on him too. Needing to feel him. Needing him to ground me.

"Good."

Then, he's kissing me again, and it's the

best kind of kiss. He lifts me up and I lock my legs around his waist. His palm skims up the outside of my thigh. My breath freezes in my chest when his hand slips beneath the skirt of my dress, cups my left butt cheek, and squeezes.

I moan.

My back connects with the wall and Brady hoists me higher, never breaking our kiss. He works his hips between mine, letting me feel how hard he is. One of my shoes thuds to the floor, but we don't separate. We don't even pause. He kisses me harder as I work my hands beneath his shirt. A pained sound leaves him and before I can react, he's tearing his shirt off, throwing it behind him, and pressing himself back against me. My hands run over the bare skin of his shoulders and chest, memorizing the planes of muscle.

I missed this. I missed him. The feel of his body against mine, the thump of his heart against mine—I'm in heaven.

Brady's lips move over my neck, sending tiny thrills of heat through me. He nips my collarbone before pulling my lips back to his where he plunges his tongue roughly inside. A hand snakes up my side and his thumb brushes beneath my breast before he cups it fully, kneading it. Running his fingers over my hardened nipple, my legs clench around him. I don't know how much longer I can take this heavy petting. I need more.

It seems it's been forever since we were together like this.

I'm panting, my breath sawing in and out in an embarrassing way. I want him inside me, I want to be as close to him as I can be, yet I can't form the words to ask. I whimper pathetically, and that's all he needs.

We're moving, my back pulling away from the wall, but I barely notice. I'm too busy trying to climb inside him, on top of him, all around him. His tense muscles tell me I'm not the only one feeling the driving need beating between us.

Brady drops me onto my bed with a groan.

Grasping my ankle, he slowly runs his hand up and down my calf, his gaze focused intently on the movement of his palm against my skin. His eyes flick to mine and a crooked grin flashes across his face right before he chucks my other shoe to the floor. He leans in, hovering over me, and skims his nose along the plumped skin of my breast. Tugging my dress straps down over my arms, he bites one of my bared shoulders lightly. My head tilts back. His fingers search for the zip on my dress, fumbling their way around my waist, but I don't help.

My hands have found their way to his

waistband and I'm working the button. Frantic to get my hands on the silky hard cock I know is waiting for me. Once they're unbuttoned, I use my feet to push them down while I shove a hand into Brady's boxer briefs. I smooth my hand down, loving the feel of him.

My dress loosens and Brady tugs downward, forcing me to release my hold on him. The pretty new dress I spent so much time looking for is lost to the floor, along with his pants and one of my shoes.

I smile up at Brady as he smooths my hair back. He's working on my bra now, his eyes trained on my cleavage. He licks his lips and pulls the material away, mumbling something under his breath. My heart thumps hard in my chest as he lowers his head, his gaze never leaving mine. Warm lips brush my nipple before he opens his mouth wide and sucks. I squirm and moan beneath him, needing more. I grip him tightly in my hand, stroking him up and down, running my thumb over his tip.

"Fuck," he breathes against my skin, his breath tickles sending tingles rushing over my body.

Big hands grip my hips tightly.
Brady kisses me softly.

"I've missed you," he says against my mouth.

I kiss him back.

"Me too," I mumble.

He's rolling me over, moving me as if I weigh nothing, pulling my panties down, and positioning me on my hands and knees before him. His hands carve a path down my spine as his lips graze first one shoulder then the other. I push myself back against him, needing to feel him, only to find that he's lost his boxers. I whimper at the feel of him pushing against the wet, aching place between my legs.

His hands fumble their roaming and he grips onto my waist, letting me know this is affecting him just as much as it is me.

"Damn." He sucks in a breath. "Hold on."

He pulls away, leaving me feeling cold and smacks my ass lightly. I want to move, to turn and watch him, but I don't. There's something in the air telling me to stay put, so I do, breathing heavily and listening to the rustle of a condom wrapper.

His warmth is back, hovering over me and he plunges into me without warning. The force of his first few thrusts sends my hands scooting across the smooth material of my comforter. My back arches and I can't help the loud sound that escapes my throat. He feels so good. It's never been like this. And I know why.

I love him.

My mind races, a hazy mix of bliss and infatuation pumping through my veins. He should know how I feel. He should know what I want.

I need to tell him. It was supposed to happen at dinner, but we lost ourselves in each other and I don't think we're going to make it to the restaurant.

"Wait," I finally manage to pant.

He grunts, but stills instantly.

"Are you okay?" he asks.

I nod, trying to catch my breath. His hands are still on my hips. He's still hard inside me, and I'm wondering why I stopped him.

"Did I hurt you?"

"No, not at all. I just—"

I drop my head and take a deep breath. Gathering my thoughts, I pull away. I should be facing him for this, not ass up on all fours. He lets me move, but his hands never leave me as I roll over and pull him closer.

I kiss him and he lifts me with a hand under the center of my back, pushing us higher on the bed toward my pillows. His brow furrows in concern.

"I can't believe I almost lost this—us." I run my fingers over the scruff along his jaw.

"Never." Brady leans his forehead against mine, then pulls away to look directly in my eyes. "You never lost me."

I take a deep breath.

Saying this, telling him how much he means to me, gives him the power to hurt me. In reality, he has that power even if he doesn't know it. The only difference is, by telling him, I'm handing that power over to him. I'm trusting him with it, trusting him to take care of me and not hurt me. Even if there's no way in hell this will work, he still needs to know. I still need to tell him.

"I love you," I whisper.

"Babe." He runs his fingers over my cheek so softly as he smiles down at me. "I love you."

His lips crash against mine, and I moan. He groans as one of his big hands grips my thighs and wraps them around his hips. With one thrust, he's inside me and moving. Brady surrounds me. His bare flesh, the smell of his cologne, the feel of his breath on my neck—it's all Brady, all around me. I can't get enough as I move beneath him. My heart thumps hard and fast as his hands skim over my body wherever he can reach.

"You feel so good." His voice is deep and

husky.

"Yes," I whisper.

It seems to urge him on, my answering moan, and he thrusts harder, faster. My nails dig into his back and he slips an arm beneath my leg and raises it over his shoulder. The move sends him deeper. His cock hits just the right spot, sending me into a spiraling abyss. Orgasm rushes through me and Brady stills above me for a split second. He kisses me hard, pushes his hips into mine, and clutches me tight through his release and mine.

Brady falls to my side, pulling me close so I'm facing him, and wraps his arms around me. He kisses my lips sweetly.

His nose nuzzles into me.

"I do, Cora."

I look up into his eyes, confused.

"Love you." He smiles.

Tears burn, threatening to spill over.

"I love you, too. So much." I'm trying to hold it back, but the words come out on a sob.

Brady squeezes me and kisses my hair.

He's quiet, holding me close. After a few moments, I calm, and my tears dry. Combing my fingers through my hair, I put a small amount of space between us. Biting my lips, I stare at his bare chest before meeting his gaze.

"Tonight wasn't supposed to be like this." I sniff.

Brady folds an arm behind his head and looks over at me.

"You regret it?"

"No. Not at all," I assure him. "But we were supposed to talk. And go to dinner." I laugh.

"We've got plenty of time to talk." He smiles. "As for dinner, how about you call that Chinese place down the street? I'm thinking maybe we should stay in. And naked."

27

There's a half-naked man in my kitchen. I rub at my sleep-hazy eyes and check again. Yep, there's a half-naked man in my kitchen and I smell French toast. The sight makes my heart do a weird little skip and my mouth water. I smile as I make my way toward Brady. He hears me before I reach him and turns to give me a grin of his own over his bare shoulder. Clad in only boxer briefs, Brady mans my stove like a pro while wielding a spatula.

Once I reach him, I place small kisses between his shoulder blades and run my hands over his biceps. His skin is hot and smooth.

"Morning," I say against him.

"Morning, babe." He moves to plate two slices of breakfast goodness. My mouth waters just looking at it. My stomach rumbles and Brady chuckles. "Hungry?" He raises a light eyebrow in question.

I nod, taking the plate he offers me.

I'm still a little in shock over the events of the night before. I expected to have to convince him to give me another chance, that he'd want to take things slow. Once again, Brady knew I needed time and he's still here, even if he didn't understand or like the separation—even if he thought I was never coming back to him. My stomach rolls. I can't believe I was ever going to walk away. I can't believe I ever thought I'd never find love or that I didn't deserve it.

Brady takes a seat across from me and digs into his food immediately.

"So?" He looks up after cutting a neat corner off his French toast.

I know what's coming.

I know we actually have to talk about things.

But …

This horrible fear of the unknown has me anticipating his rejection even though he told me he loves me. I'm being ridiculous, and I know it.

"So?" I stare at my plate, dragging my fork through the syrup pooled next to my breakfast.

"Hey," Brady says softly. I wait for him to go on, but he doesn't. He's waiting for me to look at him. I can feel him watching me patiently. Giving

in, I look up. He gives me a quick crooked grin. "Let's talk."

"Fine," I grumble.

He laughs.

I'm glad he's enjoying himself.

I want to be pissed.

I can't be, though.

Happiness crinkles the corners of his eyes as he watches me. The fact that he's making light of this makes me feel better. Nothing bad is coming, but we're adults and this is a relationship. Communication is key.

Time to suck it up.

Brady's watching me and I don't know if he's waiting to see if I'm okay or waiting for me to start. If I've learned anything about him, it's that he'll wait forever for me to be ready.

I'm about to open my mouth to apologize again, but he cuts me off.

"I meant what I said last night, Cora." His fingers brush my hand. "I love you."

The look in his eyes is soft. His words, simple and sweet, send excitement and fear bursting through me all at once. The only kind of love I've known is the crazy kind. My ears burn as a stupid lump builds in my throat. I try to clear it away, but it doesn't work. I take a swipe at my stinging eyes and smile at the man before me. My heart is full to bursting, and I can't believe how much I've grown and changed in the months since he's come into my life.

"I love you," I whisper roughly.

"Babe."

Brady moves from his spot and takes the chair next to me. After he scoots as close to me as he can get, he wraps me in his strong arms and buries his face in my hair. His touch, his strength—*he* relaxes me. I sag against him and soak up his soothing energy. I pull away.

"I'm fine," I say, kissing his lips softly. "Go eat."

His eyes roam over my face, his gaze filled with concern and love.

I shoo him away.

He steals another kiss with a grin and makes his way back to his seat.

"Now what?" I ask to get this conversation going.

Brady raises an eyebrow in my direction.

"Talking."

I gesture between us with my fork. He chuckles.

Then his face turns serious.

"I need to know you're in this. With me. I

have a son, and even though I don't have him all the time, I need to know you won't run. I can't have you in his life—in my life, if you can't accept both of us."

Shame fills me. I've royally messed this situation up.

Before I can say anything, he's talking again.

"I understand, babe. What you were dealing with—I understand. But I won't have women in and out of Logan's life. I don't want him getting attached to someone who will leave him. His mom, Kendra, she's great with him, but her career doesn't leave him with a lot of stability. If I can give him that, I will."

"I want to be with you, Brady. And I want to get to know Logan." I swallow thickly. "I can't see the future. I don't know what will happen between us, but I want both you and your son in my life. I will never intentionally hurt either one of you."

He nods.

"I know you're not ready to jump all in. I know you're still healing and that you need time. I won't push. You know that, babe. But know this too," he pauses, and if it's for dramatic effect, it works. I'm about to vibrate out of my seat with the need to know what he's going to say next. Brady has my full, rapt attention. "I want that future with you. Waking up next to you, fighting with you, making up with you, the house, the rings on our fingers, and the kids."

I inhale sharply. My pulse thumps rapidly. He wants me. And all my crazy mess. His words mean so much. They fill me with want and hope and a need for something more than just the present with him, but I don't know if I can give him all those things. One in particular worries me the most.

I blow out a breath, tuck some hair behind my ear, and tear my gaze from his intense stare. I need a second to clear my head, to make sense of the thoughts rushing around my mind in a crazy, tangled jumble.

My eyes close on their own.

"I don't—I'm not sure..."

"Look at me." It's softly spoken, but it's a command I can't deny.

Eyelids instantly open, gaze trained on his, I wait. He's moving again, his lean body graceful as he quickly joins my side of the table.

Brady cups my face, eyes filled with compassion and love. Nothing but understanding radiates from this man.

"I know, babe. I know." He kisses me softly. "One day. I can be a patient man." A breath rushes out of me in relief. "Sometimes," he tacks on with a laugh, and I'm reminded of the night before.

Worry still fills me. I ache with it. Part of the reason I never thought I'd find love or another relationship was because I didn't want to rob someone of their dreams or their needs. I don't know if I'll ever be ready for a child of my own. I don't know if I could bear being pregnant. Knowing I lost one child only to bring another into the world might be too much for me. I feel stronger than I have in a long while, though. And one day, if I'm ready for more, I know I'll want Brady by my side.

Something warm and peaceful fills me with those thoughts. My worry dissipates slowly, letting me relax and take an easy breath.

This is a fresh start.

Honesty is important.

"Brady, what if I don't ever want those things?" He frowns, and I know that came out wrong. I hold a hand up and start over. "I want you. I want a future with you. And Logan. I just don't know about kids. It was scary enough losing the baby when I wasn't ready for it. When it hadn't been something I wanted …" I gulp, "I just don't know if I could ever get past that."

He hugs me tight, my face pressed into his chest.

"Slow and steady." His fingers brush over my cheek. "When the time comes, we'll talk about it. We'll face it together."

Together.

I lick my dry lips and look up at him.

"Okay."

With everything I have in my being, I hope this works between us. I need him. Yes, I would survive just fine on my own, but I don't want to.

"Don't run from me again. Talk to me. And I'll talk to you." His words are firm, not to be argued with.

I nod and scrub a hand down my face before fussing with my hair.

"Got it."

"Now kiss me," he demands, and tilts my head back with his hands.

****

I set the last dish from breakfast in the cabinet and shut the door. Brady tosses down the towel he was using to dry the counter and wraps his arms around me from behind. Leaning into his chest, I look up, craning my neck so I can see his face.

"When do you have to pick up Logan?"

Brady rocks us from side to side and kisses my neck.

"After we shower."

My body goes stiff and hot and achy.

Shower?

While that sounds all kinds of sexy and slippery, it also sounds intimate in a way I might still be too raw for. Our talk was good, I know where we stand and we both know what to expect, so hopefully there won't be any more omissions or running. But it was still hard to bring up all those things.

He lets me go and runs his hand down my arm, lacing our fingers together. He pulls me from the kitchen and leads me down the hall until we're shut inside my bathroom.

Brady busies himself with turning on the water and adjusting the temperature until he's satisfied while I stand there wondering why I'm freaking out a little bit. When he's done, he faces me and smiles. He kisses my forehead, sensing my panic. And just like always, he knows when to push and when to stop. This is one of those times he can push because my worries are silly.

Hands on my hips, he pulls me closer and waits, silently asking if this is okay. I nod, barely, but he sees and his fingers tangle in the hem of the shirt I slipped on this morning. He slips our clothes off slowly, intently, brushing his fingers against every bared inch of my skin like he can't resist. Once we're both naked and breathing heavily, he gently turns me toward the shower and nudges me forward.

Shivers climb over my body as I step away from his body heat. Warm water slides over my shoulders and down my back as I put myself beneath the spray. Brady follows and immediately wraps me in his arms. He kisses me, his lips meeting mine softly. My heart beats faster. I take a shaky breath and Brady takes the opening to slide his tongue between my lips. My hands clutch at his neck as his work their way into my damp hair. He groans before pulling away and turning me to face the water.

I watch as he grabs my body wash. He's standing so close behind me, his skin brushes mine every time he moves. He lathers his hands and places them on my shoulders, kneading. The pressure feels so good, I sag against him.

"I just needed to touch you like this," he says, sliding soapy hands down my arms. "To feel your warm, smooth skin beneath my fingers." His words rumble in my ear as his hands slide over my breasts. "To know you're with me," he finishes.

I moan as he rubs over my stomach and hips. I'm soapy and wet, in more than one way, but

I don't move. I let him finish. He needs this right now and if feels amazing. His words, his touch—it's all so, so hot.

My brain is mush. I let him make his way down my legs, then he turns me and starts on my back. He's gentle and loving, even when he buries his face between my boobs. A laugh bubbles from me and his answering chuckle leaves me feeling lightheaded.

When he's done scrubbing me, he presses his front against mine and I stretch up to wrap my arms around his neck, pulling his head down so I can press my mouth against his. I kiss him hard, prying his mouth open and tangling my tongue with his.

I pull away.

"Thank you," I murmur against his wet lips.

"Always, babe."

I push him under the water and watch as he lathers himself up.

These moments are something I've never had—the sweet, soft touches that go nowhere. He wants me, I know, because his dick has been hard since we stepped in the shower, but he doesn't make a move. He's trying to prove something. We have a closeness that doesn't need sex. It's nice.

I reach around him once he's rinsed and

shut the water off. He nips my shoulder when I lean in and I swat him. Grabbing two towels, I drop one at my feet and then begin rubbing Brady down. I swipe drops of water from the cut of his pecs and down, where water rolls down his abs. Grinning saucily, I start to go lower, but he stops me by wrapping his arms around me and somehow managing to get the towel I was using on him around me.

"Go get dressed, handsy." Brady spins me and swats my ass as I scamper to my bedroom while laughing.

We get dressed quietly and I walk Brady to the door.

"I'll call you later, okay?" He kisses me quickly, opens the door, and leans back in to kiss me deep and long.

"Okay," I breathe when he releases his grip on my hips and lets my mouth go.

"Love you." It still sounds so weird to hear.

"Love you." And even more weird to say.

28

Sweat rolls down the back of my neck and slips between my shoulder blades. My muscles burn from being pushed. It feels great. The song ends and I plant my feet into the floor, trying to catch my breath. The new playlist I made makes me push myself.

It's the best.

The thing I love most about dancing is losing myself in the music. Certain songs hold so much meaning, so much emotion, that I forget what I'm doing. I move on autopilot, pushing and spinning, nothing but the feel of the cool wooden floor beneath my feet and freedom from everything.

It's only been a few days since Brady and I officially wiped the slate clean and started our relationship. I've been a grinning, fumbling idiot since then. We haven't seen each other much, but there have been phone calls, and texts.

Oh, the texts.

He's too much sometimes. Too sexy. Too sweet. Too funny. I'd say he's perfect, but no one is. I know that better than anyone. He just fits with me perfectly.

I bend at the waist, touching my toes and wrapping my hands around my ankles. My calves sting and I start to feel lightheaded. Just as I straighten, I feel eyes on me and a knock draws my attention. Spinning, I'm met with identical green gazes and crooked grins. Apparently, I forgot to lock the door after the last student left.

I wipe a hand over my neck.

"Hi, guys." I approach slowly, unsure of how I'm supposed to act in front of Logan.

Brady and I didn't talk about whether we were going to tell Logan, or if I would even be spending much time with him. I'm going to let him take the lead on this one because thinking about it makes me feel out of sorts and lost.

"We brought you coffee," Logan says proudly while holding out a Brunette Brew to-go cup.

I take it.

"Thank you," I say before turning my attention to Brady.

He wraps his fingers around my upper arm

and pulls me to him, giving me a tight hug. I bury my face in his chest and feel him kiss my hair before he lets go.

I clear my throat uncomfortably.

"Miss Cora, do you see my shirt?" Logan asks, pulling the hem of his tee out and looking down. "It's Spiderman! He's a superhero!"

Brady chuckles.

"That shirt is so awesome!" I think for a second. "Do you know who my favorite superhero is?"

He shakes his head and taps a finger against his lips.

"Hmmm..." He tilts his head from side to side. "Is it ... Superman?"

"Nope." I lean down, getting closer to him. "It's Ironman."

He jumps up, grabbing my arms.

"I love him, too!"

His smile is a beam, a ray of sunshine. I'm instantly grinning back. This kid might steal my heart from his dad.

"Dad, did you hear? Miss Cora loves Ironman, too." He draws the 'o' out on love and giggles.

Brady ruffles Logan's hair.

"I don't think that's true," Brady teases.

"But she does. She told me," Logan pouts.

They're having some sort of staring contest, Brady's lips are quirking at the corners, and Logan's hands are on his hips.

"Daad, Miss Cora loves Ironman!"

Brady mutters under his breath, words that sound something like being jealous of Tony Stark, and holds his hands out in a placating gesture.

I laugh. I can't help it. Logan fist pumps the air in victory.

"Okay, okay. Now, what were we supposed to ask Cora?"

"I almost forgot!" I wince at the volume of Logan's shriek.

"Inside voice, bud," Brady says in reprimand.

Logan's hand instantly goes to his mouth. He peers up at me with big, worried, green eyes.

"Sorry," he says quietly.

My lips curl up at the corners.

"What are you going to ask me?" I say. "I'm so curious."

He latches onto my hands with his much smaller ones and jumps up and down.

"Do you want to go to the zoo with us tomorrow? We can see monkeys and tigers. And they have giraffes. And—Dad," he turns to Brady,

"what are those one things that I hate? They're fuzzy and gray."

Brady looks up from his son and raises his eyebrows in amusement.

"Koalas?"

"Yeah those, they're so creepy," Logan says with a huff. "So, anyway, do you want to?"

His excitement is contagious and freeing.

Brady chuckles as I look at him.

"No pressure," Brady says, landing himself a jab in the leg with a tiny elbow from Logan.

"Are you asking me on a date?" I tease.

"No way!" Logan says at the same time Brady nods and smiles at me. "That would mean you're my girlfriend, and I'm not old enough for a girlfriend. My mom says I'm gonna be hell on wheels when I'm older if I'm anything like my dad is with the ladies."

His little voice and smile are smug and I bark out a laugh, even though the last thing I want to think about is Brady and the ladies.

"Okay, bud, that's enough. We don't want to scare Cora away."

They both turn to face me and I'm stunned into silence by matching mischievous grins. I look away, shaking my head before I answer their pleading eyes.

"I'd love to go to the zoo with you."

Logan's fist pumps through the air again and Brady smiles at me slyly.

We make plans and say our goodbyes. It's much later, after I'm home and tucked into bed, that I think about how much I wanted to kiss Brady, to touch him, but I don't know how much he's told Logan, or how much he wants him to know. I held back because I don't know how much Brady trusts me to stick around. I hope he knows the last thing I would ever do is hurt a child intentionally. If I had any doubts about my relationship with Brady, I wouldn't put myself in a position to be around Logan.

My phone dings on my nightstand and my heart leaps when I see Brady's name. I swipe open the text and am instantly relieved.

Brady: I wanted to kiss you so badly earlier. I've never had a woman around my son and I didn't want to shock him. The way I want to touch you is anything but innocent.

****

Picking at the cuticle on my thumbnail, I slump further into Brady's couch.

The zoo was great.

Logan was fun.

And Brady was distracted.

The day started perfectly. I was nervous, but quickly fell into a role I'd never expected, holding Logan's hand and telling him things about the animals. At some point, Brady checked his phone and the entire atmosphere around us chilled. The rest of our day was filled with something I couldn't name.

He was present.

He was smiling.

His mind was somewhere else.

We're at his house with plans to watch a movie and I want to bolt. The problem is, I've promised him and myself I wouldn't do that, so I'm sticking it out, batting down old insecurities while he tucks Logan in. If he didn't want me here, he wouldn't have asked.

Right?

I'm staring blankly at the TV that isn't even on when Brady enters the living room. He clears his throat and rubs a hand over the top of his head. My eyes narrow in on the movement—a sure sign something is on his mind.

"All tucked in?"

"Yes. I had to convince him three times that he didn't need to come get another goodnight hug from you."

He chuckles, but it sounds hollow, forced.

Tension lines his face as he approaches me, causing me to watch him warily. My thoughts are derailed as he moves closer. I'm in the dark and that ugly fear of rejection is rearing its head. I start thinking maybe he's changed his mind, maybe he's having second thoughts. Maybe he's breaking up with me. Maybe I did something wrong while we were at the zoo.

Brady lowers himself next to me and tugs me over so I'm lying against his side, his arm around me. I relax into him and he sighs, his chest heaving against me.

The runaway train inside my head slows. I need to get a grip.

I look up into his face and search his eyes—for what, I don't know. Some sign or spark of what's going on. I swallow the nerves crawling up my throat and prepare to take a bite out of whatever this issue is. I'm meeting it head on instead of waiting.

"What's wrong?" I drag my fingers over his unshaved jaw.

Warm lips press into my forehead before he pulls back and looks down at me. His gaze bores into mine. He too, is looking for something. I can only hope I'm showing him whatever he needs to see, whatever will put him at ease.

"We need to talk."

I hate those words. Ice grips my heart instantly.

I try to lean away, but his arm holds me close.

"Well, that's an awful statement."

"I'm sorry. I know. I know I ruined the day."

Frustration echoes in every one of his words.

"You didn't ruin the day. You were just … off."

He leans in with apologetic eyes and kisses me softly.

"I love you."

"I love you, too," I say with a frown. "You aren't really easing my fears here."

I place my palm on his chest and push away so I can see him better.

Another huge sigh leaves him and I sit up, tucking my legs beneath me. I stay close, but I'm getting the feeling this—whatever it is—is heavy, and I need some space. I also want to give him my whole, undivided attention, and let's face it, Brady's lean, hard body is distracting when it's pressed all up on me.

Trepidation fills his eyes. I sense that he's worried about how I'm going to react and I give him a small smile, hoping to ease his worries.

He clears his throat.

My fingers twist in my lap until he wraps one big hand around mine.

The air around us carries a foreboding feeling. I've never seen Brady this way. Not during any of the bullshit I put us through has he looked at me like I'm going to take off running and screaming—or worse. I dread whatever is about to come out of his mouth. If it's enough for him to have that expression, then it must be bad.

"There's a possibility Logan will be with me for the next year."

My rigid posture eases and I wait for the rest, for the explanation—for more. Brady watches me carefully, studying my reaction.

"Okay," I say when he doesn't go on. "What else?"

"That is not the reaction I expected."

I purse my lips and peer at him through narrowed eyes.

"I told you I was in this. I said I wouldn't run. We said we'd talk about things. You really thought I'd walk away just because Logan would be here all the time?"

It stings, but I won't let it show.

I hold my head up, keeping my gaze on his.

Brady leans forward, resting his elbows on his knees. His hands cradle his head as he blows out a breath.

"I don't what I thought. This is a big deal. It's a big deal for me." He looks up, piercing me with his gaze. "I'm sorry."

I sigh. It's not worth it. This fight. I'm not mad, I'm hurt, and I know Brady well enough to know he didn't mean to hurt my feelings. Besides, he's right, this is a big deal. I can see the fear in his eyes. One on one full-time with his son has to bring on some pretty heavy feelings.

That's where I need to put my focus.

"So, tell me what's going on."

Brady leans back into the couch cushions and his thigh brushes mine.

I need to comfort him. The uncertainty on his face pains me. It's so unlike him. I take his hand in mine, threading our fingers together. Giving his hand a little squeeze, I shift closer to him.

"Logan's mom got offered a pretty big modeling gig. She's going to be the face of some fancy European designer. The entire campaign will be all about her. It's the break she's been looking for since we met. It's also what she needs before she's too old for the modeling world. She can't— she won't pass it up."

I nod.

"Sounds like a great thing for her."

I don't know much about modeling, but I'm sure being the center of a campaign for a big designer will do it for your career. I can't blame her for not passing it up.

"Yeah, it is."

"She doesn't want to take Logan with her?"

From what Brady's told me about her, she's a great mother. I can't imagine her not wanting her son with her.

"No, it's not that. She'll be working so much on and off, it won't be a consistent lifestyle for him. She's worried about schooling and stuff like that."

"Makes sense. So he stays here with you?"

"It'll be easier on him—better for him." Brady looks over at me. His fingers brush my cheek as he smiles softly.

"I think you're right."

"We're going to talk to him, see what he wants to do, and then make a decision. We want him to have some say, but we also want him to have a normal life. Not one filled with foreign schools and private tutors. I just wanted you to know. If it's too much, you can walk. I won't hold it against you."

I look at him.

Really look at him.

From his slumped posture to the distraught look in his eyes, the determination in his locked jaw.

Taking his chin in my hand, I turn his face toward me and press a kiss to his lips.

"I'm not going anywhere. Whatever you guys decide, I'll be here."

Brady's hand brushes over my cheek. He tucks some of my hair behind my ear and settles his palm across the back of my neck. His eyes stay trained steadily on mine as a few seconds tick by. It seems like the longest moment of my life. Then, he pulls me into his arms and hugs me close, pressing my face into his chest. I breathe a sigh of relief.

"It's gonna be okay," I say into the material of his shirt.

He squeezes me tighter.

I wait for the panic, the worry, the need to get away from the situation to consume me, but it never does.

This is right.

Britni Hill

29

Breaking down the last box, I lean it up against the others I have stacked in the hallway. I smile as I look around. The Christmas tree we decorated on Thanksgiving crowds the corner of Brady's house—our house. My things are scattered amongst his now, and as much as I worried it would freak me out, it doesn't.

When Brady first brought up the idea of us living together, he wanted to buy a new house. Something that would be ours together, but I love his house, and we decided, for now, it would be fine for us. I didn't want to uproot Logan anymore than he already had been, though he's pretty resilient and took to living with Brady like it was nothing. He misses his mom, but he doesn't let it get him down.

I'm glad she's in town for Christmas, even if it means we won't have him here with us for the entire day. He needs her the same way he needs Brady. The front door opens and Brady comes toward me with a smile.

With a hand on my hip, he kisses me softly on the lips.

"Are these the last of the boxes?" He gestures to where the stack of cardboard sits.

I nod.

I turn back toward the kitchen to finish putting things away in there. A playful slap on my backside stings through my jeans. I rub a hand over it and peer over my shoulder at Brady. He's grinning that cocky grin of his.

He grabs the boxes.

"I'll just take these out to the garage," he says as he disappears through the door.

In the kitchen, I start pulling things from the cabinets and try to reorganize so we have room for everything. After a few minutes, I hear the door open again.

"Logan," Brady calls through the house, "your mom is here."

"I'm coming!"

Feet thunder down the hall and Logan appears next to me, grinning from ear to ear. His coat hangs from one arm as he struggles to get the other in its sleeve while still gripping a Spiderman action figure tightly.

A laugh slips from me.

"Let me help."

I pry Spiderman from his grip and set him aside while holding the coat up for Logan to slip his arm through.

"Logan," Brady calls again.

"Okay." I ruffle his hair. "Zip up. It's cold out."

He tucks his tongue between his lips as he lines up the zipper and pulls upward. It's too cute. As soon as he bundled up, he launches himself at me, wrapping his tiny arms tightly around me.

I squeeze back.

"I love you, Cora."

He lets me go and backs toward the door.

"Love you too, bud."

"I'll see you on Christmas. At night." He pulls the front door open and turns back to pin me with a look. "Don't open my presents."

"Go." I shoo him away, still shaking my head when the door closes behind him.

****

Strong hands wrap around my hips and pull me back into a warm, hard chest. Brady nuzzles into my neck, his breath tickling as his lips graze over my ear.

"We're alone," he mumbles into my ear.

"Alone?" I whisper.

He kisses down my neck, pulling the collar of my shirt away from my shoulder.

"Mmmhmm."

A small moan falls from my lips. His hands climb beneath my shirt, grazing my sides. I arch back into him. It feels so good not to have to worry about Logan bursting in at any moment. Or whether we have enough time to get all our clothes off or not.

"I'm gonna get you *so* naked."

"What?"

I can't help it. I start laughing uncontrollably. My sides ache as Brady spins me around, but my laughter dies on my lips when I see the heat in his eyes.

"I think I'm losing my game," he says with a crooked smile.

"We have a few days. Let's see if you can get it back."

I launch myself at him, kissing him hard. Pulling his shirt over his head, I run my hands over his warm skin. I get to work on his belt and the buttons on his pants, but he pulls back, stilling my hands.

Brady's hands run over my curves, stripping

me of my shirt and brushing his mouth over the flesh spilling over the lacy top of my bra. He grips my ass, pulls me against him, then wraps his hands around the back of my thighs, and boosts me up onto the counter. My skinny jeans are peeled off with a snap. Brady's mouth and hands cover every inch of bare skin they can find. His eyes are heated and determined, a possessive look taking over his face.

Shivers roll through me as desire heats my blood.

I love this side of him.

The side that knows exactly when to take over.

Before I know it, I'm naked against the cool counter and Brady's pounding into me with fierce tenderness. I'm panting and sweat glistens on his forehead. His groans fill my ears. This is rough and wild and perfect. I don't want it to stop, but my body has other plans. Every touch and thrust drives me higher and higher.

Complete, total, shocking bliss rips through me as Brady slams into me harder and harder. His fingers dig into my hips and I relish the bit of pain added to the pleasure he's giving me. I meld myself to the counter as I come down and Brady holds us steady through his own release. We're both panting and exhausted in the best possible way.

****

My head is pillowed on Brady's arm as we face each other in bed, our legs tangled together, his arm curled over my hip. It's intimate and cozy. Words bubble on the tip of my tongue. Brady's eyes meet mine and I decide to go for it. To say what's been on my mind since I unpacked the last box.

"So, I was thinking …"

"Oh, yeah?" His voice is husky with sleepiness.

Warm fingertips trail over my arm.

"We don't have a lot of space."

"You don't like my house?" he asks, laughter in his voice.

"I love your house. Remember, I was the one who wanted to move here?"

"Mmmhmm … and?"

"I really do love it here, but in the future, we might need more room, so it wouldn't hurt to keep an eye out for something we like, right?"

"Okay." He hesitates. "What are we going to need more room for? You have a shopping problem I don't know about?"

I suck in a deep breath. Here goes nothing.

"Well, I don't think Logan's going to want to

share a room with any brothers or sisters that might happen to come about."

I smile into the darkness.

Brady's quiet, but he pulls me into his arms, wrapping me up in his warmth.

We relax back into the mattress.

"So, tell me what kind of house you want."

His voice is warm and soft, a low murmur.

"What kind of house do you want? I ask.

"The kind filled with you and our kids."

My heart thumps.

"Brady, that could be any house."

He's ridiculously cheesy, but his words are perfect.

I close my eyes and start to lose myself to sleep when Brady's voice breaks the silence.

"You know I'm buying a ring tomorrow, right?"

There he is. The man who knows just when to take over. The man who always knows just what I need. The one I almost never found.

The End

Britni Hill

Acknowledgements

I still wake up every day amazed by the fact that I get to share my stories. So thank you, to all of you. Thank you to everyone who has read one of my books, to everyone who has listened to me talk about my books, and to everyone who has supported me through this journey.

To my Besties: you know who you are! Thanks for being there. Thanks for sharing your taste in books, and for all the hot guy pics. Thanks for letting me pick your brains and most of all thanks for being fantastic.

Tera and Andrea: Thank you for answering my questions and helping me get certain medical things right.

Samantha: Thank you so so much for taking the time to read my story, for getting to know Cora and Brady, and for letting me be your first. ;)

Morgan, my baby sister: I thought about you a lot while writing this book. You influence me more than you'll probably ever know. I'm so proud of the woman you've become. You are brave and strong.

You are amazing!

Thank you to my FAB girls for always encouraging me.

To all the fantastic bloggers I've met. Thank you!

Angie J: I couldn't survive without your memes and all the laughs you bring. I can't wait until I can squeeze you again.

Kate Roth (get ready for the mush): I love you with all my heart! You're the constant in my life. Thank you for being the best critique partner and soul mate I could ever ask for. Most of all … thank you for being a friend.

And that guy I live with, the one I love, the one who plays Fallout for endless hours just so I can write and edit …thank you!

So much love and thanks to give! It's amazing, all the people I'm surrounded by and how much they mean to me. Whether we've just met or you've been there for years, you mean the world to me. So thank you friends, family, readers, bloggers, and everyone in between.

About the Author

Britni Hill is a new adult and contemporary romance author. She spends her days as a hair stylist, and her nights with the characters in her head striving to write real, page turning romance.

Britni lives in Indiana where she was born and raised. She has a rescue pup she adores and an unhealthy love of binging on cheesy, teenage dramas. If she isn't writing, she's reading or watching horror flicks with her boyfriend.

Britni Hill

Other Books by Britni

The **Hollow Oaks** series

Tears in the Rubble

From the Rubble

The **Western Palm** series

Hushed

Revealed

Loved

Standalones

Taking a Gamble

Runaway Feelings